FLEECED!

Lisa Thompson was born in northern Tasmania. She grew up in a haunted house on a beautiful farm where a lot of things died in mysterious circumstances. An actor, playwright and screen-writer, Lisa has studied in the US, Australia and Brazil. She played the role of Maria-Elena Holly in the long-running musical *Buddy – The Buddy Holly Story*. Her experiences as a sheep-drencher and salsa-dancer inspired her to write *Fleeced!*, which is her first novel.

lisa thompson

FLEECED!

PENGUIN BOOKS

Penguin Books

Published by the Penguin Group
Penguin Books Australia Ltd
250 Camberwell Road, Camberwell, Victoria 3124, Australia
Penguin Books Ltd
80 Strand, London WC2R 0RL, England
Penguin Putnam Inc.
375 Hudson Street, New York, New York 10014, USA
Penguin Books, a division of Pearson Canada
10 Alcorn Avenue, Toronto, Ontario, Canada M4V 3B2
Penguin Books (NZ) Ltd
Cnr Rosedale and Airborne Roads, Albany, Auckland, New Zealand
Penguin Books (South Africa) (Pty) Ltd
24 Sturdee Avenue, Rosebank, Johannesburg 2196, South Africa
Penguin Books India (P) Ltd
11, Community Centre, Panchsheel Park, New Delhi 110 017, India

First published by Penguin Books Australia Ltd 2003

3 5 7 9 10 8 6 4 2

Copyright © Lisa Thompson 2003

The moral right of the author has been asserted

Designed by Nikki Townsend, Penguin Design Studio
Typeset in Sabon by Post Pre-press Group, Brisbane, Queensland
Printed and bound in Australia by McPherson's Printing Group, Maryborough, Victoria

National Library of Australia
Cataloguing-in-Publication data:

Thompson, Lisa.
Fleeced.

ISBN 0 14 300046 2.

1. Man–woman relationships – Fiction. I. Title.

A823.3

In memory of Tony Williams, literary agent

1936–2002

part one

GREATER EASTERN REGIONAL SHOWGROUNDS, VICTORIA

If you're going to play the organ, you've got to have good feet. Pliant, flexible, flying feet. Melanie's gold jiffies flew across the pedals of the Galaxy Home Organ at dizzying speeds, her hands pounding out show tunes on the illuminated double keyboard. 'Melanie Plays the Galaxy!' screamed the banner above her head. The banner was strung between two posts, flanking a raised platform where Melanie was on display. She wore a red sequined evening gown which hugged her five-foot-two body and showcased her generous breasts. Of Irish stock, Melanie had hazel-green eyes and her long fine hair was a deep chestnut; today it was swept up in a French roll, adorned with a white silk orchid. Her glo-mesh earrings jiggled furiously as she hurtled through a samba.

Inside the sprawling Trades Pavilion, a crowd of farming types had gathered around her, clapping and hooting their approval. Two Galaxy sales reps mingled with the avid listeners, clutching their clipboards and taking a steady stream of orders. When it came to home organs, Melanie Francis was the undisputed queen of the agricultural show circuit.

At a country show, you've got to crank up the volume. There's always plenty of competition in the pavilion – the incessant buzz of the crowd moving herd-like through the building; a chorus of reps flogging water pumps and electrified fencing and the latest in TV satellite dishes; the bleating of animals in the petting pen, as they fend off exuberant toddlers.

After two hours of non-stop playing, Melanie's show-girl smile was starting to fade. She signalled to her colleagues. 'Ten minutes,' she mouthed over the din, holding up both hands and arching her eyebrows. Grudgingly, the senior rep agreed. Pushing back the seat, Melanie freed herself from the flashing console and made for the exit, turning a few heads along the way; in a sea of overalls and Akubras, it was hard to miss a woman in a low-cut spangly dress.

Emerging into the daylight, Melanie was greeted by the roar of new-model tractors, the frantic thudding of the woodchopping events and a blast of seventies music from Sideshow Alley. Breathing deeply, she took in the country air – a blend of cow manure, diesel fumes and sizzling sausages. She slipped a pair of gumboots over her jiffies and left the pavilion behind her; it was just past 2 p.m. on a warm summer's day and, as she walked, her red sequined dress glittered in the sunlight.

'Two minutes to place your bets. You have two minutes,' a voice boomed out across the PA, announcing the start of the Bunnalup Valley Stakes.

Hoping to find a decent coffee, but knowing the odds weren't good, Melanie turned left at the ferris wheel and headed across an open field towards the Show Society Refreshment Tent. As she walked, she heard someone shouting in her general direction. Kids, she thought. Don't turn around, it'll only encourage them.

'And the gee-gees are lining up for the big one, folks . . .' crackled the PA.

'Hey! *Hey*!' More shouting. Damn kids. Haven't they seen cleavage before?

'Diablo Dame, a feisty filly out of Fitfora King . . . *crackle, crackle.*'

Suddenly the shouting was very loud and didn't sound like kids at all.

'Hey *you*!'

Melanie spun around to see a huge woolly ram with massive horns galloping towards her. Chasing the ram was a big blond man. He was yelling at Melanie and waving frantically.

'Giddout! *MOVE*!!'

Terrified, she tried to get away, but the slim-fitting gown made it impossible to run. She looked behind her – the ram was gaining ground. She reached down, grabbed the hem of her dress and yanked it up past her thighs, ripping the seams and leaving a trail of red sequins. Clutching the torn fabric to her chest, she was now striding like a sprinter instead of mincing like a geisha. In liberating her thighs, she'd also exposed her ample bottom, which was encased in Nearly Nude pantyhose and a black G-string.

'Melanie Francis, brazen hussy!' howled the Sisters of St Jacobs, clasping their respective bosoms. Thanks to her Catholic school education, Melanie was still haunted by a fearsome band of nuns, who occasionally loomed up from her subconscious to confirm any self-doubts she may have been entertaining.

Ignoring their cries, Melanie focused on her legs. 'I'm Michael Johnson,' she panted. 'I'm Cathy Freeman in the 400 metres . . . I'm the Scottish guy in *Chariots of Fire*.'

Mud and manure were spattering her legs; her French roll had collapsed and clumps of knotted hair, spiked with metal hairpins, whipped her face with every stride. Melanie shook her head as she ran; she was trying to shift the clumps to one side so she could see where on earth she was going. Stumbling and weaving about, Melanie was losing speed. She could feel the ram closing in on her, snorting and heaving and spitting.

This is it, she thought, this is my glorious demise: face-down in shit, trampled to death by a car-seat cover. No choir of angels, no serene, celestial harpists to mark the occasion, only a mob of screaming kids on the Giant Raptor Ride, and Alice Cooper rasping 'School's Out Forever'.

But just as the slavering, woolly beast was taking aim at Melanie's Nearly Nude buttocks, the big blond man intercepted. Flexing his muscles, summoning all the strength at his disposal, he grabbed the runaway firmly by the horns and wrestled it to the ground. Then he pinned it down with a well-placed knee to the chest. Squirming on its back, legs flailing, the enraged animal had met its match – but only for a moment. Twisting and turning with remarkable ferocity, the ram managed to break free and quickly rounded on its attacker, snorting and stamping with a terrible fury. As the big blond man scrambled to his feet, the beast suddenly charged, anchoring its hard, cruel horns in the soft, yielding flesh of the poor man's crotch and flinging him some distance into the air.

GREATER EASTERN REGIONAL HOSPITAL, MOUNT MALABAR

Melanie hovered around the casualty department as they wheeled her brave knight errant along the corridor. To cover what was left of her dress, she'd pulled on a plastic bin liner – not a useful jumbo, double-strength bag, but a flimsy kitchen tidy affair, which kept tearing to reveal sequins and bare flesh. Still, it was all the ladies at the Show Society tent had to offer. Between the plastic mini-bag and the top of her gumboots, Melanie was still showing a lot of leg, which didn't go unnoticed by the orderlies.

Outside casualty, the senior Galaxy rep was waving at Melanie through the sliding-glass doors. He stabbed an angry finger at his watch, then at the company van. The junior rep was sitting behind the wheel, inspecting his new hair implants in the mirror and revving the van's engine.

'One minute, okay?' Melanie mouthed to the first rep. She ignored his mimed response which warned of her imminent strangulation, and flagged down a passing nurse.

'Excuse me, could you tell me the name of that patient?'

'Sorry?' The nurse looked up from her clipboard and frowned at the vision in white plastic, who appeared to be shedding sequins. Some tart who worked on the mechanical rides, no doubt. You could always spot the show people. She'd had a catfight in a sauna, this one. Clothes all ripped, hair like a fright wig, cheap foundation running down her face. Bloody itinerants.

'What is it, dear, what do you need?' asked the nurse, with a well-rehearsed air of detachment.

'Um, the blond guy over there,' Melanie pointed at her own Sir Lancelot, who was lying semi-conscious on a trolley, waiting to go into theatre. 'Do you know his name?'

How very odd, thought the nurse. Everyone knew Gary. He was practically farming royalty. Still, what would a tart in a bin liner know about men with class?

'It's Gary,' replied the nurse, with a hint of superiority. 'Mister Gary Quartermaine.'

High on pethidine, Gary had lost all sense of time and place. He was dimly aware of being shifted sideways onto the operating table; there was a strong white light overhead and the movement of people around him. He felt a mask descending over his face and someone – a woman – was telling him to count to ten. A man in a green gown was peering intently at Gary's groin, prodding him with a blunt instrument. The last thing Gary heard was the man's voice. 'These look a bit dodgy,' the surgeon intoned. 'We may have to lose one. Nurse . . .'

Gary inhaled sharply, then everything went black.

Early next morning, a flock of twittering sparrows hopped around the hospital lawn, trawling for insects in the dew. Sunlight filtered through the venetian blinds into Casualty, where the night nurse was dozing at her desk.

There was a deafening shriek from Ward C. The sparrows fell silent and the night nurse leapt to her feet as the man's voice rang out, reverberating through the corridors.

'I've got *two*!' he roared. 'Thank you, God, I've got *TWO*!!!'

THE MAGELLAN HOSPITAL, EAST MELBOURNE

Checking that the coast was clear, Jacqui whispered across the aisle to Melanie. 'So what are you gonna do?'

The two women were sitting at their desks, ignoring their allotted tasks. They were dressed in the office uniform: white long-sleeved blouse with Peter Pan collar, knee-length navy skirt and flat navy shoes.

'He's waiting for a sign – you've got to do something!' urged Jacqui. At forty years of age, Jacqui McGlade was six years older than her friend Melanie. Her eyes were lilac-grey and her shoulder-length hair a light caramel, cut in a feathered style which matched her soft demeanour. She was taller than Melanie, with a heavier build. At home she liked to float around the kitchen in her paisley-print dresses, quaffing Fanta and making tabouleh with the Hare Krishna chef on SBS.

'I dunno, I can't just . . . call him,' Melanie whispered back. 'I mean, what do you say?'

'Send him some flowers.' Jacqui's face lit up as she pictured the scene. Dashing Farmer on remote property receives lavish bouquet from City Girl, hand-delivered by Handsome Doctor-Pilot (carrot-red hair, emerald eyes), who must fly off again to save stranded feline with broken foot. Farmer is left to roam long, lonely verandah, gazing at beauteous blooms and thinking . . .

'You reckon?' Melanie frowned, unconvinced. In her experience, men weren't impressed by overt displays of interest. Better just to ignore them; they seemed more comfortable with that.

'Send him some tiger lilies.' Jacqui beamed. 'Men *love* tiger lilies.'

The tiger lily is indeed a man's flower. It comes in strong primary colours, it's robust, and in a certain light it even looks fierce. When you send a man tiger lilies there's no risk of emasculation.

'Just think – he actually saved your life.' Jacqui stared out into space. 'That is so – incredible . . .'

Jacqui was a hopeless romantic. How she ever expected to meet a beau was anyone's guess, given that her social life revolved around her cat, a brown Burmese called Leroy.

'Ladies! I do hope we're not keeping you from your chat.' The supervisor appeared from nowhere, sporting padded shoulders and narrowed lips.

'No, Mrs Van Asch,' muttered Melanie and Jacqui, scrambling for their headphones.

'*Click . . . whirr.* The deceased is a well-nourished Caucasian male, seventy-four years of age, one hundred and eighty-two centimetres long . . .'

Melanie and Jacqui worked at a large city hospital called the Magellan. They worked in the hospital's typing pool, along with twenty-two other women of varying ages, shapes and sizes, all wearing their blue skirts and white blouses. They sat at individual desks, four across, six deep, each with a computer, a tattered copy of *Dorland's Medical Dictionary* and a transcriber. The transcribers were customised tape players, which were operated with a foot pedal. You tapped the right side of the pedal to play the tape (press right: fast forward), the left side to skip back (press left: fast rewind), and the centre of the pedal if you wanted to stop the tape.

Clattering away on their keyboards, their feet tapping and pausing and pressing, the typists churned out a mountain of work. There were clinic reports, surgery notes, autopsies, memos, general correspondence – the lot. All over the hospital, from Dermatology to Intensive Care, an army of doctors would record their daily findings on their dictaphones then dispatch the mini-cassettes and relevant patient files to the ladies in the pool.

The typists' challenge was to understand what on earth the doctors were saying. The doctors muttered, they lisped, they spoke in accents so thick as to be impenetrable. They dictated their reports in varying stages of drunkenness, or rage, or fatigue, or all three. You needed the skills of a linguist to make any sense of it.

The Magellan typing pool was run by Mrs Van Asch,

'the VA', a high-maintenance blonde of indeterminate age. She was a formidable woman with a taste for bullying and an extensive knowledge of Latin. She would have made a good nun, except she was far too glamorous.

'Keep it simple,' whispered Jacqui, leaning over towards Melanie. 'Yellow tiger lilies with a bit of foliage – give it some height. He'll love it.'

THE CRYSTAL PRINCESS, CAULFIELD, MELBOURNE

'So, this guy saved you from a sheep?' asked Richard, barely containing his amusement. Richard Cohen, forty-one, was tall and lanky with curly brown hair, dark, gentle eyes and the thinnest of goatee beards. He was sitting at a small, round table in a cavernous reception centre called the Crystal Princess. A torn piece of cardboard reading 'Band' was wedged between the condiments and an empty carafe.

Sitting with Richard were Melanie and Andy MacDougall. Andy, the young lead guitarist, was short and stocky, with sandy-coloured hair and rugby player's thighs. Born in Glasgow and raised in outer Melbourne, Andy looked like an extra from *Braveheart*. 'Just whip on the kilt, slap on the paint . . .' Melanie would tease him. 'Whip *off* the kilt, don't ya mean, darlin'?' he'd reply with a wink. Far too cheeky for a lad of nineteen.

The band table was at the back of the reception hall, near the kitchen. A line of waiters trundled past, carrying two hundred plates of chicken Kiev and grumbling about some party in St Kilda they were missing. Richard was nursing his beloved tenor sax. He wet a new reed with his tongue and attached it to the mouthpiece with a dexterity born of many years' experience.

'It wasn't a sheep,' Melanie replied defensively. 'It was a ram. A very big . . . male . . . ram, with big horns – huge horns. And he was all slobbery.'

'Ooooh, sounds pretty scary,' said Andy, as he tightened a string on his guitar.

'Wouldn't want to meet that in a dark alley,' added Richard, running a cloth around the bell of the saxophone.

'Yeah,' said Andy, 'you might even trip over it.' He plucked at the guitar string and released it with a ping.

'You'll keep,' muttered Melanie.

Milos, the trumpet player, and Sarita, the percussionist, approached the table.

'One set to go. Come on, guys, you can do it!' urged Milos, in his strong Czech accent. When he wasn't playing music, the forty-something Milos worked as a professional swimming coach for a private girls' school. He was tall and dark-haired with cheekbones to die for. 'Sweet and symmetrical but rather dull' was Melanie and Sarita's verdict after checking Milos out at the inaugural band meeting four years earlier. Hardly surprising; you couldn't look that good and be fascinating as well.

'Okay, team!' called Milos, as if he were poolside at 5 a.m. with a herd of somnolent teenagers. 'Time's up! Come on, everybody. Shake your booties!'

Dragging their collective feet, the Salsa Kings made their

way to the stage. They arrived from several directions: from the designated band table; from the Swinging Chandelier Bar, where they'd been chatting up the bridesmaids; and from the leafy Gondola Garden, where they'd been puffing on a longed-for cigarette. With a line-up of twelve musicians, the Salsa Kings was a veritable League of Nations. There were players from Europe, New Zealand, Asia-via-Narre Warren, Scotland-via-Wonga Park and, of course, Chile, which gave the band its salsa credibility.

The leader of the band was José Torres, a thin, hatchet-faced man of fifty. His hair was short and wiry, greying at the temples. José played bass – after a fashion. An aggressive and resourceful manager, he always kept the band in work, so they forgave him his lack of musical skill. Richard, who did the arrangements, would write inanely simple bass lines for José, with minimal changes in rhythm. When José did make the inevitable mistakes, the horn section could drown him out with a well-timed blast, and the audience would be none the wiser.

José's cousin, Ferdinand, fronted the band on vocals and hips. Ferdie was a simple soul in his late thirties, a barrel-chested man with black shoulder-length hair and a drooping moustache, a man who was hungry for attention. He was no Enrique Iglesias but he could hold a tune – and hold it in Spanish, which was central to the band's Latino image. And he could execute a figure eight with his pelvis while shouting 'olé!', which never failed to impress.

In addition to playing keyboards, Melanie sang backing vocals in the band. She'd like to have sung more, but

Ferdie would have none of it. He was fiercely protective of his role as lead vocalist (it was printed on his business cards, next to a pair of maracas). He needn't have worried, Melanie had no plans to usurp his position; she just wanted more stuff to do, to help her stay awake.

The band played regular gigs for the Latin American community. Tonight, at the Crystal Princess, it was a large Colombian wedding with cousins aplenty. After a big church ceremony and a long, boozy dinner, the crowd was getting tired and emotional. There was a lot of carousing and backslapping and teasing about the honeymoon – all in Spanish, but you got the gist of it. Weddings were weddings.

Melanie tugged at her leotard, which was lime green and decorated with plastic fruit. Miniature apples, bananas, oranges and grapes were sewn in along the V-shaped neck-line, accentuating her breasts. She fluffed out the layers of multi-coloured silks and satins that made up the long train, then she smoothed down the tiny flip skirt attached to the front of the costume. Checking for runs in her stockings, she slid into her platforms, adjusted the plastic-fruit headdress and clambered onstage. The rest of the band wore black trousers and floral shirts, but for Melanie it was the full Carmen Miranda, Brazilian Bombshell.

Of course the Salsa Kings didn't play any Brazilian music – no samba or bossanova or chorro or forro. They played salsa, cumbia and merengue – the music of Cuba, Puerto Rico, Chile and Colombia. Nothing to do with Brazil. But José wanted the costume. According to him, the punters saw Carmen Miranda with all the fruit, they thought 'Latin America', they remembered the band. And Melanie's tits were always good for business.

'Psst! Hey.' Sarita leant across the congas, a row of bangles jangling on her slim brown wrists as she beckoned to Melanie. Sarita had been born in Goa and raised in Melbourne. She was twenty-six, though she looked about fifteen and was a petite creature with almond-shaped eyes and jet-black hair. Her hair was cropped short and streaked with pink, in open defiance of her Uncle Nazim. A small diamond stud nestled into the side of her nose.

'Mel,' Sarita hissed, finally getting Melanie's attention. 'You gonna tie the knot one day? Put on the big white meringue?'

The bride and groom stumbled towards the dance floor for the final bracket.

'Sure,' replied Melanie. 'As soon as I meet a nice rich banker.'

'Hey! What's wrong with a nice poor musician?' protested Andy. Andy loved listening to the girls talk and joined in whenever possible. He was particularly puppyish around Sarita, who didn't appear to mind.

'Two in the same family? I don't think so.' Melanie smiled. As she turned to check the volume on her amplifier, she caught Richard's eye. He seemed a little wistful.

Melanie pushed a plastic banana out of her eyes and wedged it back into the headdress. She liked Richard, she always had, ever since she'd met him at the second Salsa Kings gig – the night he'd filled in for the original sax player and ended up staying with the band. She liked his wry sense of humour and his lanky body and his soft dark

16

eyes. Years back they'd almost become an item, but there was the small matter of a wife, whom Richard had neglected to mention. Okay, there were extenuating circumstances and he was divorced now, but the damage had been done and Melanie's suspicions about the inherent fickleness of male musicians confirmed. (Female musicians were, of course, noble, true and totally blameless.) Besides, it didn't make sense for two musicians to get together. Unless one of you was a pop star, you'd both end up stony broke.

Melanie was counting on marriage to bring her some kind of financial stability – not wealth, necessarily, but she wanted to see two names on a mortgage one day, one of them belonging to a solvent person. Someone she loved, of course. Love was essential and so was reliability. Melanie had spent a lot of time with unreliable men during her twenties (she referred to her twenties as 'the lost years' or 'the formative years', depending on her mood). But now, in her mid-thirties, she'd become a little more pragmatic. She was tired of the doe-eyed dreamers, with their hearts full of hope. Hoping is a laudable activity but it rarely generates cash. While he's searching the heavens for a sign, you're left scratching around for the rent. Melanie wanted children, so she needed a man with tangible assets, a salt-of-the-earth, weather-any-storm kind of man. A man who would throw himself onto crazed livestock, if the situation demanded.

She sat down at the electric piano; it was a Fender Rhodes called Felix. The last owner had left a faded sticker on the side – Felix the Cat – thus the appellation.

Felix weighed a ton and Melanie needed the lads to help her with him. There were lighter, digital models on the market, but they didn't have weighted keys, so you didn't get the same action. Nothing like sinking your fingers into a Fender Rhodes. For corporate gigs – short, splashy affairs – she'd use a portable keyboard with half the notes. She'd strap it around her neck, enabling her to dance while she played. But for standard sit-down gigs, like tonight's wedding, it was Felix and the full seven octaves.

Melanie arranged the train of her costume so that it cloaked the piano stool and spilled down onto the stage. She was thinking about Gary, wondering whether he got the flowers she'd sent him. I should've written my number on the card, she chided herself, pumping out 'La Bamba' for the thousandth time. There'd been no problem getting Gary's address, the Greater Eastern Show Society had been happy to oblige. They'd given her his phone number too. She hadn't asked, they'd just volunteered it. Security was clearly not an issue in the country.

But she wasn't going to call him. She'd wait a few weeks, then write him a short note, inquiring after his health. She'd include her own number in the note – discreetly, in small print – so that Gary could call *her* if he wanted to. Or not. No pressure, no expectations. Anyway, so what if he didn't call? She wouldn't care, she wouldn't give a monkey's – hell, she didn't even know the guy, he might be a total jerk. She'd only sent the flowers because that's what a person does when another person behaves in a chivalrous and life-saving manner.

She sighed. For God's sake, Melanie, get real. He's

bound to be married. Or, at the very least, betrothed. They marry young in the country. They get promised to someone at birth.

CORAL TREE LANE, SOUTH MELBOURNE

'OOOOeeeee! I saw your map of Tasmania!' squealed Marshall from somewhere down the hallway.

'You did not!' Melanie shouted back.

Standing in the lounge room, Patrick ignored all the squabbling and continued setting the tea trolley. It was late on a Sunday morning and he'd been the first one out of bed, as per the household custom. Melanie had a gig most Saturday nights, so she'd generally sleep in on Sunday. Marshall slept in seven days a week. 'Sleep and bottled water – you can never have enough,' he'd call from under the covers.

Patrick had already taken his morning constitutional up to the markets, collecting the paper and treats from the patisserie on the way home. After a few yoga stretches on the sundeck and a quick shower, he was now padding around barefoot on the shag pile, looking casually stylish in cream chino pants and an aubergine button-up shirt.

Marshall glided into the lounge room, a young Noel Coward in his maroon silk smoking jacket and leather slippers. He waved his hands about, teasing Melanie in a sing-song voice, 'I saw your map of Tasmania! I saw your ma-ap, I saw your ma-ap!'

An aggrieved Melanie shuffled behind him, tripping on her pink candlewick dressing-gown ('the walking bedspread', Marshall called her). 'Marshall,' she whined, never at her best in the morning, 'don't barge in when I'm in the shower.'

'*Barge in*?!' Marshall clapped his hands to his face. 'And *who* didn't lock the door, Missy? D'you think I'd deliberately expose myself to such a terrifying sight?! Ooh, I'm in shock. I've got that post-traumatic . . . trauma thingy.' He raced to the gilt-edged mirror above the china cabinet, inspecting his face for any new lines. 'Patrick, how do I look?'

'Peaky as always, my love,' replied Patrick.

'Liar!' Marshall wrapped his arms around Melanie, blowing raspberries into her neck so she couldn't be cross.

Everybody loved Marshall Jovich. He was thirty-three but a teenager at heart: vain, affectionate and a terrible flirt. He'd have Patrick and Melanie in stitches when he did his soap star impressions, or danced elaborately to Kylie, narrowly avoiding the furniture. Marshall ran his own hair salon, working miracles on his devoted clients, who paid generously for the privilege. His broad, five-foot-seven body was well sculpted from regular workouts, and his olive skin was waxed smooth.

Patrick Kellerman was Marshall's long-term, long-suffering boyfriend. Willowy and soft-spoken, he was six inches taller and ten years older than Marshall. While Marshall was dark-haired and solid, Patrick was fair and fine-boned, with an air of vulnerability. Patrick's idea of a nice night's entertainment was sitting on the couch with a glass of port and reading the latest Ruth Rendell with a Brahms concerto on the stereo. He enjoyed the company of other people but, unlike his show-pony lover, he didn't crave their attention. Patrick was a Visual Merchandising Supervisor (in lay terms, a window dresser) at Leo Dunne's, a large retail chain with stores throughout the country. He'd collected many beautiful things over the years (in addition to Marshall): furniture, paintings, sculptures, exotic rugs and porcelain, all arranged around the house with the skill of a professional.

Being of limited means, Melanie hadn't acquired many possessions of her own. She enjoyed living among Patrick's treasures, and gave him total control of the decor. As she freely admitted – and the boys were quick to agree – she had no eye for decorating. She was good on the aural, bad on the visual.

For the past five years, Melanie, Marshall and Patrick had lived in a cosy terrace house in South Melbourne. A veteran of share-housing, Melanie had decided that single girls should always live with gay men – they're tidy, they're funny and they buy expensive unisex cologne, which they leave on the bathroom sink. In addition, Marshall did Melanie's hair for a tiny fee ('I'm an artist, darling, I have to charge you something'); and Patrick, a whiz on the Singer, with unlimited access to quality fabric, designed and stitched Melanie's costumes for free.

Marshall raced up to his bedroom and bolted back down with a fluffy toy sheep. 'Run, Mel, run!' He pretended to attack Melanie with the sheep, but she wasn't in the mood to play. She pushed Marshall away and he wrestled the sheep to the floor.

'Look out, it's going for the goolies! Eek! That's right, Mel, just run off. Forget about me, you selfish cow, just look after yourself!' He flailed around with the hapless toy, nearly up-ending the coffee table.

'Cup of tea, ladies?' Patrick interrupted, rescuing the sheep from Marshall's clutches.

'Yes please,' replied Melanie, picking up the newspaper and sitting on the couch.

'Yes please,' echoed Marshall, inspecting his knees for carpet burns. 'You're so lucky, Mel – big tough bloke saving your life. Was he good-looking?'

'I think so, it was hard to tell.' Melanie leafed through the paper, looking for the 'piffle pages', as her mother used to call them. Maybe the social section would have photos from a b & s ball, or similar country-style knees-up, where Gary had been snapped with a bunch of jackaroos, all looking deliciously uncomfortable in their tuxedos.

'Oh, go on, give him a call,' pleaded Marshall, desperate for excitement.

'I don't have his number,' Melanie lied, scanning the full-colour spread. There was a fundraiser for the Ancient Egypt Society – a slave girl bursting out of a lamington pyramid, cheered on by numerous Cleopatras. There was an opening-night party at the Merle Oberon Playhouse – bleary-eyed patrons guzzling tequila after five long hours of *Sayonara Fagin-san*, a kabuki reworking of *Oliver Twist*. There were several twenty-firsts, two ruby wedding anniversaries and a very debauched Hawaiian night at the

Fox 'n' Weasel. But no bachelor and spinster ball, and no Gary. Melanie closed the paper and picked up her teacup (fine bone china, Leo Dunne's employee discount).

'Go on, Mel,' whined Marshall, 'you have to *call* him!'

'Not everyone's as brazen as you, Mister Minx,' Patrick scolded, handing out the macaroons. 'Though I must say, Melanie, I am intrigued.'

'I bet they shot the ram,' declared Marshall. 'I bet it was in all the country papers – "Homicidal Ram Goes On Killing Spree".'

'I told you, nobody got killed.' Melanie bit into her biscuit.

'God, it's all so *butch*!' Marshall swooned and collapsed onto the couch.

WYLLANDRA, MAYBURY

In the driveway outside his house, Gary's soon-to-be-ex-wife, Carla, was loading books into the back of a silver Mercedes. Gary hovered, saying nothing.

A pair of pink-and-grey galahs, perched high in a she-oak, started to squawk excitedly. Gary looked up and sniffed the air; like the birds, he could smell the rain coming. He gave it six minutes.

Carla slammed down the boot and moved to the front of the car, Gary trailing behind her. She hopped into the driver's seat and pulled the seat belt across her body with a resolute tug.

'If you find anything else, send it to my lawyer,' she snapped, firing up the engine.

Gary watched the silver sedan as it sped off down the driveway, leaving a cloud of dust. Slowly, he hobbled over to his white Holden ute and drove to the farm next door.

IRON-BAR HOMESTEAD, MAYBURY

Col and Dorothy Quartermaine lived in a grey weatherboard place, built in the twenties. It was functional and drab, belying the considerable wealth at their disposal. The stables in the yard provided a clue: they housed a dozen sleek thoroughbreds whose success on the track had made Col a small fortune. Having a generous cash flow set Col apart from most other Maybury farmers, who were asset-rich but struggled to pay the bills.

At four o'clock each morning, the farm would come to life as a dozen local stablehands pulled up in the driveway. Under Col's watchful eye, they'd ride, groom and care for the horses, prepping them for the big-time professional jockeys in Melbourne, who'd take the reins on race day.

Col Quartermaine was a lean, weather-beaten man in his early sixties. He was a skilled trainer, a knowledgeable farmer and he worked like a Trojan. Col was respected but not particularly liked; he could be hard and unforgiving, and his temper was legendary.

Gary parked the ute under the carport, beating the downpour by a matter of seconds. Gingerly, he made his way to the front door, eased off his boots and dropped them onto the mat. He limped along the hallway, which was covered in flock wallpaper and lined with pictures documenting Col's racing career.

Col had been winning on the track for over forty years. There were wide-shots of his horses galloping to victory (in one race, a stunning trifecta); a jubilant jockey in the winner's circle, hurling his cap into the air; and a giggling Miss Spring Carnival, 1973, feeding daffodils to a sweat-stained filly. There was a smaller black-and-white shot taken in the sixties – a fresh-faced Col, flanked by a couple of race callers. Col was clutching a trophy and smiling broadly, a mop of brown hair falling across one eye. Gary paused to look at the photo, trying to connect this effusive young man with the Col Quartermaine who was sitting in the next room.

Col was at the kitchen table, reading the stock market pages in the *Greater Eastern Gazette*. The morning had gone badly: Green-Bay Lad had pulled a tendon and Shiralee Storm was down with colic. The vet would be over soon. Once he'd sorted out the horses, he'd have the planting to do (a new strain of lupin he was experimenting with), he'd fix the fence-line near the dam, meet the Ag Department bloke about the herbicide and check the stock. Then, after dinner, he'd call the new jockey Ted Mangan had recommended, and eventually he'd start on the paperwork.

Dorothy was standing at the old gas stove, pouring boiling water into a teapot. She wore a blue gingham pinafore over her tracksuit. Tucked under the collar was a delicate gold chain – a gift from her husband. The once luxuriant blonde curls were now grey and thinning, but her blue eyes still shone brightly. They were the eyes of a young beauty who, over forty years ago, had stolen Col's affections.

'Hello, dear, how are you feeling?' Dorothy greeted her son with a quick hug.

Dorothy's day was as busy as her husband's. She had risen early, making a strong pot of coffee for herself and Col. He'd gone off with the horses, down to the race track he'd had built on the property, and she'd gone to the shed to milk Gertie, the jersey cow. Then she'd started on the housework. She'd made a big, hot breakfast for Col and the troops – they'd all turned up as usual after training, at around 8.30.

She was much loved by the stablehands – the troops, as she called them. When they came in for breakfast she'd give them icepacks and liniments for their cuts and bruises and, once Col had left the room, dispense motherly advice on matters of the heart. Later in the day, after feeding the hens, geese and goats, and after a few more hours of cooking and housework, she'd visit them in the stables where they were cleaning the tack. She'd bring them freshly baked scones with lashings of butter. Dorothy's softness was an essential balance to Col's tough line; theirs was a combination that had worked effectively for several decades.

'Hello, Dad.' Gary tried to sound cheerful.

Col grunted, eyes on the page.

'You buying or selling?' Gary nodded at the *Gazette*.

Col said nothing. Folding his arms, he leant back in his

chair and looked straight ahead at the kitchen wall. Dorothy carried two mugs of tea and a plate of lamb sandwiches to the table, then returned to the kitchen bench, where she was making some bread.

'It doesn't look good,' Col spoke in a low, angry voice.

Gary spooned some sugar into his tea.

'That's two wives in ten years.'

Gary pulled his chair closer to the table. The rain was pelting down; he'd have to check on the poddy calves later.

'And there's your cookin' and cleanin' . . .' Col continued.

'I can cook. I like cooking,' Gary protested.

'No job for a man! And don't expect your mother to look after you. She's got enough to worry about.' Suddenly, Col pointed at the refrigerator and addressed his wife: 'Broken gate, bottom paddock.'

Dorothy moved to the fridge door, where a sheet of butcher's paper was secured with magnets. It read: 'Dottie – To Do'. She added 'gate' to the list, then returned to the bench, pounding out a lump of dough with more zeal than was necessary.

'You better find another one, quick smart,' muttered Col.

Gary inspected the chutney in his sandwich.

'Farmer needs a wife,' Col continued, glancing at Dorothy to see how far he could push it. ''Specially you.'

'Uhuh.' Gary wouldn't be drawn.

Dorothy rattled the cutlery drawer.

'She was a good little earner, our Karen.' Col tapped a healthy incisor with his finger. 'She did a good job on m'teeth.'

'Carla, Dad. Her name is Carla.'

Col probed around in his mouth, certain he'd found a cavity in a back molar. 'Guess she won't be doin' m'teeth no more.'

Dorothy dropped a chopping board into the empty sink.

'Guess not.' Gary shifted in his chair, trying to get comfortable. The painkillers were starting to wear off.

'Well, you better start lookin',' muttered Col.

'Yes, Dad.'

'Clock's tickin'.'

'Yes, Dad. I know.' Gary's voice was strained.

Dorothy turned from the sink and glared at her husband. Col gave a grunt and looked down at the *Gazette*, pretending to read the weather chart. Gary drank his tea in silence, listening to the rain as it clattered on the roof.

LINGA-LONGA CAROUSEL, CRANBOURNE

In a vast suburban shopping centre, the Salsa Kings were 'screwing zee big boyce', as José liked to say. Weddings brought a reasonable return, but a corporate gig meant serious money, particularly a product launch like today's. It was a busy Saturday morning, around 11 o'clock. The band was playing on an elevated stage under the centre's much-lauded glass atrium. In keeping with the centre's Easter theme, the musicians had added fluffy white rabbit ears to their standard costume of floral shirts and black pants.

Melanie struggled to keep the ears in place, as they waved cheerily from the top of her Carmen Miranda headdress.

Dotted around the stage were gaudy, free-standing placards advertising 'Tropitang – A carnival in the fridge!' A row of matching posters was tacked to the wall behind the band. Tropitang was a carbonated yellow fruit drink which came in a pineapple-shaped bottle. To enhance the tropical mood, a blanket of lime-green balloons covered the stage floor, the amplifiers were draped with yellow streamers and a rig of overhead lights flashed orange, yellow and red.

In the middle of the stage, towering over the musicians, was a giant mechanical pineapple, more than eighty feet tall. The long green spikes were waving like tentacles, rotating on the fixed yellow base. Melanie kept her distance, worried that the spikes would fly off and come crashing down on her head. She'd escaped the ram, she wasn't going to be done in by a pineapple.

Hundreds of shoppers milled around the centre, pushing trolleys filled with Easter eggs, groceries, new socks and jocks, and various kitchen appliances. They battled their small, protesting children, who kept dragging them back towards the big pink koala, the one handing out the chocolate bilbies.

They rode the lifts and the escalators to pricey boutiques on the skylight level, sports stores and computer dealers on the mezzanine, and bargains in the basement. On ground level – supermarkets, keycutters and salsa bands – the shoppers formed queues along Fast Food Alley, attracted by the smell of deep-frying. Watching Saturday football on the overhead monitors, they occasionally glanced over at the band; a few people bobbed their heads, one woman moved her hips. An excited toddler spun around in circles, squealing with delight as he fell to the floor.

After playing for an hour, the Salsa Kings took a break. Melanie and Richard sat on some cartons at the back of the stage, swigging bottles of Tropitang and surveying the scene. Teenage girls in Tropitang T-shirts, frayed denim shorts and rabbit ears were handing out free samples. The MC grabbed a mike and called for the crowd's attention. Wearing an ill-advised yellow jumpsuit, he darted around the stage like a featherweight boxer.

'Yes, folks, it's a ticket to the tropics! It'll put a spring in your step and a tingle in your nose. People, you know what I'm talking about – I can see it in those beautiful shining faces!' Weaving in and out of the Tropitang placards, the MC held up a bottle of product. 'On the count of three . . . What's the brand new drink for the new millennium?! Everybody just *scream* it out. Here we go, now – one! . . . two! . . . three! . . .'

The crowd stared back in silence, munching on their fish bites and mini donuts.

The MC was undeterred, twirling the mike and going in harder. 'Come on, people, I *know* you can do this!'

At the back of the stage, Consuela Torres appeared, clutching two pay packets. One she handed to Richard, the other she threw at Melanie's feet, hissing abuse in her Chilean-Australian patois. Then, pulling her black cardigan tightly around her shoulders, she spun on her heel and marched off.

'I don't think she likes you,' observed Richard.

'Oh, I don't know,' said Melanie. 'At least she didn't spit on me.'

'This is true,' said Richard, nodding as he watched Consuela depart. Remarkable, he thought, how someone could radiate so much hostility through their back.

Consuela was José's wife – a short, round woman with blue-black hair and suspicion in her eyes. She was convinced that every female in town, including Melanie, was after her husband. This had always struck Melanie as a curious concept, born of blind devotion or too much sangria – or both. She wouldn't have put the words 'José' and 'attractive' in the same sentence. It wasn't only his physical appearance; he had the soul of a rattlesnake.

'Excuse me.' A voice from the crowd. Probably another punter wanting a free T-shirt. Melanie stood up and delved into the carton she'd been sitting on.

'Excuse me, are you Melanie?'

She turned around and there he was.

'I'm Gary Quartermaine.'

Taller than she remembered. Good teeth.

'Yes, of course. Hello.' Melanie blushed furiously, hoping she still had some lipstick on after that last bottle of fizz. 'Oh, heavens. Gosh,' she stammered. 'Well, fancy that. It's you. Gosh, last time I saw you, you were lying on a trolley.'

'Yeah, now I'm pushing one!' Gary declared with a grin.

'Oh. Yes.' Melanie laughed nervously, glancing at the mountain of groceries. Could one man eat this much? He's shopping for the family – gotta be. Wife and ten kids, by the looks of it. Unless he's stocking up. They do that in the country – they stock up . . . Aha, no wedding ring. Of course, he could be married to a European, so he'd wear it on the right hand . . . Nope, both hands vacant. But maybe farmers don't wear a ring, even if they are married. It'd get in the way when they're shearing, or birthing lambs, or whatever they do.

'I like the outfit.' Gary surveyed the fruit on Melanie's head, taking in her lycra-clad breasts and stockinged thighs with his peripheral vision. Today she was wearing the 'Tangerine Dream' version of her Carmen costume with 'extra gardenias to frame the bosoms, darling'. Patrick had made the same design in seven shades of loud.

'Oh, do you?' Melanie blushed again. 'It's, uh, Carmen Miranda.'

'The famous Queen of Salsa,' Richard chimed in, vying for an introduction. Richard was always on the alert for potential rivals. Gary was male and breathing, ergo – threat.

'Oh, right . . . um.' Melanie collected herself. 'Gary . . . Quartermaine . . . this is Richard, Richard Cohen. He plays in the band – saxophone.'

'Great. Love the sax.' Gary shook Richard's hand vigorously. 'John Coltrane, right? *Giant Steps* – great album.'

The country boy had heard of Coltrane? Shaking back with equal vigour, Richard gritted his teeth and refused to be impressed.

'And now, shoppers, here they are – the Tropitang Tappers!' boomed the MC, leaping to one side. A troupe of papier-mâché pineapples on legs thundered into view. The audience perked up considerably.

'So, um, what are you doing in town?' Melanie asked. Too late, the words had left her lips and she was power-less to retrieve them. What does it look like he's doing, the can-can? That's it, now he *knows* you're an idiot.

'Just doing a shop, you know,' said Gary. 'I come up about once a month. We've got shops down home but, you know, it's a lot cheaper up here. There's more stuff you can buy.' Gary's denim shirt brought out the cornflower blue of his eyes. The shirt was half tucked into a pair of faded jeans, which clung to his sturdy thighs and showed off his trim waist. His blond curls caught the sunlight shining through the glass atrium and created a halo effect. Richard eyed him with mounting concern. He was a strapping fig-ure of a man. Damn it, the guy was a prince, and Richard had no option but to hate him. Hate, loathe and despise.

Melanie was struggling to think of questions, fazed by Gary's presence. Of course – the accident. But how could she broach the topic? Surely it's not polite to talk about the man's testicles at this stage of the game. She decided to be diplomatically vague. 'Are you, um . . . are you feeling better?' she inquired, keeping her gaze well above waist level.

'Oh, yeah. Thanks,' muttered Gary, with a grimace. He was suddenly back on the operating table with the knife-wielding surgeon. Then he brightened, recovering his confident swagger. 'Listen, uh, Melanie, that was really nice of you, sending the flowers.'

Flowers?!! Richard's ears pricked up, quick as a

Doberman. She'd sent the guy *flowers*? She'd never sent *him* any flowers, not even when he had his wisdom teeth out. Okay, she'd brought him the jelly and custard – big deal.

'Oh, heavens, that's all right,' cooed Melanie. 'It's the least I could do.'

'I've never been given flowers before,' said Gary, clearly impressed by the gesture.

Melanie's face was warming under his tender gaze. 'Well,' she replied, 'you did save my life.'

'Oh, get away.' Gary looked down and nudged the trolley wheel with his foot. 'Anyway, it'd take more than a sheep to kill you.'

'So *you're* the sheep guy,' said Richard, looking highly amused.

Melanie shot him a look and continued her conversation with Gary.

'I suppose they had to put him down,' she said, determined to establish the seriousness of the episode. 'I mean, a dangerous animal like that.'

'He isn't dangerous – he's just frisky,' replied Gary, not helping her case any. 'Anyway, they're not going to shoot that fella. He's worth over sixty grand.'

'Sixty thousand dollars?!' Richard gasped.

'Yeah, it's big bikkies,' said Gary. 'Well, it's really the sperm you're paying for.'

'Really?' Richard was intrigued. Despite his simmering jealousy he was curious about the professional stud scenario. An entire industry revolving around sperm. As a sperm producer himself, he felt compelled to pursue the topic. 'So, how does that work?' he inquired, trying not to sound too interested. 'I mean, the sperm – selling it and everything?'

The music blasting out of the speakers suddenly got louder. Richard and Melanie sat down on the edge of the stage to get closer to Gary, so he wouldn't have to shout.

'Well,' said Gary, 'first you milk the sperm out of the ram . . .'

'What – you do it yourself?' asked Richard.

'Me and Dad,' said Gary. 'Or one of the strappers, they'll give us a hand. The vet showed us what to do. Once you get the hang of it, it's dead easy.'

'Right,' said Richard, not sure he'd want that particular skill on his CV.

'So you bring in a ewe,' continued Gary. 'The ewe's in season, of course. You get the ram interested, then you deflect the penis into a nice warm AV.'

'Deflect the penis,' thought Melanie, that's a phrase you don't hear too often. It had a certain musicality.

'An AV? That'd be an Artificial . . .' Richard baulked at saying the word.

'That's the one,' Gary saved him. 'It's about eight inches long, and it's made out of poly-piping. You slide in a rubber sleeve, then you fill the space between the outer casing and the sleeve with warm water – that fills out the sleeve, makes it nice and snug. Then there's like a disposable fitting that catches the sperm. So when the boss is done, you remove the fitting, dilute the sperm, pack it up and send it off.'

'Where does it go?' asked Richard.

'Well, we do a lot of business in Argentina – some in China, but mainly Argentina.' Gary was enjoying his superior knowledge. He couldn't play the sax, and he didn't have a hip goatee beard, but he knew about farming.

'So how do you dilute the sperm?' asked Melanie, almost as curious as Richard.

'It's like a glucose kind of fluid. You get it from the vet.'

'And how do you pack it up?' asked Richard.

'Very carefully,' said Gary. 'You pour it into glass straws, then you put the straws into a thermos. It's full of liquid nitrogen – keeps it frozen.'

'Pretty boring for the ram,' mused Richard. 'Whatever happened to leaping around the paddock?'

'Don't worry,' said Gary, 'the old boy gets plenty of action. The señoritas get the frozen stuff, but the local girls get it fresh.' Gary winked. 'Home delivered, if you know what I mean.' Lowering his voice, he looked Richard in the eye. 'You ever see a ram's testicles up close?'

'Ah, no. Can't say that I have.'

'They're *huge*, mate. Bursting at the seams. There's gallons of the stuff. Just let him loose and watch him go. You see, your stud ram, he's a loving machine. He'll service a hundred ewes a day, during season.'

'Wow.' An image flashed across Richard's mind – a hundred voracious women lining up for sex, and one day to get them all pregnant.

'Yeah,' laughed Gary, reading Richard's mind. 'Makes you tired just thinking about it.' Now Richard was laughing too.

Gary suddenly stopped and turned to Melanie. 'Oh,

I'm sorry.' He seemed genuinely contrite. 'I hope I haven't offended you.'

Offended her? Here was a man expressing concern over her tender sensibilities – he obviously didn't know her very well. Still, it was strangely flattering.

'Oh, heavens,' she blustered, dismissing the notion with a wave of her hand.

'Melanie's used to rough talk,' said Richard wryly. 'We play a lot of weddings.'

'Oi! Mel! Richard! Hurry up!' Andy called out from the other side of the stage. The ambulating pineapples were taking their bows and the band was about to start up again.

'Sorry, Gary, we have to go.' Standing up, Melanie picked up her portable keyboard and placed the strap over her head.

'Um, can I call you?' ventured Gary.

'Oh . . .' *Clunk*. Defences in place. Who was this guy anyway? Maybe he wanted to deflect the penis into a nice warm city girl, then run back home to the wife. Maybe he planned to sue her over the ram fiasco. Maybe he belonged to a smock-wearing agrarian cult who were gearing up for a night of fiendish rituals and needed a female of child-bearing age to complete the Satanic circle . . .

Milos played a riff on the trumpet. The band was waiting. Gary held Melanie's gaze, waiting for a response. He looked endearingly hopeful.

She smiled. 'Yeah, sure. Why not?'

Gary reached into his shirt pocket and produced a pen. 'Here,' he said as he handed it to Melanie, 'give us your number.' Then he took a box of Special K out of his shopping trolley. 'Write it on this.' He offered her the cereal. 'Write it under "Special".'

She blinked at him. He smiled. She took the cereal, scribbled down her number and handed it back. Wait, she thought, I'll give him the mobile too – but by then Richard had grabbed her arm and he was bundling her across the stage.

'Hurry up, Mel, they're all waiting,' Richard said gruffly. The thrill of the sperm conversation had passed and he was back to feeling plain old jealous. 'Anyway, you know the rules. You can't go fraternising with the punters.'

'Yeah, right.' Melanie smiled. 'Like you don't. Anyway, he's sweet.' She was revelling in all the male attention, excited by Gary's overtures and surprised by Richard's take-charge behaviour – he was normally so placid. She felt like Anita in *West Side Story*, overseeing a punch-up between the Jets and the Sharks. 'I get so *hot* when zee men start to fight' – or whatever the line was. As a self-proclaimed pacifist, Melanie was bewildered by these primal stirrings. It was *Gladiator* all over again: sitting in the Multiplex, watching Russell and co. and their sweaty, leather-bound chests; all that girding of loins and charging into battle . . .

'Yeah, he's sweet.' Richard rolled his eyes. 'And you're "special".' Joining the other horn players, he stood waiting for the count, muttering to himself. 'Write it under "Special"' – puh-lease. He'd never get away with a line like that. Bloody hick farmer.

Sarita struck four beats on the cowbell and the band launched into a merengue. As she played and moved around the stage, Melanie scanned the Saturday crowd, but her Denim Prince was nowhere to be seen.

CORAL TREE LANE, SOUTH MELBOURNE

By Tuesday night, three and a half days had gone by and Gary Quartermaine still hadn't called. Melanie was soaking in the bath, listening to Marvin Gaye on the radio. Her hair was tucked up inside a plastic grocery bag, ingesting a hot oil treatment; a bright blue seaweed–oatmeal toning mask was setting on her face.

'Eleven minutes past eight o'clock, and tonight we're ridin' the *soullll* train,' crooned the DJ. 'Slidin' into cruise control with Tony Joe White – he's the *maannn* . . .'

Melanie inched further down into the water, closing her eyes and planning the rest of the evening. After her bath she'd work on a couple of new tunes, iron a blouse for work, cook up a heap of popcorn and join the boys on the couch for the late-night movie.

The boys had already installed themselves in the lounge room, where they were nursing their hot chocolates and consulting the TV guide. Marshall had one eye on the phone, which was attached to the wall in the corridor, midway between the lounge–kitchen area and the bathroom.

'Comin' up to eight fifteen, guys and gals, and we're givin' Miss Aretha Franklin a whole lotta *R-E-S-P-E-C-T*.'

Topping up the bath with more hot water, Melanie reached for a tub of hand cream and scooped out a sizeable amount. A blend of coconut oil and vaseline, the lotion was thick and greasy and worked a treat. She massaged it deep into the joints, soothing away the day's typing, making her hands soft and pliable for piano practice later on.

She was thinking about Gary's hands, trying to recall their exact shape and dimensions. They were long hands, she remembered. Long, large, muscular hands – broadened, no doubt, by all that whip-cracking or wrangling or whatever it was that farmers did. She wondered what it would be like to have those hands on her skin – those strong, brown hands caressing her face and neck . . . cupping her soft, white breasts . . .

Suddenly the phone rang. Marshall was out of his seat like a greyhound bursting out of the stalls. Melanie's heart was pounding but she stayed where she was. If it was Gary calling, better that Patrick or Marshall answered the phone so she didn't seem too eager. Sitting up in the bath, Melanie craned her neck towards the door, straining to listen.

'Ah, g'day. It's, uh . . . it's Gary Quartermaine calling . . .'

Marshall put his hand over the mouthpiece and hissed to Patrick, 'It's him! Quick, go and get her!'

Patrick jumped to attention. Marshall resumed his conversation with Gary, adopting a honeyed tone. 'Why, hello Mister Quartermaine, this is Marshall speaking. That's Marshall of Marshall's Style Soirée, but my friends just call me . . . *Irresistible*.'

As Patrick passed by, he gave Marshall's buttock a good, firm pinch.

'Owww!' squawked Marshall. 'Oh, I am sorry,' he purred into the phone. 'Just the manservant accosting me again. Honestly, you can't get good staff any more.'

On hearing Gary's name, Melanie had leapt out of the bath. But she couldn't move her face – the mask had set rock hard. She tried to tear it off, but her hands were still greasy from the coconut vaseline and she couldn't get a decent grip. There was a rap at the door. Melanie grappled unsuccessfully with the doorknob.

'Aye aunt o-hen eet!' she grunted.

Patrick pulled open the bathroom door to find a wet, naked, blue-faced woman with a Coles bag on her head.

'It's him!' Patrick whispered, pointing towards the phone.

'Aye aunt alk!' Melanie jabbed at her face.

Patrick threw a towel around her and started pulling at the seaweed-concrete mask.

Gary wasn't sure he had the right number. 'Look, mate, I was hoping to speak with a young lady called Melanie Francis. Is this –'

'Oh yes,' Marshall interrupted him, 'they *all* want to speak with Melanie. But the thing is, does Melanie want to speak with them? You know, the phone never stops – ring ring ring – I mean, what's a girl to do?'

Marshall was spun around by the shoulders. Seeing an angry Patrick and a half-peeled Melanie staring him down, he let out another squawk.

'Oh, do forgive me,' Marshall gushed into the phone. 'A creature from the Island of Doctor Moreau has just broken into the house, but it's all right, the manservant is showing her off the premises. I'll get Miss Melanie for you. Bye-ee.'

Melanie snatched the phone away from Marshall. 'Hello?'

'Melanie?'

'Yes. Gary, hello.' Hearing the farmer's voice, she suddenly became nervous and started stumbling over her words. 'Um, yeah . . . right . . . look, sorry about that, um . . . about him – you know . . . Marshall, I mean.'

Marshall clutched at his chest as if he'd been knifed in the heart. Patrick herded him out of the house for an unscheduled evening stroll.

'He lives here,' Melanie was gabbling. 'Him and Patrick, there's three of us – friends. Well *they're* not friends – of each other – I mean, they're a couple. Patrick and Marshall – they're together, I'm the friend.' She ran out of breath. There was a brief silence.

'Well,' said Gary, sounding very amused, 'I'm glad we sorted that one out.'

'Yes.' Melanie laughed, the tension now evaporating. 'So am I.' Gary's voice was warm and blokey. He was a cheeky sod and she was liking him more and more.

'Listen, Melanie, it was good to finally meet you.'

'Thanks.' Melanie leant back against the wall. 'You too.'

As she and Gary chatted, Melanie drew patterns in the shag pile with her toes. She felt like a schoolgirl again, and Gary was the handsomest, most popular boy in town, calling to invite her to the Year Twelve ball.

Of course, they hadn't had balls at St Jacobs. Not proper ones. No glamorous gowns or big hair or dancing

42

to a live band under flashing disco lights, like the rich Protestant kids at Bridgedale Ladies' College. At St Jacobs they'd had dreary school socials (jeans and jumpers) in draughty gymnasiums with harsh fluorescent lighting. They'd shuffle about in their desert boots with the lads from St Benjamin's, everyone looking jaundiced under the lights and feeling horribly self-conscious. At regular intervals a team of nuns would go out on patrol. Armed with sticks and torches they'd flush out the 'sirens of Beelzebub' (aka 'Lucifer's dark legion', aka the Year Nine boarders), who could usually be found near the science block, hitching up their skirts and luring 'good boys' into sin.

Back in the gym, the novice priests from St Benjamin's would be operating the portable record player and handing out the party pies and ginger beer. These angelic young men always looked wistful and distracted, as if they were questioning their vocation. At least, that's how they'd looked to Melanie, who was baffled by their choice of career. Why would they opt for a cold, lonely life in the seminary, sleeping on a plank and putting bromide in their tea, when they could have a cosy marital home, a libidinal wife and a king-size bed? It made no sense.

Of course, the priests from St Benjamin's had been the kind ones – quite different to Melanie's teachers, the nuns – the 'Little Sisters of Assault and Battery'. Trained in the ways of the cane, with a natural flair for ridicule, those women could damage your body *and* your soul.

In Year Seven you got Sister Jean-Claude. She had had huge, scary, knotted hands (arthritis, Melanie later realised, with a glimmer of compassion), but she had still been able to grip a long wooden cane and give you ten of the best. Jean-Claude and Sister Philomena were the craziest. Their careers had screamed to a halt when they bullied a student with connections. They'd been banished to a nuns' retreat in a distant suburb, where they remained to this day, stitching altar cloths and mysterious nuns' undergarments, Melanie imagined.

Prior to their forced retirement, Sisters Phil and Jean-Claude had coached the A-grade hockey team (displaying utter contempt for non-sporty girls like Melanie). They'd get into a real lather at the inter-school matches, especially when St Jacobs played the 'heathens' from Bridgedale. They'd race up and down the oval with their long black robes whipping in the wind. 'Get 'em, girls!' they'd scream. 'Get the damned Proddies! Get 'em in the side! Work that stick, Mary-Ellen! Flick that ball, get it high! Get it high!' The A-girls were trained to disable their opponents with an elbow to the ribs, a stick to the shins and, if they could get away with it, a hockey ball to the cranium. Nothing like a head injury to sort out a non-believer.

Sister Jean-Claude had had one human weakness – she'd succumbed to a crush. It was a sad infatuation with a priest from St Ben's who was half her age and oblivious to her interest. He was Father Coughlin (aka Father What-a-waste), a dark-haired dreamboat who'd visit Melanie's Year Seven class to talk about Jesus and teach the girls the recorder. On Friday mornings he'd arrive at the classroom door. Sister Jean-Claude would drop the Cane of Death and start brushing her robes with her twisted claws in a strange act of grooming. 'Ooh, Father

Coughlin,' she'd bluster, her cheeks turning a bright cerise. The girls would save their giggling for the shelter sheds at recess, thus avoiding ten sharp whacks or a *Yellow Pages* to the head.

Father Coughlin, unlike the Sisters of No Mercy, had actually been *fond* of children – in the purest, noblest sense of the word. He'd been kind to the girls; he hadn't threatened them with the laminated posters of hell which graced the classroom walls and still lived in Melanie's nightmares. He'd spoken gently about caring for your neighbour, he'd made jokes and drawn pictures of cartoon characters on the blackboard – Goofy and Donald Duck and Road Runner – which had made the girls beam with happiness.

Father Coughlin was the first man who'd ever been kind to Melanie, the first man to make her laugh, to tell her she was special (admittedly, he'd told all the girls they were special – they were all 'God's sunbeams'). She'd sit at her desk gazing up at him, knowing that one day she'd marry a man just like him. Someone big and gentle and funny and kind – someone who made her feel safe.

'And the band was great,' Gary was saying. ''Specially you, in all the gear and everything. You looked great up there.'

'Oh . . . thanks. Well, it pays the bills,' Melanie stammered. She was thrown by the compliment. She never knew how to handle compliments. 'But you know, I've been wondering, how did you know it was me? '

'Sorry?'

'At the shopping centre,' said Melanie. 'You knew it

was me, you came right up to the stage. But at the show-grounds, you didn't see me – not properly. I mean, you didn't see my face.'

'Yeah, well, you were heading in the other direction.' Gary chuckled.

'God, don't remind me.' Melanie cringed at the thought of her stockinged bottom wobbling violently as she fled the charging ram.

'No, you're right,' said Gary. 'I did see you before – before that time with the ram, I mean. It was at the Mount Malabar Show. I walked into the Trades Hall and there you were, playing the organ. It was great. It was great watching your feet.'

'Right, the feet.' Melanie smiled.

'They're bloody fast,' said Gary. 'Stick you in a barrel of grapes, you'd be pumping out the beaujolais.'

'Yeah, well,' she said with a laugh, 'I do have my uses.'

'My cousin Fraser, he got himself one. One of those Galaxy do-dads,' said Gary, 'with the flashing lights.'

'Right.'

'About six months ago. He showed me that photo of you – the one in the brochure.'

Melanie groaned. 'I hate that photo.'

'Rubbish, you look great. Fraser liked it so much, he stuck it on the fridge. But Deb – that's his wife – Deb got stroppy, took it down.'

'Good.'

'Mind you,' Gary continued, 'you're better in the flesh. I mean, the picture's great, but you . . . well, jeez, Mel, you're beautiful.'

Melanie felt fluttery and girly and silly. Strange, she thought, how a simple remark from the right person could resonate through your entire body, activating all those long-dormant receptors.

'I dunno,' she said. 'You country lads, you're pretty smooth.'

'Yeah, smooth as bloody gravel!' Gary laughed. 'Anyway, listen, Saturday week I'm having some mates over for a meal. I was hoping that maybe you could come too.'

'Well, yeah. Yeah, that sounds great.' No gig that Saturday. The forces of destiny were on her side.

''Course, you can bring a friend. You know, share the driving.'

'Sure. That would be . . . good.' A friend? Did he mean a male friend? Was this a couples thing? 'So, uh, how far is it?'

'About two hours, give or take, now they built the freeway. It's pretty easy to find. Tell us where you live, I'll send you a map. And don't forget your PJs, we've got plenty of room down here. Sunday we'll give you the big tour. You can take a look at a working farm.'

Melanie was a little disturbed by Gary's repeated use of the term 'we', but she gave him the address, thanked him for the invitation and said goodnight. Then she washed her hair and scrubbed off the remnants of the mask. Emerging from the bathroom in her dressing-gown, she found the boys were back from their walk and ensconced in the sofa. They greeted her with eager faces.

'Well?!'

'Dinner party Saturday week. His place. Staying the night.'

'Way to go, Miss Pussy-Galore!' Marshall bounced up and down on the cushions.

Patrick was more circumspect. 'I don't know, Melanie, isn't that a little presumptuous? I mean, a gentleman would never –'

'No, it's nothing like that,' she replied. 'There are plenty of spare rooms, apparently. He asked me to bring a friend.'

'Woo-oo, threesome! Threesome!' Marshall bounced higher.

'Stop it, Marshall, you'll break the springs.' Patrick sighed.

'To share the driving,' continued Melanie. 'He said, bring a friend to share the driving. Do you think he's married? Do you think it's a couples thing?'

'No, dear, you've misunderstood,' Patrick replied. 'Why would a married man ask a single girl to a couples thing?'

'To set her up!' declared Marshall. 'Blind date! He's setting her up with some hairy old wart-hog.' He started snuffling and snorting till Patrick reached over and pinched his nostrils together.

'No, Marshall, I don't think so.' Melanie frowned. 'But it's funny, he kept saying "we". "*We'll* show you around", "*We've* got plenty of room . . ."'

'Oh, Mel,' said Patrick, 'that's how they talk in the country. They're all terribly . . . collective. It's just a figure of speech.'

'Has he got big hands?' asked Marshall. 'Big feet? Big nose?' He loved winding Melanie up.

'He's got a big property, that's all that counts,' said Patrick.

'Maybe in your universe, darling.' Marshall batted his eyelids then switched his attention to a male news-reader on the television. 'Look, look. It's a rug! You see? It's a rug.'

'Anyway, I'm off to do some practice,' said Melanie. 'Give me a hoy when the film starts.' She headed towards the stairs.

'Mel, dear, I think it's wonderful,' said Patrick.

Melanie paused at the bannister as Patrick swivelled in the couch to face her.

'Just think,' he enthused, 'a dinner party in the country! Everyone staying in the guest rooms . . . It's like a week-end with the royal family! All the bright young things off to Sandringham, everyone drinking Pimms and trotting about on the ponies. Very civilised.'

'No, Patty-Pie,' said Marshall as he commandeered the remote. 'They *marry* the ponies, remember?'

Melanie smiled and climbed the stairs. Practice went extra well that night.

THE MAGELLAN HOSPITAL, EAST MELBOURNE

'*I jumped a train in Hilver-su-uh-um* . . .'

The VA's mandatory exercises were in full swing. They'd been designed by a hospital physiotherapist to prevent Repetitive Strain Injury – the scourge of typing pools and tennis courts the world over. Standing at their desks, the typists performed them to music, every hour on the hour.

'*Won't go back to Rotter-da-a-am . . .*'

Mrs Van Asch strode up and down the aisles, singing along at high volume. She always played her son's demo tapes for the workouts. Her son Maarten fronted the Dutch Caps, a retro-grunge-rockabilly outfit in the Netherlands, who'd attracted a small but devoted following.

'*I caught a ride in Gronin-ga-a-an . . .*'

'Come on, ladies, keep up the pace!'

The music was loud and pumping, in stark contrast to the exercises, which were small and low-key, targeting the hands and wrists.

Melanie and Jacqui waited till the VA was out of range.

'So, are you going?' Jacqui was drawing little circles with her index fingers.

'Of course I'm going, but you have to come with me,' replied Melanie, abducting and adducting her thumbs.

'*I found my girl on the Snel-we-geh-eh-en . . .*'

'One-two, one-two. Come on, ladies, stay active, stay attractive!' boomed the VA in her fruity headmistress voice.

'But you're going on a date,' Jacqui insisted.

'It's not a date.' Melanie squeezed her right hand into a fist and pulsed. 'It's a dinner party. There'll be heaps of people.'

'But what about Leroy?' bleated Jacqui. She pushed her palms together, then opened them out, repeating the action, as if closing and opening a book.

The VA strode by. 'Keep those joints lubricated, ladies!' she bellowed.

'Oh, come on, Jacqui,' Melanie hissed. 'You can leave him on his own for *one* night. Maybe he'd like some space.'

Jacqui ignored her, making small rotations with her wrists.

'Look,' Melanie continued, the VA now a good distance away, 'Gary said to bring a friend, and we can stay the night. He's got plenty of beds.'

They pulled in their chins, then relaxed them. In again, relax.

'So . . . what – you're not going to sleep with him?' said Jacqui, her jaw retracting into her Peter Pan collar.

'*Sleep* with him? On a first date?!' Melanie tried to look indignant.

'Ahah! So it *is* a date!' Jacqui smiled triumphantly.

They fanned out their fingers to full stretch, held them for the count of five, then shook their hands violently.

'Flicking off a spider's web! Come on, ladies, flick, flick, flick!' shouted the VA.

The music ended abruptly and the typists dropped to their seats. The VA went into her office and emerged holding a large cardboard box. Proceeding up the aisle, she glared at Melanie and Jacqui, who were far too self-assured for her liking. The younger girls were much easier to intimidate.

'Miss Francis, Miss McGlade . . .' She delved into the box. 'Something for your listening pleasure.' She placed a file and a mini-cassette on each of their desks, then continued along the row. 'Susan, Cardiovascular. Ros, Orthopaedics. Helen, Ophthalmology.'

Melanie looked at the tape and frowned. 'Autopsy.'

'Me too,' said Jacqui.

It wasn't the gore so much, it was the din. An autopsy is a noisy procedure, with high-speed drills and electric saws cutting through bone, and the pathologist shouting over the racket, 'The spleen weighed one hundred and seventy grams and showed extensive capsular sclerosis . . . *grang, grang, grang* . . . the parenchyma was mushy . . . *grang, grang, grang* . . . Oi, Derrick! Whack his liver on the scale, would ya, mate? . . . *grang, grang* . . .'

Jacqui opened her file and winced. 'Can we swap?' she asked. 'I know this man, he used to live on our street.'

'Sure, I'll take it.' Melanie dropped the tape into the transcriber. 'Did you know him very well?'

'Not really. Kind of.'

Melanie adjusted her headset, tapped the pedal and started typing.

'Trevor,' said Jacqui, to no-one in particular. 'Nice old bloke. He had a fig tree in his yard. He used to make lovely jam. Not too sweet. We'd all get a couple of jars.'

'His brain weighed eleven hundred grams,' Melanie reported from under her headset.

'Right,' said Jacqui. She gave a little sigh. 'Thanks, Mel.'

DONOVAN'S DEN, RICHMOND

Donovan's Den was a jazz club on Beverley Street, a short tram ride from the centre of town. Beverley Street was still in the process of gentrification, comprising an even spread of the newly renovated and the slowly mouldering. The club was in the cellar of a red-brick warehouse. The warehouse stood between a silvery art-deco cinema and a seedy no-star hotel.

Donovan's was owned and operated by Brian Donovan, an easy-going, avuncular man in his late forties. Brian was in good physical nick, thanks to years of playing amateur cricket, and still had a full mane of hair, which was greying and shaggy and made him look like a seventies DJ. Brian was friend and confidant to many a Melbourne musician, including Melanie, Richard, Milos, Andy and Sarita. The five players belonged to two different bands: the Salsa Kings, which was the money gig; and the Morangos – a five-piece combo they'd put together especially for Donovan's Den. The Morangos ('the Strawberries', in Portuguese) performed at the club on Thursday nights, presenting an all-Brazilian repertoire. For the musicians, it was a welcome change from reception halls and shopping centres, and with José out of the way, Andy got to play bass guitar instead of lead. Donovan's was an ideal venue for the band, offering an intimate atmosphere, good acoustics and a civilised clientele who refrained from shouting over the music.

The Morangos played a lot of tunes by Tom Jobim – not only 'Girl from Ipanema', but many of his lesser known, equally beautiful creations. They played contemporary tunes made famous by Gal Costa, Caetano Veloso, João Bosco, Elaine Elias and Gilberto Gil – there was a stockpile of Brazilian gems to choose from. They explored the rich harmonies of the bossanova, the vibrancy of the samba, the poignant melodies of the fado.

It was a Thursday night, around ten o'clock. The band was playing 'Agua de Beber' (Water to Drink), a sensual bossa by Jobim. Brian was leaning against a pillar behind the bar, enjoying Richard's solo on tenor sax. Brian preferred tenor to alto – it was a warmer, more full-bodied sound. Thank God he didn't play soprano, thought Brian. If there was one thing that set Brian's teeth on edge, it was the soprano sax. Whoever invented it should be tied to a bench and forced to watch mime artists.

Melanie was playing on the club's piano, a cheap and cheerful upright that had spent most of its life in a dockside pub and had the scars to prove it. Melanie liked playing electric, but it was good to get back to the real thing, even if Brian's piano wasn't exactly a Steinway. And it was good to get out of the costume – no Miss Miranda fruit basket tonight; instead, her hair was hanging down, with the ends slightly curled. She wore a crushed velvet little black dress (House of Patrick) with a faux-pearl choker and a pair of black stilettos.

Melanie sang as she played. She'd picked up some basic Portuguese from a set of language tapes and from listening to Brazilian vocalists. You didn't need a big voice to sing Brazilian; there were no seismic vibratos or booming crescendos. It was a subtle style – light and conversational – and it suited Melanie's smaller, more lyrical voice.

Campbell Walsh, a long-term customer, proffered his empty glass. A senior manager at Veterans' Affairs, Campbell was a good-natured, phlegmatic man in his fifties, his ample girth testament to his love of fine ales. Working with elderly gentlemen, as he did, Campbell was well acquainted with the perils of the comb-over, so rather than cling to his last few strands, he'd shaved his head completely – to the delight of his wife, Eve, a big Yul Brynner fan. Eve was elsewhere tonight, out with her musical theatre appreciation group. She liked show tunes; he liked jazz.

'She's a nice player,' Campbell remarked to Brian, nodding towards Melanie. 'Mellow. She can sing all right too.'

'Yeah.' Brian sighed and filled Campbell's glass. 'Just wish I could buy her a decent piano.'

'Well, mate, you know what to do.'

'Campbell, it's a jazz club. I am not having naked bar-maids.'

'They aren't naked, Brian, they're "scanty". "Scanty ladies" – you'll make a fortune.' Campbell took his beer and pocketed the change. 'All right, clothed ladies. Anything but your ugly mug.' Sipping some froth from the glass, he looked back at the band. 'You know, Melanie and that Richard – they sound good together. They kind of blend, you know? Very cruisy. Are they . . . you know . . . ?'

'You're a nosy bastard.' Brian smiled, hauling a tray of glasses out of the washer.

'Well, you know me.' Campbell reached for the tandoori peanuts. 'Just taking an anthropological interest.'

'But Your Majesty, it's perfect!' Marshall sank to his knees and held out a feather boa, thick with yellow plumes. He offered it up with great reverence, as if it were made of spun gold. Getting no response, he started to whimper.

'No, Marshall.' Melanie was standing firm. 'I'm not wearing it. It's a dinner party, not a street parade.'

'But it's a first date!' Marshall shook the boa impatiently, causing several feathers to dislodge and float to the carpet. 'You've got to make a good impression!'

'Exactly.' Patrick's icy tone put an end to the matter.

The household had gathered in Melanie's bedroom. The boys were in their tank tops and shorts, ready for their Pilates class at Brace Yourself Ladz, a ritzy male gym in Prahran. Melanie was in her bra and Cottontails. They were there to choose an outfit for Melanie's forthcoming social engagement – dinner at the Quartermaine estate – or, as Marshall put it, 'Mel Roots the Ram-Guy'. Despite Marshall's predictions, and her own track record, Melanie was determined to employ restraint. She'd conducted a straw poll at work, her colleagues all agreeing that a lead-in time of ten weeks was fair and reasonable. 'Till you get to know the guy,' came the familiar chorus. Melanie had secretly halved it to five weeks. Maybe three. After all, it'd been a long time between drinks (fourteen months, but who was counting?).

Still clutching the boa, Marshall climbed to his feet, poked his tongue out and plonked himself down on her bed. 'You are a dull little thing,' he said with a scowl.

'Nonsense. She has excellent taste, don't you, dear?' Patrick scooped up the dress he'd selected – olive-green jersey and nicely stitched. One of his best. 'I'll give it a press.'

'You're an angel.' Melanie stood on her toes and kissed Patrick on the cheek.

'Don't encourage him,' Marshall groaned, scratching at the paint on the bedhead. 'He already thinks he's Mother Teresa.'

'That's Father Teresa to you,' trilled Patrick, arranging the dress on a hanger with his elegant hands.

Melanie pulled on her dressing-gown, then sifted through a tray of earrings, deciding against the small hoops and opting for the 'faux-diamond drops' (Patrick made everything sound stylish, even plastic jewellery).

'What d'you think, Mister Dark and Handsome?' She held up the earrings for Marshall's approval, but he just frowned and said nothing, continuing his excavations on the bed.

'Oh, ignore him,' said Patrick, 'he's sulking. One of his clients made him do a spiral, so now he's taking it out –'

'Aaarrghhh!' Marshall interrupted with a shriek, 'Spiral perm!' He leapt to his feet, jabbering, 'I didn't want to do it, Mel, but she made me!' He shook Melanie's shoulders to make his point. 'She forced me! She's cruel and mean – she's a witchy-poo from hell, and she'll never look anything like our little Nicole.' Releasing Melanie, he shook his fist at the ceiling. 'D'you hear me, Mrs Blencowitz? *Never*!' Marshall leant heavily against the wall. 'God, I feel so . . . *violated*.'

'Darling, you were violated long before Mrs Blencowitz hit the chair,' said Patrick, pursing his lips.

Catching his reflection, Marshall suddenly brightened. 'Look, Mel, I'm dark, handsome – and toned!' Marshall rushed to the full-length oval mirror and threw the feather boa around his neck. Preening and pouting, he flung out his muscular arms – which were a little on the short side, though no-one would ever say it. 'All right, Mister De Mille,' he gushed, 'I'm ready for my close-up.'

'Yes, and I'm ready for my cup of tea,' said the willowy Patrick. 'Off you go, Gloria.'

Marshall huffed and tossed back his head. 'Cecil!' he trumpeted, 'I'm working with amateurs . . .' His voice trailed off as he sailed down the stairs.

'He's thrilled about your new fella,' remarked Patrick, checking the dress for any loose threads. 'He's already planning the wedding – your hair is going to look fabulous.'

'Hmm.' Melanie was perusing the shoe rack for something chic yet casual. 'A tad premature, wouldn't you say?'

'Just a tad.' Patrick smiled at Melanie fondly, then he left to join Marshall in the kitchen.

Melanie kept hunting for shoes. She still wasn't sure about Gary. Was he married or single? He hadn't mentioned a wife, but there were plenty of men who didn't mention their wives – the wives who were conveniently away, up in Sydney on business, or down at the hospital giving birth, or back in the old country, nursing a dying relative. The wives who'd eventually return, by which time you've been given the flick and he's had the entire house dry-cleaned to remove any trace of his indiscretion. These were the men, unfettered by conscience, who could compartmentalise their brains into 'short-term', 'long-term' and 'prospective' and slide each hapless female into the corresponding slot.

Melanie's father, Jack, had been a prime example. As a real estate agent it had been all too easy: an abundance of female clients, often in the throes of divorce; irregular working hours ('Don't know when I'll be home, honey'); and a swag of keys to empty apartments. Jack had been an arrogant, ambitious man, always trying to clinch the best deals, drive the hottest car, bed the most women. And his drinking had made him very unpleasant to live with. Melanie's mother, Claire, had put up with it for years, as good Catholic wives were encouraged to do, but had ultimately filed for divorce when Melanie was twelve. Claire had died seven years later from an aneurism. The doctors had told Melanie it was just one of those things, a structural weakness that couldn't be detected. But Melanie had always blamed Jack. While Claire had certainly died from a pre-existing condition, Melanie saw her father as the trigger. Thanks to Jack's appalling behaviour, Claire had been living with constant stress. That kind of relentless anxiety must certainly weaken the immune system, activating all kinds of health problems. If Claire had married a kind, decent, caring man, she'd still be around today – that's how Melanie saw it. She resented Jack deeply for taking her mother away, and she felt she could never forgive him.

He'd never been a proper dad, not like Michael Landon in 'Little House on the Prairie' – Melanie's benchmark for good fathering. He'd never scooped her up, laughing with joy, when she skipped home from school with her lunch pail and her long, swinging plaits; he'd never listened adoringly to her gabbled stories while pouring her glasses of ice-cold milk; he'd never arranged cosy family meetings to discuss Melanie's education and general wellbeing, like Michael did for Laura Ingalls. 'Pick me!' Melanie would shout at the TV. 'I'll come and live on the prairie. Pick me!'

Jack had rarely engaged with Melanie, apart from eyeing her suspiciously and muttering, 'Just like your mother.' He hadn't approved of Claire 'wasting money' on the rented piano and Melanie's weekly music lessons. Melanie had worked hard at her music and she had done well at school academically, but that hadn't impressed Jack, who'd enjoyed reminding her that she was 'crap at sport'. The only activities that had met with Jack's approval were 'pouring Dad's beer' and 'washing Dad's car'.

Maybe Gary had been married at some stage, thought Melanie, but he could easily be divorced by now. A lot of men get divorced. Like Patrick always said, women over thirty shouldn't be fazed by all that 'left on the shelf' palaver. Just look at the stats, he'd say. With a forty per cent divorce rate, a girl could always rely on the Second Round of Offers. It's only a matter of time before another wave of men come stumbling out of their houses, clutching their suitcases – you just have to drive up and grab 'em.

Melanie was tired of being alone. She could survive well enough, but she craved a little warmth in her life. Someone who'd step in and say, 'Hey, mate, that's my wife you're hassling. Back off.' Someone who'd smile adoringly and make her cups of tea while she rambled on about nothing. Someone who'd take her in his big, comforting arms and waltz her around the dance floor till she felt like the Queen of Sheba. He didn't have to be a sporting legend or a rock star or Richard Branson. Just a good, kind man who knew how to make her laugh. It didn't seem like too much to ask.

MAYBURY

Maybury was a farming district in the Greater Eastern region, about one hundred and fifty kilometres south-east of Melbourne, down on Bass Strait. 'Where the Bush Meets the Beach', as it said on the glossy brochures. The dramatic coastline was popular with photographers, inspiring numerous coffee-table books and a cameo in *National Geographic*. Wild seas battered the rocks and sprayed the ancient, towering cliffs at Breakaway Point; the waves flowed onto white beaches, depositing kelp and seashells onto the sand; powerful ocean winds kept shaping and reshaping the dunes.

Beyond the dunes there were vast expanses of bushland. Tiny bush rats and big Eastern Grey kangaroos moved through the dense scrub towards open pastures, attracted by the lupins and maize. Thanks to an abundance of rainfall, the farmland in the region was lush and fertile.

Maybury's human population changed with the seasons. For most of the year it numbered five thousand, but for ten weeks over summer it swelled to more than thirty thousand, as city dwellers flocked to the coast, filling the guesthouses and caravan parks, splashing in the surf and boosting the local economy.

Maybury was primarily a sheep and cattle region, producing wool, lamb and beef. Two large dairies supplied milk and cream to Mount Malabar and Melbourne.

In the township there were two pubs, a post office, a small supermarket, butcher, baker, newsagency, hair salon, barber, coffee lounge, Chinese restaurant and video store. There was no actual cinema but the Barking Shark ran film nights in the ladies lounge, or in the beer garden in summer. (Barry, the publican, was a George Kukor enthusiast and screened *The Philadelphia Story* at every opportunity.) There was a small medical centre, a community hall and two primary schools. Secondary students were bussed up to Mount Malabar. The town was built around the glistening waters of Maybury Bay; a flotilla of dinghies, fishing boats and yachts lay anchored in the harbour. On the pier was Bella's Seafood Emporium, justifiably famous for the best calamari rings in the southern hemisphere.

According to Gary's map, it was an easy run to the farm. '2–2½ hrs max' he'd scrawled in the margin. After four hours on the road, Melanie and Jacqui were starting to worry. Several wrong turns had taken them to a quarry, a football field ('Home of the Mighty Goannas', apparently) and a yabby farm. One track looked promising; they followed it for forty minutes, finding only a broken windmill and a half-filled dam. Attempting to leave, they came bumper-to-snout with a huge feral pig.

'Razorback!' gasped Jacqui. She'd seen one before on the telly.

Melanie revved the engine and blasted the horn, but the pig wouldn't budge, so she switched off the car and they waited. Eventually the pig got bored and wandered off, and the two women fled the scene at high speed.

When they finally arrived at Gary's, it was past nine o'clock. They pulled up at the letterbox and Jacqui leant out of the passenger window with her key-ring torch.

'Wyllandra,' she read. 'G Quartermaine, RMB 129, Maybury. Yep, this is it.'

But Melanie didn't answer – the view had rendered her speechless. Directly ahead was a long, steep driveway, lined with elegant she-oaks. At the end of the drive, illuminated by floodlights, was a magnificent two-storey home – a contemporary building constructed with natural timbers, bluestone and a sea of glass. A short distance from the house there was a small bluestone cottage. The cottage walls were covered with yellow climbing roses and ivy. Tall lavender bushes framed the porch.

Jacqui whistled in admiration. 'Location, location.'

Proceeding up the drive, Melanie parked her trusty blue Laser next to two white utes, a sporty black four-wheel drive and an elderly brown station wagon. A well-scrubbed Gary emerged from the front door and strode towards them, throwing out his arms in a gesture of welcome. His blue eyes were shining and his blond curls gleamed under the floodlights.

'Mel, he's gorgeous!' Jacqui gasped.

He wore a sports jacket, pinstriped shirt, moleskin trousers and RM Williams boots, and looked very dashing – every inch the wealthy Australian farmer. Jacqui was in her favourite Laura Ashley paisley print and Melanie wore the House of Patrick green jersey. Looking at Gary's attire, they were glad they'd opted for a slightly formal look. As Patrick always said, there was nothing like a well-cut frock to highlight a girl's assets (and camouflage the rest).

'You made it! Good trip? Come in, come in.' Gary took the cat box and the overnight bags out of the car and ushered his visitors towards the house. On the way they passed a large tin shed, and Gary paused for a moment at the shed door.

'You wanna see me girl?' He motioned for the women to take a look.

Melanie's heart froze. His 'girl'? With her luck, there'd probably be a half-starved milkmaid inside, chained to a pillar. She exchanged a nervous glance with Jacqui, and together they peered into the shed. To their mutual relief, it was only a tractor.

'Vintage model,' said Gary proudly. 'Nineteen-fifty-nine TEA20 Massey Ferguson. Restored her myself.'

'It's, um, a nice colour,' said Melanie, who knew nothing about machinery.

'Yes,' added Jacqui, who knew even less. 'It's very . . . red.'

From inside his wicker basket, Leroy started to hiss and spit. Alarmed, Jacqui leant down to look through the basket's wire grill. 'What is it, boy? What is it?'

'Oh, sorry, ladies,' said Gary. 'I was gonna tie him up.'

A dark shape lumbered into view; it was a brown-and-white springer spaniel. Stopping at Gary's feet the dog looked up expectantly.

'It's only Marmite,' Gary explained. 'He's just scrounging for food. Git, boy!' he growled at the dog. 'Git!'

Marmite hauled his generous girth back towards the verandah, where his mattress and blanket awaited.

Gary took the two women into the house and down the corridor to their rooms, where he unloaded the luggage. There were folded towels and little guest soaps at the end of each bed, and a sprig of lavender on the pillows. Jacqui stayed back for a moment to reassure Leroy, then she joined Gary and Melanie, who were now in the lounge room.

It was the largest room in the house, with a high ceiling and exposed wooden beams. In one corner there was a wooden staircase leading up to even more guest rooms. The centrepiece of the lounge room was a large bluestone fireplace with a stained jarrah mantel. A log fire was crackling in the grate.

Gary pushed open a set of sliding doors, which led into the dining room and kitchen – an open-plan affair. As in the lounge room, the windows were floor-to-ceiling. There were five guests at the dining-room table, though it could easily seat a dozen. Behind a marble workbench was the kitchen area, with a casserole simmering on the stove and freshly baked bread warming in the oven.

'Here they are, folks!' announced Gary. 'Our intrepid travellers. Melanie and Jacqui, this is Brendan, Rosalie,

Simon, Pip, Blodwyn.' There was much hello-ing and standing and scraping of chairs. Melanie apologised for being late, explaining they'd lost their way.

'We got bailed up by a razorback!' said Jacqui, still recovering from her brush with nature.

'Yeah? Whereabouts?' asked Brendan.

'We were driving along a track,' Melanie explained. 'It was near a windmill.'

'Ah, that'd be ole Trotsky,' said Gary.

'Dan Carmody's pig,' said Brendan. 'Brought him back from Darwin.' Brendan Buchanan was a big shambling man, aged around fifty, with a thick grey ponytail and a bushy beard. He was wearing a windcheater and faded jeans.

'Trotsky likes scorched almonds,' said Rosalie, Brendan's wife. 'If you feed him scorched almonds, he's as gentle as a kitten.' Rosalie, also fifty-ish, was a large, rotund woman, blessed with luxuriant tresses of long, henna-red hair. She wore a bright floral kaftan and around her neck hung numerous strings of clattering wooden beads.

Next to Rosalie was the smaller, slimmer Simon O'Reagan. In his mid-twenties, Simon wore a brown crumpled suit and steel-rimmed glasses. He looked rather like an accountant. Simon's partner, Pip Webster, was a sporty, toothy girl with a blonde bob, also in her mid-twenties. She wore a pastel-blue tracksuit and a perpetually sunny expression, contrasting markedly with the gaunt, surly woman sitting next to her – Blodwyn Platt. Blodwyn looked to be in her late thirties and was dressed in a baggy black shirt and black jodhpurs. She was pale and thin, and her coarse, brown hair was cropped close to her head. She reminded Melanie of a whippet.

Jacqui popped out to the bathroom and appeared a few minutes later in the doorway, holding Leroy. She admitted she'd been anxious about leaving him in the bedroom on his own, so she'd gone back to retrieve him. Oblivious to the assembled humans, Leroy began casing the joint for other felines. Realising he was the only cat within cooee, he swaggered about with renewed confidence, claiming the territory as his own.

After a round of vodka and tonics, dinner was served. Sweet potato soup with warm sourdough bread was followed by Mongolian lamb and basmati rice – all of it delicious. At short notice, Gary had whipped up a cheese soufflé for Jacqui. Melanie had forgotten to mention that Jacqui was a vegetarian – unlike Leroy, who was now sleeping in front of the fire with a bellyful of Maybury mince.

As the evening progressed, Melanie and Jacqui learnt more about the other guests. Brendan was Maybury's all-purpose handyman, Gary explained, and he could fix pretty well anything, from kitchen blenders to combine harvesters. Rosalie worked as a volunteer ranger, caring for injured and abandoned wildlife. The mild-mannered Simon was a self-described 'eco-warrior'. He worked for a government agency called SLUDGE – Salinity, Land Utilisation and Degradation in the Greater Eastern. Perky Pip was a food technologist with the Sheep Board and was very excited about her current project: developing flavoured sheep yoghurts for the primary-school market.

Despite the 'Baa-nana' debacle, she still had hopes for the Choc Mint. Blodwyn was a high school teacher who taught up at Mount Malabar but lived in Maybury. Her partner couldn't make it that evening, which may have explained her sullen demeanour. She only picked at her food, which Melanie couldn't understand – Gary's cooking was fantastic.

Gary was topping up the red wine, while a sozzled Brendan held court.

'Bloody Wenn-eyes, they're the worst,' Brendan said as he waved his fork around. 'Move down here an' all they talk about is "Wenn-eye was in Melbourne . . . Wenn-eye was in London . . . Wenn-eye was in bloody Timbuktu." If it's so good, why don't they go back, eh?'

'But you're both Come Overs,' Pip explained, addressing Melanie and Jacqui. 'We like Come Overs.'

'Yep, you girls pass the test,' said Gary, walking behind Melanie's chair on his way to the kitchen.

Melanie looked up at him and he smiled – a gorgeous, corn-fed, knowing smile that made her tingle all over.

'We saw a beautiful pub on the way in,' said Jacqui, interrupting Melanie's reverie. 'The Barking Shark – it looks pretty old. Is it Georgian?'

'It's heritage, I know that much,' said Simon. 'Barry can't change a light bulb without consulting the National Trust.'

'Good thing too,' declared Rosalie.

'Blodwyn, you're the history teacher,' said Gary. He manoeuvred a hot baking dish out of the oven. 'What year did they build the Shark?'

'Wouldn't have a clue,' said Blodwyn coolly, fingering her wine glass. There was an uncomfortable pause.

'Blodwyn – that's an interesting name,' said Jacqui, trying to rescue the mood. 'Is it Scandinavian?'

'Welsh.' Still icy.

'The kids love it,' Brendan guffawed. 'What do they call you? "Blod the Plod"?'

'Yes, and they call you big fat stupid Brendan,' countered Rosalie. She patted Blodwyn's hand and continued, 'You ignore him, dear, it's a fine Celtic name.'

Gary arrived at the table with a steaming dessert.

'Sticky toffee pudding! Yummo!' Pip brandished a spoon and reached for the whipped cream.

After dinner they moved to the lounge for coffee and Sambucas. Pip and Simon had already left – they'd be planting trees the next morning, somewhere up the coast. Jacqui had called it a night. It'd been a long drive and she wanted to get Leroy settled with some warm milk. Blodwyn and Brendan were leaning against the mantelpiece, warming their hands on the fire and arguing about the Crimean War. Melanie was sitting on a long dove-grey leather couch, in between Gary and Rosalie.

'We get heaps of bottle-nosed dolphins,' said Rosalie. 'And Southern Right whales – they come right into Breakaway Point. Gary, we should take her out on the boat one day! Would you like that, Melanie?'

'Well, yes.' Melanie beamed, imagining herself on the

bow of the boat, wrapped in Gary's arms as the marine life frolicked around them. 'Yes, that would be great.'

'No worries.' Gary smiled at her. 'I'll have a talk to Ted, see if –'

'Ooh!! Guess what?!' Rosalie leapt to her feet. 'Gary's got a fat-tailed dunnart!'

Melanie paused, unsure of how to respond.

'It's a beastie,' said Brendan with a laugh, on seeing Melanie's expression. 'A local beastie, like me.'

'Much nicer than you, you big lug,' said Rosalie, then she smiled at Melanie. 'It's a dear little native animal that lives around here.'

'A rat,' said Brendan. 'A big ugly rat.'

'Excuse me, Brendan, it's very handsome!' Rosalie pretended to be annoyed with her husband. This was clearly one of their favourite arguments. She turned to Melanie and Gary. 'Come on,' she said, grabbing her shawl, 'let's go take a look.'

As Rosalie made for the verandah, Gary found a jumper and some gumboots for Melanie. They both followed Rosalie into the night, collecting a torch on the way out. Blodwyn and Brendan topped up their Sambucas and took over the couch.

The party of three ambled across the paddocks, a big orange moon (and the torch) helping to light their way. Melanie couldn't amble too gracefully in Gary's big gumboots, though she liked the way he caught her when she tripped.

'You see, your fat-tailed dunnart,' Rosalie was saying, 'he stores food in his tail – like a camel stores water in its hump. Hence the fat tail.'

They reached a large area of scrub. Rosalie put a cautionary finger to her Frosted Orange lips.

'There's a burrow in here,' she whispered. 'You have to approach in a zigzag. If you zigzag towards an animal, they don't pick up your scent.'

Thanks to too much good wine, the trio's attempts at zigzagging soon degenerated into circular stumbling, Gary and Melanie trying to stifle their laughter.

'Sssshhh!' Rosalie feigned annoyance, but before long she was giggling too.

'Over there!' Gary had spotted something. But it wasn't a dunnart, it was a spiny anteater. Or, as Rosalie corrected him, a 'short-beaked echidna'.

Gary moved the torch in closer to get a better look. Alarmed, the echidna took action. At high speed, it burrowed into the earth with its powerful claws, the dirt flying up as it gradually sank from view.

'That's amazing!' Melanie gasped. The ground had literally swallowed it up.

'It's a good trick,' said Gary.

'Did you see the spurs on its back legs?' asked Rosalie. 'That means it's a male. They use them to fight with other males. Very nasty, those spurs. They can do a lot of damage. '

'Ah yes,' said Gary, 'it's the old story: boy meets girl, boy kills other boys . . .'

'Not always,' said Rosalie, resting her well-padded body against a rock. 'Sometimes it's the girls who kill the boys. Like the yellow-footed antechinus.'

'The what?!' laughed Gary. Melanie laughed too. She

was happy and light-headed and everything seemed funny tonight.

'It's like a hedgehog and a mouse mixed together,' said Rosalie. 'When they have sex, it goes on for twelve hours straight – twelve hours of non-stop bonking. Then the male drops dead.'

'I'm not surprised!' exclaimed Gary. 'I think I'd drop dead after that kind of effort.'

'Hmm.' Rosalie put her hands on her hips. 'That's not what I've heard, ducky.' She winked at Melanie.

'Yeah, yeah, enough of that,' Gary said with a grin. 'Don't listen to this woman, Mel, she's an inveterate liar.' He put his arm around Rosalie's waist, her wooden beads clattering as she responded with a generous hug.

Melanie looked on, smiling to herself. In a few short hours she'd learnt a lot about Gary: he was an affection-ate man, he could laugh at himself and he didn't make other people feel small. He was different to a lot of the men she'd met lately, the men who'd talk to you at parties and keep looking over your shoulder for the people they should be impressing.

They returned to the house, Melanie kicking off her gumboots and leaving them on the verandah. Blodwyn had already departed in her zippy four-wheel drive and Brendan was now snoring on the couch. Rosalie poured her husband into the station wagon and they headed off down the drive. This left Melanie and Gary, alone, stand-ing in the semi-darkened lounge room. Melanie surveyed the scene: gorgeous man and big, inviting couch in front of smouldering fire – way too risky.

She pulled off Gary's bulky jumper. 'Well,' she said, handing it back to him, 'better call it a night.'

'Oh.' Gary couldn't hide his disappointment. 'Really?'

'Early start in the morning.' Melanie tried to sound convincing. 'Long drive back to town.'

Gary smiled. 'It's only two hours.'

Melanie smiled back. 'Yeah, right,' she said. 'Two hours on your map, four hours on mine.'

'You know,' said Gary, trying to buy some time, 'it isn't really that late.' He motioned towards the couch. 'We could sit down for a while, have a couple of ports. The fire looks good . . .'

'Yeah, it does.' Melanie paused for a moment, then started backing out of the room. 'But I really have to get some sleep. Thanks anyway. Goodnight.'

'Night.' Gary watched her as she disappeared down the corridor. He proceeded to lock up the house. He switched off all the lights, put the guard in front of the fire and eventually retired to the master bedroom at the end of the corridor, not too far from Melanie and Jacqui.

After a shower in the guest bathroom adjoining her bedroom, Melanie climbed into her flannelette pyjamas. She opened the bedroom window and drew back the curtains so she could see the moon. Then she switched off the lamp and got into the single bed. But she didn't sleep – she was a bit drunk and pleasantly aroused by the memories of Gary brushing past her all night. And there he was in his big soft bed, only metres away, naked probably, all alone and hungry for affection. Ignoring her natural impulses, Melanie snuggled deeper under the bedclothes.

For some reason, possibly connected to rogue DNA from the Neolithic, men still needed The Chase – Melanie knew this. Without The Chase, they wouldn't value The Conquest. Silly, really, this struggle to appear unattainable. Here she was, an experienced woman, affecting a virginal coyness for the purposes of entrapment. Still, as Patrick always said, 'Whatever it takes, darling, whatever it takes.'

There was a gentle tap at the door.

'Yes?' said Melanie, sitting up in bed. For a moment she thought it might be Him. No, she decided, it'll be Jacqui, wanting to talk. What happened after dinner? Did he kiss her goodnight? Do cats have nightmares . . . ?

Slowly the door opened. Standing in the hallway, resplendent in the moonlight, was her host, the delectable Gary. Still in his shirt and trousers, but minus the boots, he leant against the doorframe.

'Hi.' He spoke in a whisper, aware of Jacqui in the next room. 'Is everything okay?'

'It's fine,' Melanie whispered back, her pulse racing.

'Do you need any more towels?'

'No thanks, I'm fine.'

'I'm glad you girls could make it down. It was a good night.'

'We had a great time. You're a terrific cook.'

'Thanks.' Gary paused for a moment, unsure of what to do next. He looked over at the bedroom window. 'Right. I just gotta . . .' He crossed to the window and closed it tight.

'Oh, can't you keep it open?' asked Melanie. 'The breeze is lovely.'

'Yeah, sorry,' replied Gary, searching for an excuse. 'But, well, at night you gotta lock everything up.'

'But isn't it pretty safe round here?' Melanie pulled up the doona to hide her unprovocative pyjamas.

'Sure,' said Gary, flicking the lock. 'But we get some big goannas. Clever buggers. They can open a window in ten seconds.'

'Right.' That's a new one, she thought. House-breaking goannas.

Moving back towards the door, Gary paused at the end of the bed. 'May I?'

'Um, sure. Okay,' replied Melanie, with all the coyness she could muster.

Politely, Gary perched on the bed. He picked up a small satin cushion and kneaded it with his large, strong hands. 'It was a good night, eh?'

'Yeah,' said Melanie, 'it was great.'

Gary shifted further up the bed. Melanie caught the alluring scent of his pheromones, mixed with a dash of aftershave. Dropping the cushion, he took Melanie's hand. His skin was warm. She tried to stay focused.

'Listen, Mel, thanks for coming to see me,' he murmured.

'That's all right,' she murmured back.

Very gently, he leant in and kissed her on the mouth. It was subtle and sweet. She felt a soft, exquisite thrill. He kissed her again, pulling her closer. She could feel the blood heating in her veins, the warmth enveloping her body. He continued kissing her for some time – languid and teasing, exploring her lips, her face, the side of her neck.

Then he lowered her head onto the pillow and, very slowly, started moving on top of her, kissing her all the while. She sighed, revelling in the sensation. To feel the weight of a man's body again, after such a long, lonely time – she'd forgotten how truly sublime it could be. She reached out to cradle the back of his head, then slid her hands along his muscular back, down to his waist. Gary's body stiffened in response. He groaned and kissed her mouth deeply, caressing her breasts through the pyjamas, freeing the buttons with consummate ease.

Melanie was slowly slipping into delirium when, suddenly, a bunch of typists were shouting in her head. 'Wait till you get to know the guy!' they roared. And there was Patrick, tapping his foot and wagging his finger. 'Man the Hunter, Man the Hunter . . .' They were right, of course. She had to remember The Chase. It was absolute bloody rubbish, but there it was. She rallied her dwindling defences.

'Um, this is lovely,' she whispered. 'In fact, it's wonderful . . . but . . .'

'Hmm, s'wunnerful.' Gary's mouth was on her breast, his body pressing into hers with increasing urgency.

Melanie took a deep breath and struggled to sit up, pulling at her pyjama top. 'I'm sorry,' she gasped, doing up the buttons. 'It's fantastic, but, well, you understand . . . it's just . . .'

Reluctantly, Gary sat back up on the bed. His face was flushed and his blond, choir-boy curls were damp with sweat.

'You're right, you're right,' he said, not really meaning

it. He raked a hand through his hair. 'Wasn't thinking. Got a bit carried away.'

'Look, I'm sorry.' Mel was pulling up the covers. 'I shouldn't have . . .'

'No, don't apologise. It's me. *I'm* sorry.' Then he smiled – that knowing, corn-fed smile. 'Well, I'm not sorry, but, you know . . .'

Melanie couldn't believe she was doing this. She was drunk, she was happy, she was virtually naked with this big hunk of wranglin' man, and she was saying *no*?!

Gary was gazing at her now, brushing her cheek with the back of his hand. She went to speak and he pressed a finger to her lips.

'It's okay,' he whispered, 'there's plenty of time.' His voice was warm and kind. 'Plenty of time.'

TIVOLI GARDENS, ALBERT PARK

Up in the city, another dinner was in progress. It was a modest affair in a small, humble flat rented by Milos Novotny, Salsa Kings trumpet meister, and his girlfriend, Renata Cerná. The building was owned by Art-House Inc, a charitable trust providing low-cost accommodation for musicians, actors and dancers. There was a long waiting list for the flats. Entry by audition.

It was a dinner for three – Milos, Renata and Richard Cohen. Richard, who lived upstairs on the third floor, was a big fan of Renata's cooking. It was Eastern

European, like the food his mother used to make. Roszika, Richard's mother, was a pianist from Budapest, who'd migrated to Australia in the fifties. She met Richard's father at Jazz Centre 44, a club in St Kilda. Larry was a shy, blue-eyed accountant from Romania, who'd bravely approached the young pianist and asked her if she knew any Cole Porter. These days Larry and Roszika lived on the Gold Coast, in a retirement village called Maison Mazeltov. There, Roszika ran a swing band for seniors and Larry cheered her on from the front row. Richard was tall like his father, with the same dark curls, but he had Roszika's gentle brown eyes and her talent for music.

Renata Cerná was a small, sensible woman of thirty-eight, with olive skin and shoulder-length mousy hair. She and Milos had been sweethearts since school, more than twenty years ago. Milos was always the first to leave a gig so he could hurry home to his little 'Natka'. Richard liked being around his two friends, but there were times when he envied them their happiness.

Tonight Renata had prepared her standard menu – schnitzels, potatoes, blintzes, dumplings and creamed spinach – all tasty and substantial. She brought some bottles of Pilsener from the kitchen and bustled around the table, ladling food onto plates.

'It's okay, I can do this.' Richard took over serving and Renata sat down.

'So, where is Melanie tonight?' she enquired.

'Oh, she's gone off to the country – some kind of dinner,' replied Richard, trying to sound indifferent.

'A romantic dinner?' Milos piled potatoes onto his plate.

'No,' said Richard, a little too quickly. 'It's just a friend. Some . . . farmer, I dunno. She's probably selling him a keyboard. You know Mel, she does all those gigs in the country. At the shows.'

'Shows?' queried Milos.

'Agricultural shows,' explained Richard. 'Cows and monster trucks. Horrible.'

'A farmer?' Renata was impressed. 'Is good to find a man with property.'

'Like me!' Milos squeezed Renata's hand. 'I have beautiful Falcon car.'

'You know this farmer?' Renata had taken a keen interest, much to Richard's annoyance.

'I've met him,' Richard muttered, pouring himself a beer.

'Is nice, a man who work on the land. They have . . . grunt,' said Renata, her eyes lighting up.

'Grunt?' Richard wasn't familiar with the concept.

'Is good to have grunt,' said Milos.

'Just a bit – not too much,' added Renata.

'Do I have grunt?' ventured Richard.

Milos and Renata exchanged a look and Renata reached for Richard's plate.

'Schnitzel?'

The following afternoon, Melanie and Richard and the rest of the Salsa Kings were playing a Sunday wedding – a last-minute booking. Melanie and Jacqui had driven up from Maybury early that morning. There had been no time for a tour of the farm, as originally planned, and barely enough time for coffee. Leaning in through the car window, Gary had wished them both a safe trip, then, *sotto voce* to Melanie: 'I'll call you.' Jacqui just wanted to get out of there before Leroy got taken by one of those giant goannas.

Inside a fancy white marquee, the Kings were playing an up-tempo version of 'Auld Lang Syne', as the guests bade farewell to the bride and groom. It had been a constant battle to keep sand out of the instruments. Beach weddings were romantic but they could ruin your equipment. The guests trundled down to the shore, where there was the usual scuffle over the bouquet. The newlyweds boarded a speedboat and rocketed through the surf, bound for connubial bliss.

The musicians started packing up their gear. Consuela was at the mixing desk, pulling out leads. Melanie was grappling with her keyboard stand, trying to fold it back up.

'D'you want a hand?' Richard took over, as per their ritual.

'Thanks, Richard. Oh, excuse me – José!'

'Sí?' José turned around, hoping to find that cute waitress he'd had his eye on, but much to his annoyance it was only Melanie.

'Consuela keeps turning down my foldback,' said Melanie. 'I can't hear what I'm playing.'

'Ees new for her,' said José. 'Everybody make mistake sometime.'

'She does it deliberately. You know she does.'

José turned his back on Melanie, ignoring her pleas. 'Ricardo,' he said, 'take zee gear back to shop.' He handed Richard a small brown paper parcel. 'Here ees money, okay? For Antonella. You give to her.' Then he left to confer with the bride's father, who was busy writing out cheques.

'He is such a pig.' Melanie shoved some leads into a plastic bag.

'Yep, that's José.' Richard slid the parcel into his jacket pocket. 'Mind you, he's getting better. He played four songs in the right key today.'

Melanie smiled despite herself. 'That's gotta be some kind of record.'

'See you at Donovan's?' asked Richard hopefully.

'No, I can't tonight,' replied Melanie. 'We're having a thing at home – one of Marshall's little evenings. Bitchin' Bingo, he calls it. Take-away Thai, too much beer and half a dozen hairdressers screaming "Legs eleven!".'

'Sounds like fun.' Richard smiled.

'It is actually.' Melanie smiled back.

Richard picked up an amplifier and hauled it out of the tent. Pausing at the entrance, he called back to Melanie, 'If you change your mind . . .'

GOOD VIBRATIONS, ESSENDON

Richard lurched into the hire shop with the amplifier. A young woman with short dark plaits was leaning against the counter, flicking through a magazine and snapping gum. She wore baggy jeans and Doc Marten boots. Her T-shirt read: 'Don't ask me about my thesis.'

'Hi Richard.'

'Hi Antonella.'

'Nelly.'

'Nelly. I'll put this one out the back, okay? There's more in the van.'

'Need a hand?' she asked, not looking up from the magazine.

'I'm right. How's your dad?' Richard wheezed, negotiating a tight corner.

'He's okay.'

Richard disappeared behind the counter into one of the storerooms.

The bell on the shop door tinkled and two men sauntered in. It was the Sciarelli brothers: Australian-born from Calabrian stock. Michael, in his late thirties, was very much the older brother, the caller of shots. Johnny, in his mid-twenties, took orders from Michael and knew his place. They were big men, well over six foot and solidly built. Both wore dark suits, neatly pressed and several years out of date, and Saint Christopher medals on thin silver chains. They were clean-shaven and sweet smelling, with short blue–black hair and baby-soft skin.

The instant Nelly saw them she reached into the till and

pulled out a white envelope. Anxiously, she handed it to Michael. He peered into the envelope then looked up at her with an angry, accusing face.

'Dad said to tell you that's all there is,' Nelly explained, her breathing becoming more rapid.

Richard emerged from the storeroom door, just behind Nelly. He didn't see the two brothers – Nelly was blocking his view. Unaware of her predicament, Richard reached into his pocket and took out the brown-paper parcel José had given him. 'Here ya go.' He handed it to Nelly.

Michael leapt on the parcel and snatched it away from her. 'I'll take that.'

'Oi!' Richard shouted.

'It's okay, mate,' said Michael. 'Just settling an old account.'

Johnny moved a step closer to Richard and puffed out his chest. The Sciarellis were doing business and pesky interlopers would not be tolerated.

'It's okay, Richard. Really, it's okay.' Nelly didn't want any dramas in the shop; there was valuable gear on the shelves.

Michael ripped open the parcel. It contained a clear plastic bag, filled with premium-grade marijuana. He opened the bag and sniffed, then he showed it to Johnny.

'That's dope.' Johnny was clearly surprised.

Richard was as surprised as anyone.

Michael eyed him suspiciously. 'What else you selling?'

'Nothing! I thought it was cash – cash to pay for the sound gear,' jabbered Richard.

'Richard didn't know,' said Nelly hastily. 'It's for my dad. He takes it for his arthritis.'

'Really, does it help?' asked Johnny. He turned to Michael. 'You know, Auntie Emmy's got bad arthritis, maybe she should take it too . . .'

Michael silenced his brother with a fierce glare. Then he lunged at Richard, grabbing his collar and hauling him across the counter. He spoke quietly and angrily into Richard's face.

'Now listen, mate, the only dealers in this neighbour-hood are the Sciarelli brothers, ya got it?'

'The Sciarelli Brothers – isn't that a cabaret band?' Richard ventured unwisely.

'That's our cousins!' Johnny beamed, then he sighed mournfully. 'We never got to learn instruments.'

'Shut up!' Michael barked. Then he turned back to Richard and pulled his collar tighter, cutting off the air supply. 'I'm gonna be watching you. You got that?' He pulled Richard even closer, till their eyeballs almost met, and repeated his threat in a low growl. 'I'm gonna be watching you.'

Then Michael released his grip and slowly backed away. He pointed a menacing finger straight at Richard and continued pointing as he reversed out of the shop.

Richard stayed frozen to the spot. He didn't move a muscle or take a breath till he heard the tinkling of the bell on the shop door. The coast was clear. The Sciarellis had left the building.

Richard sat at the bar with Brian and Campbell, downing a succession of whiskies in an attempt to calm his nerves.

'I told him a hundred times, don't use dope to pay your bills. I said to him, "José, it's illegal. Not legal. As in, against the law."'

'Crazy,' Campbell mumbled into his beer.

'I had no idea I was carrying the stuff.'

'My friend the drug-runner.' Brian handed him another shot – a double.

'What if the police had pulled me over? What if the school had found out – what about my teaching job?!'

'Yeah, well,' said Brian, 'that's the thing with schools. They take a dim view of capital crime.'

'But you know the worst thing,' the colour was returning to Richard's cheeks as the alcohol kicked in, 'I was really scared. It's pathetic.'

'I've heard of the Sciarellis. Aren't they musicians?' asked Campbell.

'That's their cousins,' Richard muttered.

'Two guys bail you up, threaten you. Crikey, I'd be scared to death,' said Brian.

'I was shakin' like jelly.'

'No grunt.' Campbell nodded.

'Exactly,' Richard concurred. 'I have no grunt.'

'Oh, come on,' said Brian.

'It's true,' Richard insisted. 'It's why women don't respond to me.'

'What a load of crap.' Brian took a full bottle of

whiskey off the top shelf to replace the empty one. 'Women respond to you. They're always asking me for your number.'

'Yeah?' Richard looked doubtful. 'Like who?'

'Like . . . that woman, Judy,' said Brian. 'You know, the redhead.'

'Right, Judy,' Richard sighed and leant his chin on his hands. 'She wanted music lessons for her son.'

'Yeah, right.' Brian winked, then he realised Judy had, in fact, wanted music lessons for her son. He decided to change tack. 'Well, what about Melanie?'

Semi-sedated now, Richard picked at the edges of a beer mat and said nothing. Brian had struck a nerve.

'Have you asked her out?' Brian asked, prodding him in the shoulder.

'Look, I told you, she doesn't go out with musicians,' Richard mumbled.

'So get a real job,' said Campbell, always less than helpful after a few ales.

'Very funny.' Richard slumped on the bar stool. 'Look, we nearly had a thing, but I screwed up, okay? The fact is, she's pretty keen on this . . . farmer.'

'Well, it's the whole country thing, isn't it?' said Campbell. 'Horses, cows, Hank Williams on the radio – a lot of women find that very appealing.'

'Yeah, that's the ticket,' said Brian. 'Get yourself some of those cowboy boots, an' a beat-up guitar.'

'Brian, I'm a nice Jewish boy from the suburbs. Hank Williams and big leather boots – these are not part of our tradition.'

'Oh, come on,' Brian jollied him along. 'I can see you now, striding across the paddocks, the sun coming up . . .'

'Big metal spurs janglin' away.' Campbell rattled his keys, clinking them against a glass.

'K-chhhh!' Brian cracked an imaginary whip. 'Get along now, little doggies. K-chhhh!'

Richard slid off the bar stool. 'Right, check ya later.'

'Yeah. Rightio, mate,' said Brian. 'Get yourself some sleep.'

'Ya gotta get up real early now, boy,' said Campbell. 'Ya gotta wrassle them steers, tote them bails . . .'

'You know, Campbell, it really doesn't help,' said Richard, then he headed out the door in search of a taxi.

THE MAGELLAN HOSPITAL, EAST MELBOURNE

It was lunchtime in the hospital gardens. Melanie and Jacqui sat on a long wooden bench, eating their sandwiches and taking in the sun. A few of the patients were taking their catheters and drip poles for a spin, padding along the path in their corduroy slippers, bags of saline swinging overhead. Other patients sat in their wheelchairs with rugs over their laps, knitting or reading or just enjoying the fresh air, relieved to be out of the ward. In the middle of the gardens there was a small lake with a gushing fountain. It was bordered by weeping willows and lined with thick reeds. Nurses and orderlies and lab technicians and typists were sitting on the grass around the lake, feeding crusts and assorted tidbits to the resident birdlife.

Peals of laughter rang out across the lawn; they came from a group of interns, who were sitting around a wooden table underneath a pergola. They were young, with bright eyes and white coats, and their shiny stethoscopes were on prominent display, either hanging around their necks or draped across a shoulder.

Jacqui nodded towards them. 'There, you see that?'

'What?' Melanie glanced over, not sure what she was looking for.

'Half the new interns are women.'

'Ah. Yes.'

'And they're pairing off with the other half, who are men. So all the young eligible doctors, they're marrying other doctors.'

'Serious earning capacity,' said Melanie, grappling with the childproof lid on her orange juice.

'So what's left for the nurses and the secretaries, eh? You gotta spread the wealth around.'

'But look at those guys, they're boys.' Melanie gestured towards the pergola, where the fresh-faced interns were busy impressing one another. 'They're way too young for us.'

'But they're so sweet,' said Jacqui. 'They're always flirting with me.'

'Yes,' Melanie frowned at her, 'and why do younger men pursue older women?'

'Why?'

'To learn everything they can about sex,' replied

Melanie. 'Then they take the jewels of knowledge you've bestowed upon them and give them to some girlie half your age.'

'You reckon?'

'Listen, Jacqui, dating a younger man, it's like taking on an apprentice.'

'Sounds like fun.' Jacqui shrugged.

'What, training up a bloke for another woman – you call that fun?'

'Well, you don't have to worry.'

'Oh, come on,' replied Melanie, her heart warming at the mere thought of Gary. 'It's early days.'

'What a guy,' sighed Jacqui. 'He can cook *and* he owns real estate.'

A couple of stray ducks approached the two women and looked hopefully at Melanie's crusts. She separated small pieces and dropped them onto the lawn, where they were quickly guzzled.

'He wants me to go and stay with him,' Melanie tried to sound casual. 'Just for a couple of days.'

'Wow!' Jacqui exclaimed. 'Mel, this is serious! I bet you're gonna meet his parents.'

'Maybe, I dunno. It's no big deal.' Melanie was playing it down, not wanting to get too excited. She knew that getting too excited was bound to tempt The Fates.

Despite their allegiance to the One True Church, the nuns at St Jacobs liked to cite Greek mythology – anything to inspire fear. Melanie had learnt all about The Fates: the three vengeful Sisters sitting in the clouds somewhere (not heaven, presumably) watching out for hussy mortals who were getting too big for their boots. When they spotted one, they'd pull out their giant scissors and snip that hussy's length of string, thereby ending her run of luck – or possibly her life, Melanie couldn't remember. Either way, it was bound to hurt.

'No big deal? Are you kidding!' Jacqui was suddenly distracted. 'Oh my God!' She sat bolt upright on the wooden bench. 'There he is!'

A striking-looking man with green eyes and carrot-red hair had walked out of D Block and was fast approaching them via a nearby path.

'Doctor Gorgeous,' whispered Jacqui, tremulous.

'Ahhh, so that's the guy.' Melanie cast an appreciative eye.

'Thirty-nine, a specialist – and single,' said Jacqui. 'What are the odds?'

Doctor Gorgeous walked past the two women and disappeared into B Block. Melanie's mobile phone started to ring; she fished it out of her bag.

'Hello?'

On the other end of the line, Consuela had placed a tissue over the mouthpiece, in an attempt to disguise her identity.

'When you dance,' she hissed, 'you look like a *whore*!'

'Hi Consuela,' replied Melanie cheerily. 'Sorry, gotta go.' She pressed the 'end' button and dropped the phone into her bag.

Consuela's lips tightened with anger. She slammed down the receiver and screwed up the tissue in disgust.

Melanie and Jacqui rose from the bench and reluctantly

headed back towards the office. Two young carpenters in their work shorts and singlets passed by. As they walked, their well-developed thigh muscles rippled impressively.

'Men in shorts,' Jacqui sighed, 'ya gotta love 'em.'

'Yeah, legs are okay,' said Melanie.

'Just *okay*?'

'They're not the best part.'

'Oh, come on, you think there's something better than a man's thighs?'

'Ohhh yes.' Melanie glanced around her and lowered her voice, as if she was divulging a state secret. 'It's the forearm. In fact, the lower half of the forearm.' She traced a line along her arm from the elbow down towards the wrist. 'There,' she said, 'just before the arm meets the wrist. Sometimes you can't see it properly, you know, if they're wearing long sleeves or a big watch.'

'I never noticed it before,' said Jacqui.

They were suddenly overtaken by the red-haired, emerald-eyed Doctor Gorgeous, who was striding towards the hospital car park.

Jacqui's heart skipped a beat and she leant on Melanie's shoulder to catch her breath.

'Can a person die of unrequited lust?' she gasped.

'I'll look after Leroy when you're gone,' said Melanie.

'You're a pal.'

Swinging a sports bag across his shoulder, Milos thumped on the door. 'Come on, Superfish, time to go!'

Still groggy with sleep, Richard emerged from his flat. He was clutching an old school bag and a faded bath towel.

'Okay, we hit the water!' Milos slapped Richard's back gleefully.

'It's four o'clock in the morning,' Richard grumbled. 'I wanna hit the bed.' Dragging his feet, Richard followed his energetic neighbour down the stairs. Despite the early starts, Richard was grateful to have Milos as his very own personal trainer, free of charge. To win back Melanie's heart, he knew he'd have to be fit – as fit as the farmer. And Milos was the man for the job.

Twenty years earlier, in the former Czechoslovakia, Milos had been regional backstroke champion and a contender for the Olympic squad – the first child in his family destined for something bigger than the Brno shoe factory. But at nineteen, Milos had decided to defy the Iron Curtain and he'd made a break for the West, taking Renata with him.

His cousin Karel had driven a postal van and made regular trips across the border. Karel had hidden Milos and Renata in his mail sacks, bribing the guards with denim flares so they wouldn't search the van. Then, via a few refugee camps in Germany and Switzerland, the couple had finally made it to Australia. Australia had been the logical choice, given Milos's sporting prowess and Renata's craving for sunshine. They were now fully fledged citizens, their certificates hanging on the lounge room wall next to a faded poster of Roxette.

With all the time lost in transit, Milos had bowed out of Olympic contention, which was fine by him. While he enjoyed swimming, Milos didn't have the killer instinct that propelled elite athletes to Olympic glory. And being a coach instead of a contender gave him more time to play the trumpet, which was his true passion, along with Renata.

Richard was very fond of Milos; he was a good friend, a fine musician, and a highly respected coach, by all accounts. Maybe Milos was the one to help Richard find his grunt.

CORAL TREE LANE, SOUTH MELBOURNE

At around six in the evening on Friday, Melanie was packing clothes into a small vinyl case. Moving to the dresser, she took some new lingerie out of the drawer – lingerie was one of her necessary luxuries, in the absence of real estate, stocks and shares, job security, etc. The new satin bodysuit was exquisite; it was a subtle ivory colour with delicate lace panelling. Melanie held it against her face for a moment, then popped it into the case with the T-shirts and jeans. Closing the lid, she pulled the zipper across and grabbed the handle. Collecting the rest of her luggage along the way – canvas travel bag, plug-in rollers, beauty case, handbag and snacks for the journey – she headed down the stairs and along the hallway, depositing her bags onto the Leo Dunne Turkish mat just inside the front door.

'Guys, I'm going!'

Patrick and Marshall were in the lounge room, watching *Lady Windemere's Fan* for the hundredth time. The boys' video collection comprised Oscar Wilde and soft porn, nothing else. If it wasn't *Lady Windemere's Fan* or *The Importance of Being Earnest*, it was *Romping Naked Firemen* or *Demitri Does Dallas*. Marshall leapt off the couch and raced up the corridor.

'Now, Missy, you know what you said.' He gave her a kiss on the cheek.

'Marshall, it was a joke.'

'But you promised!'

'I didn't promise anything.'

'Say it.'

'Don't be silly.' She took the car keys out of her handbag.

'Melly-Jelly, you have to say it!'

'Oh, all right,' Melanie sighed. 'I will name my first-born son after you.'

'"Mister Marshall Quartermaine"! Lovely!' Marshall did a pirouette and promptly stubbed his toe on the brass doorstopper. He started to wail.

'Bye darling,' Patrick called from the lounge room. 'I won't get up – it's the part where they find the fan.'

'Okay, see you!' Melanie called back, picking up her bags.

Limping theatrically, Marshall opened the front door.

'The second boy,' he whined, 'you have to call him Oscar.'

'*Two* boys! Gimme a break.'

IRON-BAR HOMESTEAD, MAYBURY

Col was sitting at the kitchen table, with his head in the paper. Dorothy was at the sink, chopping rhubarb and apples for tonight's fruit crumble. Gary stood in the doorway, eating a piece of toast and looking out into the yard. He was watching Melanie, who was collecting eggs from Dorothy's chook pen.

'So what does she do?' asked Col, hoping for another dentist.

'I told you, Dad, she's a musician,' replied Gary.

'Say what?'

'Melanie's a musician.'

'A *musician*?!' boomed Col. 'What kind of selfish, time-wasting damn fool thing do you call that?' He slammed his fist on the table. 'This is Australia! We don't need musicians. We need engineers, nurses . . . people who are good in a flood!'

Melanie waved to Gary, holding aloft a speckled brown egg. Gary waved back, giving her the thumbs-up.

'Hmmph, I s'pose we could use her at the primary school.'

'No, Dad, she's not a teacher. She's a musician. She just . . . plays.'

Dorothy stood behind Gary and peered over his shoulder. Melanie was sprinkling pellets on the ground, inciting a feeding frenzy amongst the hens.

'The chookies seem to like her,' said Dorothy.

'Oh well, the bloody chookies know everything, don't they?' Col grumbled into his paper. 'Prob'ly read the bloody stock market too. Tell ya what, Dorothy, I'll just fire the accountant and ask the bloody chookies, all right?'

'Well, I think she's a sweetheart,' said Dorothy.

'Hmmph,' grunted Col. '"Sweetheart" doesn't pay the bills.'

Gary squeezed his mother's hand and she smiled up at him, a conspiratorial gleam in her eye.

Melanie waved at Gary and Dorothy, who were watching her from the doorway. Dorothy seemed nice, but Col was a bit gruff. Maybe he was having a bad day. She was pleased to see that Gary got along with his mum. It was men who hadn't resolved their anger towards their mothers who could give a girl problems, and Melanie had known a few. Like the vet guy, George, who'd fly into violent rages during his sleep. He'd thrash around in bed, shouting abuse at his Greek mother, who'd refused to let him go prawning with the non-Greek boys in Grade Five, apparently, thereby destroying his social credibility. In his waking hours, George would peer at Melanie suspiciously, imagining that she, like his mother, was planning to sabotage his happiness. Or Ross, the IT guy, who'd spent their one and only date, at Melanie's favourite Thai restaurant, speculating loudly about the lemongrass fish and how exactly it would manifest itself as a bowel movement. When challenged about the appropriateness of such comments, Ross had burst into tears, revealing that his mother had forced him to keep a daily record of his bodily functions, till he'd run away from home at the age of thirty-two. And who could forget Gadget Boy – he of the numerous devices – who'd attributed his need for conjoining plastic bits during sex to the complete absence of Lego in his early life, courtesy of his cruel and despotic mother.

But Gary seemed pretty normal. There'd been no talk of the large intestine, or temper tantrums in Greek, or plastic building sites being assembled around her thighs in anticipation of Mister Sling-it-up (a faceless toy engineer operating a modified crane). No, Gary was normal. More than normal. He was fantastic.

Her weekend break had turned into four glorious days. Patrick had phoned the Magellan on Monday morning, advising the VA, in solemn tones, that Melanie was far too sick to come to the phone, much less the office. The man was a born actor. Melanie knew the hospital wouldn't care; she was only a casual, so they wouldn't have to pay her. Anyway, she didn't have time for clinic reports or memos, she was far too busy getting to know Gary.

In the mornings, they'd gone across to his parents' place to feed bottles of warm milk to the poddy calves. The calves gazed up at Melanie as they drank, sending her maternal urge into overdrive. Then they'd zipped around both properties on the ATVs (All-Terrain Vehicles, as Gary had explained – like a motorbike with four wheels), checking the water troughs and rounding up Gary's sheep and Col's cattle. They'd ridden horses together at dusk, ambling along the shoreline in a quiet cove – for Melanie, a plodding retiree called Flash; for Gary, a spirited brumby called Banjo, whom he handled with consummate ease. On Sunday they'd set up the telescope on the long, wooden verandah and together they'd explored the vast night sky. Gary seemed to know a lot about astronomy; displaying considerable patience, he'd helped Melanie to find the Great Nebula in Orion and the beautiful Alpha Centauri double stars – the pointer stars to the Southern Cross.

And then there had been the sex.

After the mandatory evening in separate rooms, nature had taken its course – far too early, of course, but Melanie had been forced to revise her original schedule due to the lust factor, which was clearly beyond her control.

She'd enjoyed a range of lovers in her time, some of them delightful, others eminently forgettable, but Gary was remarkable. When the spirit moved him – and it moved him several times a day – Gary was like a man possessed, generating enough energy to light up a small town. Some men could be coy about certain aspects of intimacy, but not Gary. Sex for him was a rapturous celebration of the spirit and the flesh, fireworks included. Maybe it came from growing up around animals – all that fornicating livestock. Everywhere you looked, something was on heat. Or maybe it was living near the sea, with the pounding of the surf – those big angry waves crashing onto the rocks.

On the fourth day, after dinner, they were relaxing on

the couch in front of the fire, drinking cognac and trying to see pictures in the flames. For one scary moment Melanie saw the VA looming up at her, waving a mini-cassette – a reminder that she'd have to drive home the next day. Gary seemed subdued tonight, not his normal boisterous self. Eventually he broached what was clearly a difficult subject.

'Melanie,' he began, in ominous tones, 'there's something I have to tell you.'

Melanie's heart sank. Here we go, she thought, this is where he tells me about the manslaughter charge or the inherited madness or the fact that he's an orthodox Mormon and would Melanie like to join the other wives – she'd get him Tuesdays and Sundays. She readied herself for a quick getaway, trying to remember if the car keys were in her bag or her coat pocket.

'The thing is . . .'

He couldn't even look her in the eye. God, she thought, it must be bad.

'The thing is, I'm divorced.'

Melanie said nothing, waiting for the clincher. He was divorced – and what? He'd killed his ex and buried her in the bottom paddock? He'd cooked her on the barbecue?

'And there's more. I'm not proud of this, but . . .'

He'd drowned her in the dam?

'I hope you won't think any less of me, but . . . there wasn't just one. I've been divorced twice.' He sighed heavily. 'Two wives, two divorces.' Even saying the word 'divorced' seemed to cause Gary physical discomfort.

Two divorces? thought Melanie. If that was the sum

total of Gary's transgressions, he was doing all right. Divorce was virtually part of the life cycle. Melanie knew legions of people who'd been there, including her good self – though it hadn't been a proper marriage, just a green-card scenario she'd rashly agreed to at the tender age of twenty. The man in question had been Rory McPhee, a charming Kilkenny guitarist who'd high-tailed it to Darwin the moment he got his permanent visa. Rory had implied, pre-ceremony, that he felt some level of affection for Melanie, but, as she later realised, he'd only created this illusion to clinch the deal. Bloody musicians – she should've known better. Still, what do you know at twenty? And Rory was a happy little Vegemite, running his pub in the Territory, remarried now to a Darwin girl, filling the balmy air with Irish melodies. It was hardly a sinister outcome, even if it did mark Melanie as a 'divorcee'.

She wrapped her arms around Gary, who was warm and cuddly in his bulky knit jumper. Men's clothes were heaven. 'Listen, you.' Her voice was soft and reassuring. 'Who cares? Who cares about ex-wives – or ex-anything, for that matter? Now, current wives – that would be a problem.'

Gary looked seriously relieved. 'Thanks, Mel.' He took her hand. 'I thought it would freak you out. I thought you'd jump off the couch and run away.'

'Come here, you big dag.' She laughed and kissed Gary fondly. Then she told him about Rory and he relaxed even more.

Now that the panic had passed, Gary wanted to talk

a little about his ex-wives. Melanie didn't press him, he just wanted to talk.

'The first wife . . .' he began, 'well, I was very young. It lasted about four years. She was a local girl. She's up in Sydney now. Anyway, that's ancient history. Then I married Carla.'

'The most recent wife,' Melanie teased him.

'Yeah, all right.' Gary smiled, though he was still a little tense about the subject. 'I was thirty when we got married – that's five years ago. Carla – Carla Denton – she's a dentist. She's like you, a city girl.'

'A dentist,' said Melanie. 'All that free work. You'd save a fortune.'

'Yeah,' said Gary, 'I guess. Anyway, she ran a surgery over in the medical centre, and it was good for a while, but living in the country . . . well, it isn't for everybody.'

'But it's so close to Melbourne,' said Melanie. 'It's not like you're living in the Simpson Desert.'

'Yeah, I know.' Gary smiled. 'But Carla liked the bright lights, big city. It was too quiet down here, she couldn't settle. Like I said, it was good for a while, but in the end she just felt too confined.'

Confined? thought Melanie, looking out at the rolling hills and the glistening bay beyond. How could you live here and feel confined? If you want confined, try the inner city.

THE ERROL FLYNN MEMORIAL PUBLIC POOL,
NORTH MELBOURNE

A few weeks later, Milos Novotny was pacing up and down alongside a fifty-metre, indoor pool. He shouted instructions to his squad, which was powering through the water at high speed.

'Use your legs, people! Use your legs! Watch the turn, Briony . . . watch it – no!! No good, do it again! Yes, Chloe, that's great. Great, good girl – much better. Natasha, what is that?! Please, what you are doing with your head?! You are swimming, Natasha, not watching tennis!!'

Six lanes of the Errol Flynn public pool had been roped off for the squad's 4 p.m. training session. The public was paddling along in the narrow strip of water that remained. Among them was Richard. He struggled towards the end of the lane, reaching for the metal bar on the diving block and spluttering with relief. Milos walked over to greet him.

'Superfish! You made it!' Milos beamed. 'Only ten more to go.'

Richard was emptying the water out of his goggles. 'Milos,' he gasped, 'I have to rest. Just for a minute.'

Melanie came cruising up to the end of the lane, doing a speedy freestyle. She grabbed the bar and shook the water out of her ears.

'So much swimming – must be new boyfriend,' Milos called to her.

'Huh?' Melanie shook her head again. Now she could hear.

'I said, *new boyfriend*. You have to be very fit!'

'Well, all that farm work takes it out of a girl,' muttered Richard.

'It's fun,' replied Melanie, treading water.

'Sure, great fun,' replied Richard. 'Why play the piano when you can cut the dags off sheep?'

'I can play the piano too,' said Melanie, wearying of Richard's jibes about her 'abandoning her career'. Unlike Richard, Melanie had never seen her musical activities as a career. She enjoyed playing gigs, but she wasn't a serious jazz type like Richard. Certainly she could find her way around a keyboard, but she didn't have Richard's extensive training or, she believed, his talent. After leaving school, Melanie had started off in tribute bands, playing Neil Diamond and Elton John, then she'd picked up some latin jazz along the way, which she adored, and that was enough. She saw herself as an entertainer; she played music to make people happy, be it at shopping centres or private parties or Donovan's Den. She'd never fantasised about playing Carnegie Hall, or recording be-bop tunes for ECM, or donning a beret and hanging with Thelonious Monk devotees at obscure European festivals. Music was a part of her life, but it wasn't the sole focus. There were too many other things to do.

'This farmer, he is lucky man to have gorgeous lady!' Milos declared. Then he spied a stray swimmer, straggling behind the others. 'Natasha! Twenty more, no stopping!'

Melanie turned to look at the teenage girls in Milos's squad. 'Now those girls, *they* are gorgeous,' she said.

'Too thin.' Milos frowned. 'They are like – how you

say? – eels. But you, you have beautiful bottom, beautiful bosoms. You are real woman.'

Melanie laughed, feeling flattered. It was nice when men actually admired your curves instead of telling you to lay off the cheesecake.

Richard pulled on his goggles and turned to face the other end of the lane. 'Okay, real woman, I'm off.'

'Hey, Richard!' Melanie stopped him. 'And Milos, you too. Listen, Gary's having a party Sunday week. You both have to come – Renata as well.'

'No worries, mate!' said Milos. 'We love to go to country, see many horses and cows!'

'Will we have to raise a barn?' Richard scowled.

'Only if you want to.' Melanie pulled herself up on the bar, ready for the next lap. 'Come on then, "Stay active, stay attractive".' She set off with a splash.

Milos and Richard watched Melanie swim away.

'You know, that girl, she is crazy about you,' said Milos. Then he walked off to check on his squad.

Yeah, sure, thought Richard, she's nuts about me, she's just playing hard to get. He watched Melanie freestyling into the distance. Of course, it was all his own fault. He'd blown it completely four years ago when they'd met at the Salsa Kings gig. He should have told her about Deliah straightaway, but he hadn't wanted to scare her off. They'd gone out for a coffee after the gig, and again after the next rehearsal, and the chemistry had been so exciting that he couldn't even think about Deliah. After the fourth rehearsal they'd had dinner together, then he'd driven Melanie home and they'd kissed on the front doorstep. He could still remember the softness of her mouth, and how his soul had lit up like a beacon, playing a Duke Ellington arrangement of 'Take the "A" Train'.

At the following rehearsal, Deliah had suddenly arrived, unexpected and uninvited. She'd walked straight up to Richard and embraced him in front of the entire band, as if she was marking her territory. It was a ridiculous gesture, given that the marriage had been dead for years, but a gesture that had clearly upset Melanie. Later, when Richard tried to explain to her that he and Deliah were in the process of separating and just because you still slept with your wife didn't mean that you necessarily loved her, that sometimes sex was about habit and comfort – when he tried to explain all this, Melanie had become even more upset. So much for honesty.

And when he finally did get divorced, Melanie still wasn't interested. She and Richard became good friends, but anything beyond that was off the agenda – some crap about 'once a liar . . .' God, it was only Deliah! It wasn't like he'd slept with somebody *else's* wife! Besides, he'd only ever kissed Melanie. He wasn't hopping between beds – that wasn't his style. He was a good Jewish boy; he just wanted to marry a nice girl and settle down.

When he thought about it, he knew his marriage to Deliah had been doomed from the start.

'But Richard,' she'd always complain, 'you're never at home. You go out nearly every night.'

'I'm a musician,' he'd reply, exasperated. 'Musicians work at night. What – you thought I'd be working nine to five? What am I, a clerk? I play the saxophone, remember? The big shiny thing that honks when you blow it.' It had not been a happy time.

Then one night Richard had gone to a reception hall to fill in for a mate who was playing in a large salsa band. It was there that he'd first laid eyes on Melanie Francis. She had been sitting at the piano with her long chestnut hair and the hazel-green eyes and the tinkerbell laugh. Richard's throat had gone dry and his heart had pounded and he had finally understood why men did crazy things when they met the Right Woman.

Getting to know her had only made it worse. Not only was Melanie beautiful, she was smart and funny as well – the ultimate shikse. When the two of them were at gigs together, people often thought they were an item, because they usually hung out between sets, and they must have looked very relaxed together. Richard liked it when people made this assumption. He'd do nothing to discourage the idea; he'd just stand in the background and acknowledge their quiet smiles.

She was José's secret weapon with the corporate clients. They were enchanted by Melanie. With or without the cleavage, she was great for business. Richard used to watch her as she chatted with the fizzy drink guys and the tinned fruit reps, making them feel like captains of industry. He'd watch her joking with the waiters and the cleaners at the reception halls, or the kids and the catering staff and the neighbours over the fence at whatever party they were playing. Melanie liked engaging with people and she brought out the best in them. She was feisty and vivacious, but not aggressive. She had – what did his father call it? – a 'generosity of spirit'.

Roszika and Larry Cohen had met the famous Melanie at the Ripponlea synagogue, at their niece Ruth's bas mitzvah. Melanie had agreed to accompany Richard as his 'colleague and friend'. The fact that she played the piano and dressed nicely had won her major points with Roszika. As for Larry, Melanie could play the nose-flute wearing a potato sack and he'd still adore her. Roszika's advice to her son was to stop worrying and let destiny take its course. 'Que será, será, darling . . .' But Richard couldn't stand by and wait, he had to do something to turn the cosmic tide. At least if he was fit and buffed and full of grunt, he'd stand a better chance.

As he contemplated the next gruelling lap, Richard noticed a familiar face in the adjacent lane. This guy had been coming to the pool for a few weeks now, always at the same time as Richard, and always swimming in the next lane. The stranger lifted his head to take a breath, and as he did he stared straight at Richard, right into his eyes. Suddenly it all made sense. Of course, the guy was following him! Richard was being tailed. The Sciarelli brothers had enlisted one of their goons to shadow him. Richard felt a knot in his stomach. Bloody José and his dodgy payment plans.

'I'm gonna be watching you.' The words reverberated around Richard's brain as he plodded along in the pool, performing a variation on the backstroke that had Milos on the verge of tears.

'I'm gonna be watching you . . .'

The Sciarellis had issued a warning, and Richard knew they meant business.

QUARTERMAINE WOOLSHEDS, MAYBURY

Gary's woolshed party was up and running. The large wooden shed was festooned with streamers and balloons, there were kegs aplenty and the trestle tables groaned with food. A jukebox in the corner was pumping out rockabilly favourites and the occasional ballad. About thirty people were up and dancing, others were chatting in groups or helping themselves to drinks and a feed. The party spilled out onto the grass, where Dorothy was flipping meat on a barbecue. Patrick and Marshall plied her with shandies, ferrying steaks and sausages to the tables inside.

There were about a hundred and fifty guests, including Gary's friends from the dinner party – Brendan and Rosalie, Simon and Pip and the dour Blodwyn, accompanied tonight by a plump geography teacher called Maxine. There were wool classers, stablehands, jackaroos and jillaroos; farmers and their wives; Gary's extended family, including the mob from Mount Malabar; and Melanie's friends from town.

Jacqui was dancing with a strapping young man. He held her close, and they were barely moving to a slow country waltz.

'So, you're a farmer?' Jacqui mumbled into his shoulder.

'Yeah, kind of,' the young man replied.

'Where's your farm?' Jacqui breathed in the comforting scent of lanolin. Must be a sheep farmer, she thought. The lanolin from the wool gets into their skin.

'Um, well, I, uh . . . I work on the prison farm up in Bunnalup.'

'Oh.' Jacqui stiffened.

'I'm on weekend leave. I get out in three months.' The young man smiled hopefully, Jacqui now plotting her own escape.

🥾

Richard was sitting on some hay bales with Simon and Pip, trying to look interested in the conversation.

'Forget about wheat and sheep, that's history,' declared the bespectacled, dark-haired Simon. 'You've got your crocodile meat, your water buffalo, your emu farming . . .'

'The emu is such an amazing bird!' enthused the blonde, toothy Pip. 'Did you know, Richard, the female emu can store sperm inside her body for up to six months? She just uses it when she needs it. Isn't that fantabulous?!'

🥾

Renata Cerná was at a table with Polly and Jan, two Mount Malabar ladies in their fifties. They were the daughters and wives of wealthy graziers and spoke with plummy accents acquired at expensive boarding schools.

'Of course, there's the main property,' Polly was saying, 'and I've got a dear little place on the sea, when I need to get away from my boys.'

'She means her bulls,' explained Jan. 'Polly's got a stud farm with the most gorgeous Poll Herefords. All champions, you know.' Polly's record in the semen industry was a source of community pride.

'Oh, Jan,' said Polly, feigning embarrassment, 'don't . . .'

'Really, Renata,' gushed Jan, 'you should see them, they're such beautiful boys. There's plenty of lead in those pencils!'

'And Jan has a magnificent place in Mount Malabar,' said Polly. 'Georgian. Convict-built, National Trust, beautifully renovated. The grounds go on for miles.'

'Well, we need the space,' sighed Jan. 'We collect antique horse floats. My dear, they take up so much room.'

'And what about you, dear?' Polly enquired, cocking her head to one side. She was intrigued by Renata's accent – Eastern European, a titled lady perhaps?

'Yes, dear, what about you?' asked Jan.

'Me? I have . . .' Renata thought for a moment. Then, smiling serenely, she announced, 'I have rich interior life.'

Over on the hay bales, Richard was still being assailed by Simon and Pip.

'Macadamias, Chinese broccoli . . .' droned Pip.

'Japanese green tea,' chanted Simon.

Richard was getting very fidgety. It was a party, for God's sake. Did these people always talk shop?

'And if you've got water on your place,' said Pip, giddy with the possibilities, 'well, the sky's the limit!'

'Yabbies, prawns . . .' Simon counted them off on his fingers.

'Barramundi!' cried Pip, beside herself with joy.

Richard picked the hay from his trousers and looked around for Melanie. He spotted her behind a table, fiddling about with some plates, assisted by Jacqui, who seemed to have lost interest in that young guy she'd been dancing with.

Melanie was pointing out members of Gary's family.

'The one next to Gary, see him?'

Jacqui squinted, trying to make out Gary and whoever was standing next to him. Her eyesight wasn't the best. Vanity kept her away from Ophthalmology, where the nurses kept bugging her to take a test.

'Umm, is he the one in the blue shirt, with the grey hair?'

'Yep, that's Col. He's Gary's dad.'

'Ooh.' Jacqui frowned. 'He looks like a mean old codger.'

'Yeah,' replied Melanie. 'That's what I thought, but I reckon it's all a big act.'

Gary and Col were standing on the other side of the shed, nursing their beers. They noticed Melanie looking over at them and gave her a quick wave.

'You see?' Melanie said to Jacqui, as she waved back at Col. 'He's very friendly. I talk to him about music and travelling – that kind of stuff. He doesn't say much but I can tell he's interested. He's just a bit shy.'

Melanie picked up some bread plates and handed them to Jacqui.

'I reckon Col's a bit of a dreamer – underneath,' said Melanie. 'Underneath, he's a free spirit. That's what I think.'

Jacqui looked over at Col, searching vainly for his inner gypsy.

'I like that girl,' said Col. He shifted his weight and took another swig of beer. 'That Melinda, she's gonna work out fine.'

'It's Melanie, Dad,' said Gary. 'Her name's Melanie.'

Col slapped Gary on the back. It was a solid whack, delivered with gusto. 'Son,' declared Col, 'you've done well! Nice manners, good hips,' he nodded approvingly towards Melanie, 'and just look at the way she's organising those plates.'

After a succession of chardonnays, Renata, Polly and Jan were oblivious to social barriers and were having a grand old time. Polly leant in close to Renata and nodded towards the large bearded man with the thick grey ponytail, who was about to pass their table.

'Look out, Renata, here he comes!'

'Guy with the beard,' whispered Jan.

'Get ready!' Polly covered a hiccup.

'He wears it on the left!' squeaked Jan.

'On the left!' echoed Polly.

Polly and Jan tried to contain themselves as Brendan Buchanan walked by and Renata swivelled in her chair to take a look. As she turned, Renata found herself face-to-groin with the generously endowed Brendan, who was squeezed into a pair of stonewashed jeans. He was indeed wearing it on the left.

Renata turned back to Polly and Jan with a look of such horror that they lost any semblance of control and started howling with laughter.

🔈

Jacqui had settled into a corner of the shed with Vicki, a local hairdresser and petite blonde in her early twenties. The two women were discussing highlights.

'Definitely auburn for you, Jacqui,' cooed Vicki. 'Nice and natural, it'll look like the sun is lighting up your hair.'

Jacqui loved talking to hairdressers, it was very soothing. For Jacqui, hairdressers had long replaced priests as purveyors of spiritual consolation.

A fresh-faced bloke in his late twenties approached them, grinning broadly. His sleeves were rolled up to his elbows. Jacqui was drawn to the shapely line of his sturdy ulna bone as it fused so elegantly with the slimmer radius, meeting at the carpus. Melanie was right, she thought, the male forearm is truly a thing of beauty.

'And this is my husband, Mick.' Vicki beamed.

Mick put his delectable forearm around Vicki's tiny waist and Jacqui's heart sank a little.

'Mick,' Vicki completed the introduction, 'this is Jacqui. She's a friend of Melanie's.'

'G'day.' Mick grinned, the warmth of his smile spreading down to Jacqui's toes. 'Nice to meet ya.'

'Hi Mick,' said Jacqui, thinking how unfair it all was.

'Are you a farmer too?'

'Heavens, no,' Vicki laughed musically. 'Mick's a slaughterman at the abattoir.'

'Oh,' said Jacqui, a little taken aback.

Mick gave her an understanding look. 'Are you a vegetarian?'

'Um, sort of,' she replied. 'I eat fish, but I don't eat meat or chicken. I have this little rule: don't eat anything you can pat.'

'You can pat fish,' observed Mick, not unkindly.

'Only when they're dead,' said Jacqui. 'So, if they're already dead, you might as well eat them, right?'

'Right,' said Mick, reaching for a stubbie. He could never understand these townies.

∗

Milos was in another corner, attempting a conversation with Col.

'Eh?' Col eyed the stranger closely. 'You're from where?'

'Czech Republic,' replied Milos.

'Say what?' Col's knowledge of geography ended at Longreach, Queensland.

'Czech Republic,' Milos repeated, a little louder this time. 'Used to be Czechoslovakia. Now is two country: Czech Republic and Slovakia.'

'Jeezus Christ!' Col rounded on the stranger with some hostility. 'Are you a commie bastard?!'

'No, no!' Milos tried to placate him. 'Not me! I am – how you say? – Australian citizen bastard!'

∗

Later in the evening, Gary drew a radiant Melanie to his side and called for quiet. Richard could feel his throat tightening and his stomach starting to churn. He couldn't believe what was happening, even as it unfolded in front of his eyes.

Nope, she won't do it, he was telling himself. Mel's a sensible girl, she wouldn't do anything so patently idiotic. A farmer?! Mel's a city girl, she can't marry a farmer. She's going to marry Richard Laurence Cohen. We've got the well-developed friendship, like it says in all the magazines, we've got the common values, we've certainly got the lust. Well, I've got the lust. She had the lust once. It'll come back eventually, once she's discovered her true feelings. It's only a matter of time . . .

'And then,' Gary was saying, 'I looked over, and she was sitting at the keyboard in a beautiful sparkly dress, and her eyes were all sparkly too.'

Melanie was giggling. Richard felt as if a giant anvil was crushing his chest.

'Playing one of my mum's favourite tunes – "Tico, Tico" – really fast. Bloody hell, you should've seen her feet, they were flying across the pedals!'

Everyone was laughing now. Everyone except Richard.

Gary drew Melanie closer. 'And I thought to myself, Gary Quartermaine, this is the girl for you.' He squeezed Melanie's waist. 'She's the finest damn girl that a bloke could ever meet.'

The women in the crowd gave a collective sigh, the men guffawed and Melanie nestled into Gary's shoulder.

'And I've asked you all here tonight,' Gary continued, 'to tell you that I'm the luckiest bastard on earth.'

Richard was finding it hard to breathe.

'Ladies and gents,' declared Gary, beaming with pride, 'it gives me great pleasure to announce . . .' Richard's knees started to buckle, '. . . that Miss Melanie Francis has agreed to become my wife!' Richard sank onto a nearby bale of hay, no longer able to stand.

Gary's news was greeted with cheers and applause, emotions running high after a night of steady drinking. Gary and Melanie were swept up in effusive group hugs and cries of delight. There was much charging of glasses, noisy agreement about Gary's ability to 'pick a winner', and light-hearted speculation about how many children they would produce.

Jacqui pushed her way through the crowd and threw her arms around Melanie. 'You!! You are so naughty! I had no idea!'

Melanie laughed tearfully. 'We wanted it to be a surprise.' She hugged her friend back, rocking her from side to side.

'Well, you surprised me!' exclaimed Jacqui. 'It's fantastic! God, I'm so happy for you, Mel! When did he ask you?'

'A couple of weeks ago.'

'Did he get down on one knee?' Jacqui asked breathily. 'Was there a guy playing the violin? Did he put the ring in a bowl of lemon sorbet?'

Gary crossed to Jacqui and embraced her warmly. 'Thanks for coming, Jacqui.'

'Gary! Congratulations! It's the best news. I was just grilling Melanie about the details . . .'

Gary put his arm around Melanie's shoulder. 'Well, it was a big night, wasn't it, darlin'? We had the Melbourne

Symphony Orchestra and the Channel Ten chopper, and they lowered the ring down on a big satin cushion.'

'Actually,' said Melanie, 'he was standing in the septic tank and he said, "Have a look in me top pocket, love."'

'She is such a liar.' Gary leant down and kissed Melanie's neck.

'We were having a quiet dinner at home,' she confessed, 'and he just popped the question.'

'It was the pears in red wine sauce,' said Gary, winking at Jacqui. 'Works every time.'

'Promise you'll come and visit. There's plenty of room,' Melanie insisted.

'Yes, you must,' Gary urged her. 'Stay whenever you want – for as long as you want. And bring Leroy.'

Jacqui nodded enthusiastically, but she had no intention of bringing Leroy anywhere near those marauding goannas. Tonight he was up in town being cared for by Jacqui's mother and probably feeling very cross and abandoned. She'd have to make it up to him with some of those dried liver snacks.

The only people to appear less than thrilled about the engagement were Richard and Blodwyn. And Milos, who felt sorry for his friend. Poor Richard, he'd lost his girl and he swam like a rabbit. It didn't seem fair.

Richard left the party soon after, deciding to drive home and not stay in the 'Big House' with all the other 'townies'. All that mucking in and breakfast for twenty sounded dreadful. And Melanie's happiness was too much for him to bear.

The following night Richard took refuge in the cosy confines of the jazz cellar. This was his natural habitat, his true domain. No cow shit or steel guitars or bastard bloody farmers. Looking tired and drawn, Richard hunched over the bar and rolled an empty glass between his hands. Tonight even his shiny brown curls looked limp and despondent.

'She'll never go through with it,' said Brian from behind the bar, where he was cleaning down the taps.

'I mean, for God's sake, she's only just met him,' said Richard.

'I married Evie after ten days,' offered Campbell. 'Been together ever since. Thirty-six years. Best thing I ever did.'

Richard frowned, ignoring Campbell's remark. 'I mean, what does she know about the guy? He could be a total fraud. He could be a real shyster.'

'Ooh yeah, those farmer types,' said Campbell. 'They're real slippery. Here today, gone tomorrow. Mind you, she could probably track him down if she went to . . . oh, I dunno . . . if she went to his – *farm*!'

'Oh, shut up, Campbell,' said Brian.

'People get engaged all the time,' said Andy, the lead guitarist, shifting his thighs on the bar stool and trying to sound wiser than his nineteen years. 'Doesn't mean they get married.'

'I dunno,' muttered Campbell, shaking his older, balder head. 'They find a fella with money . . .'

'I could've had money.' Richard sighed, tugging at his slim goatee beard. 'I was s'posed to be a doctor. I got into the course and everything. Mum was over the moon.'

'Get away,' said Campbell.

'Get away,' said Brian.

'True,' said Richard.

'So what happened?' asked Andy, always up for a good story.

'Well,' said Richard, 'it's the first day of uni. I'm walking along, off to the lecture, minding my own business, and I get waylaid by these two beautiful girls. They're wearing those long cheesecloth dresses – you know, see-through, no bra – and they've both got long flowing hair . . .'

'Like Daryl Hannah in *Splash*,' said Campbell.

'Yeah, kind of,' said Richard, 'except they weren't mermaids, but anyway . . .'

'Like Morticia in "The Addams Family",' said Brian. 'She had really long hair.'

'Anjelica Huston or the one on TV?' asked Campbell.

'TV,' said Brian. 'Sixties, I think. What was her name?'

'*Anyway* . . .' Richard frowned and went on with his story. 'These girls, they're studying music therapy. It was a new course, just started. They gave me the brochure, explaining it all. We get chatting over dandelion tea and rice balls and, before you know it, I've dropped out of medicine and I'm doing this bullshit course.'

'Music therapy, what's that?' asked Andy, who was looking younger all the time.

'It was big in the seventies,' explained Brian from under his thatch of grey hair.

'Before you were born,' said Campbell.

Richard didn't hear them, he was lost in regrets. '"Combine your talent for music and your gift for healing," they said. "A nice steady job in a hospital," they said. Sucked me right in. I mean, where is this place? Where is this utopia with all the highly paid music therapists?!'

'I met a physiotherapist once,' offered Andy.

'Speech therapist,' said Brian.

'Occupational therapist,' added Campbell.

'Exactly,' said Richard. 'They're all weaving baskets, but nobody's playing the saxophone.'

'What about those gigs you do?' said Brian.

'What gigs?' asked Campbell.

'Richard plays in hospitals sometimes,' said Andy. 'With Mel. You still do that, don't you, mate?'

'It's an old people's home,' muttered Richard.

'Piano and sax,' Andy continued. 'They play standards – old stuff.' Andy saw Richard bristle. 'I mean, classics.'

'They play for the diggers out at Croydon,' Brian explained to Campbell. 'In that retirement village. Poor old buggers in wheelchairs, they don't get out too much'.

Campbell turned to Richard, looking genuinely impressed. 'Mate, I think that's terrific.'

'It's no big deal.' Richard brushed off the accolade, looking embarrassed.

'No, really,' said Campbell, 'it's great. Hey, maybe you could come up to Veterans' Affairs, play for the queues?'

'Yeah, right,' said Richard, busy dissecting a beer mat.

'Well, there you go, mate,' said Brian, trying to lift

Richard's mood. 'You play music and it cheers people up – that's music therapy.'

'Yeah, whatever,' said Richard. 'But the point is, I could've been a GP by now, or an orthopod, or a neurologist – all that lovely money. I bet . . . I bet if I was a brain surgeon with a big house and ten cars, Melanie Francis wouldn't be passing me over for some idiot farmer.'

'Come on, Richard,' said Brian, 'you know Mel, she's no gold-digger. Plenty of rich bastards come in here, they see a pretty girl at the piano and they try their luck. Most of them are complete wankers, Mel can see that. She doesn't give them the time of day.'

'Yeah, Mel's all right,' said Andy.

'What rich bastards?' Richard's eyes narrowed.

'Well, I don't reckon it's about money,' said Andy. 'I think that Melanie – well, she just likes that kind of bloke. Y' know, a bloke from the bush. A blokey bloke.'

'I'm blokey!' Richard was highly indignant.

'Face it, mate,' said Campbell, 'you're a soft city boy. All that crying into your cappuccinos, wearing skivvies – it takes its toll.'

'I have never cried into a cappuccino, thank you very much. And it's not a skivvy, it's a "polo pour homme".'

'The thing is,' said Andy, 'you've gotta get in touch with the bloke inside.'

'Oh. Really. And how do I do that, pray tell?' Richard snipped, tired now and a little drunk and not sure that boys half his age should be giving him advice.

'You don't *do* anything. That's the point,' replied Andy. 'Blokeyness . . . it just bubbles under the surface.'

'Women can pick up on it,' agreed Brian. 'Like radar.'

'But they don't want to see it in action, they just want to know it's there,' continued Andy.

'I reckon you lost yours,' said Campbell, shaking his bald head sadly. 'It can happen. One day you wake up and it's gone.'

'Well,' Richard was looking a little anxious, 'assuming I've lost it – and I'm not saying I have – but, hypothetically, if I had, how would I find it again?'

'Ahhh,' replied Brian, attempting a Hollywood-Chinese accent. 'That is your journey, grasshopper.'

part two

THE MAGELLAN HOSPITAL, EAST MELBOURNE

'So, any news? Have you guys set a date?' asked Jacqui. She and Melanie were sitting at their desks, keeping an eye out for the VA.

'We're going to talk about it tomorrow,' replied Melanie. 'I think it'll be soon, he's pretty keen.'

'Oooh, Mel, it's so exciting!' Jacqui rose from her chair and moved to the printer, which was churning out a report she'd just typed.

'It's funny,' Melanie took aim at the side of her screen and gave it a good thump, which sorted out the blurring, 'some men are nervous about getting married, but not Gary.'

'There was something in the paper about that.' Jacqui resumed her seat. 'It said married men and single women have good mental health, but it's the single men and the married women – they're the ones who get depressed.'

'Right. And if you drink coffee and eat cheese at the same time you get cancer,' replied Melanie.

'Well, it was in the paper.' Jacqui slid the new documents into a folder, then paused for a moment. 'Or is it the single girls who get depressed? Can't remember.' She leant across to Melanie's desk. 'Come on, Mel,' she whispered, 'show us again.'

Checking the coast was clear, Melanie held out her left hand for Jacqui to admire. The delicate engagement ring glittered and gleamed, catching the light from the overhead fluorescents. An heirloom from Gary's great-grandmother, the ring featured a dark blue sapphire surrounded by tiny white diamonds. After Jacqui had finished her daily ritual of worship, Melanie removed the ring and put it into a velvet box, dropping it into her handbag.

'No, don't take if off,' Jacqui protested. 'It's so pretty.'

'I dunno,' said Melanie. 'It feels kind of strange. It's like all of a sudden I belong to someone, like I'm his property or something.'

'Don't be stupid. His property will soon be your property – and that's a good thing.'

Melanie frowned and busied herself with some files. 'Look, it isn't about the money.'

'I know,' replied Jacqui. 'You really like the guy and you'd marry him anyway, but as an added bonus, he's rich. Talk about landing on your feet.'

'Yeah, I know,' said Melanie. Then she looked up at Jacqui. 'I am being stupid.'

'Just a tad.'

Melanie smiled. 'It's just that . . . I get a bit jittery sometimes. You know, it's all a bit new.' Reaching into her bag, she retrieved the ring and slipped it back onto her finger. 'Marshall says he sees it all the time – at the salon.'

'Marshall's *Style Soiréeeee*,' Jacqui said with a grin.

'The *Style Soiréeeee, darrrling.*' Melanie grinned back. 'He says, they're sitting in the salon, having their hair done, it's only two hours till the wedding and they're crying like babies.'

'And that's just the men,' said Jacqui.

'Boom boom.'

Jacqui reached for the next cassette, knocking over a slim aluminium can that was perched on her desk. Melanie leant down to retrieve it.

'What's this? "Pretty Kitty"?'

'It's for Leroy.'

'Jacqui, this is spray-on mousse. You bought mousse for your cat?'

'Yeah, well,' Jacqui sniffed, 'his fur gets a little unruly.'

'But Leroy's a shorthair. He's got short hair. How unruly can it get?'

'Just leave it, okay?' Jacqui adjusted her headset and went back to transcribing her tape.

'Sorry,' Melanie muttered, putting the can on Jacqui's desk. Then she picked up a pile of patient notes and started arranging them in date order.

Jacqui became increasingly exasperated as she tried to decipher the incoherent ramblings on the tape. She frowned and huffed and leant her head to one side and screwed up her face till finally she ripped off the headset and slammed it down on the desk.

Sitting in her office, the VA's antennae shot out of her head.

'I can't understand him!' blurted Jacqui. 'I hate this job! I hate it!'

Appearing in the doorway, the VA adopted a menacing pose and glared angrily in Jacqui's direction. Jacqui lowered her head and pretended to type, looking suitably chastened.

When the supervisor had returned to her office, Melanie leant across to her friend. 'Jacqui, you're a smart girl. You could get a much better job than this.'

'So could you.'

'Yeah, but I'm only casual, I do other stuff. You're here five days a week. Tell you what, did you speak to Ericson?'

'Forget it. You want a leg up, he wants a leg over. Anyway, I'm sick of taking orders. I wish I could . . . I dunno, run my own business or something. Anything, just not this.'

Melanie leant across and took Jacqui's headset, placing it over her own ears. 'Come on then, let's have a listen.'

Jacqui operated the pedal while Melanie closed her eyes and concentrated.

'It's the accent, it's too much,' Jacqui whined.

'Sshh,' Melanie said, frowning, 'I can't hear him. Play it again.'

Jacqui tapped the pedal and Melanie listened intently.

'It's "men-in-gitic". Yep, "meningitic".' Melanie handed the headset back. 'Doctor Pasquale, he always says his 'I's' like they were 'E's'.'

'It's so confusing.'

'I know.'

Calmer now, Jacqui resumed typing. Then she spotted a visitor entering the room. 'Oh my God.' She gulped for air. 'Mel, look! It's Doctor Gorgeous!'

The doctor was consulting with Mrs Van Asch over a file he'd brought in. Jacqui gasped as he ran a manly hand through his glossy, all-natural carrot-red hair.

'Just keep breathing,' said Melanie.

'Oh my God, he's coming over!' Jacqui sat very straight, trying to look perky, alluring and efficient all at the same time.

The doctor strode over to Melanie's desk and jutted his chiselled jaw in her direction. 'Are you Jacqui McGlade?'

Melanie pointed silently at Jacqui, who was now on the point of a seizure, in a perky, alluring, efficient kind of way.

'Miss McGlade.' Doctor Gorgeous trained his emerald-green eyes on Jacqui, who was trying not to swoon. 'It's about this clinic report, the one you typed.' He flipped open the file and pulled out a piece of A4 paper, holding it up for everyone to see. 'Now, Miss McGlade. Can you tell me why this patient would have "black Dalmatians"?'

Endeavouring to think straight in the doctor's deliciously handsome presence, Jacqui stammered a reply.

'Oh, um, well, I . . . I . . . oh yes, I remember now. That was a tricky one. I thought, Dalmatians? Hmm, must be pet therapy. Psych ward. Pet therapy – it's a healing thing, right? I mean, not just for crazy people, normal people too. You pat the dog, you feel calm, blood pressure goes down . . .'

'The patient does not have "black Dalmatians",' boomed Doctor Gorgeous, the veins in his neck starting to bulge. 'The patient, Miss McGlade . . .' he was almost spitting now. 'The patient has *black bowel motions*!'

Jacqui had lost all trace of perkiness by this stage.

'And I thought the nurses were stupid!' The doctor hurled the file onto Jacqui's desk and marched out of the room, slamming the door behind him.

Jacqui sat in her chair, stunned and humiliated. Melanie reached across the aisle and touched her hand.

'Well, m'dear, mystery solved,' said Melanie, in a soft voice. 'Now we know why he's single.'

FIT 'N' FUNKY GYM, ALBERT PARK

On a Saturday morning in early June, Richard and Milos arrived at the local gym. Formerly a church hall, the pine-slatted walls and high ceilings had been softened by track lighting and apricot carpet. Posters of glamorously fit men and women in various stages of undress lined the walls.

As Richard and Milos surveyed the scene, they were hit by a blast of rhythm and blues. Richard raced over to a large mirrored studio to watch the aerobics class that was just starting. He checked his timetable: it was 'Step Up & Boogie On Down (Advanced)', led by an impossibly muscular woman in a neon-yellow catsuit.

'Way to go!' Dropping his gym bag, Richard went to join the class, but Milos grabbed his arm and hauled him back.

'No, Richard! Not today. Come on, we have to start work.' He dragged the unwilling Richard away from the high-steppin' crowd, away from the slinky neon leotards, away from the spine-tingling Quincy Jones horn arrangements.

He led him past the Swedish sauna, past the rows of Thighmaster machines and mini-trampolines, past the crèche, the solarium and the daisy-yellow coffee shop. Eventually the two men arrived at a dank, dingy enclosure. The sign above the door boomed 'WEIGHTS ROOM'. It reminded Richard of a gig he'd played in a maximum-security prison – except the prison had had better lighting. In the 'WEIGHTS ROOM', angry men with thick, mallee-bull necks and elaborate tattoos were groaning loudly, grinding down their joints in the Dickensian gloom. No music here, no driving beat to motivate the limbs, only 'Talk Radio KKK' blaring out of the speakers – a sneering shock-jock bemoaning the demise of capital punishment.

Milos turned to Richard and smiled broadly. 'Welcome to the land of grunt!'

THE BARKING SHARK, MAYBURY

In addition to running film nights, Barry Vernon, from the Barking Shark, knew how to organise a good party, and wedding receptions were his speciality. He was sitting with Melanie at a heritage-approved table in his Georgian-style ladies lounge, discussing the menu on Tuesday night. Steak for the men and fish for the ladies, Barry was advising. It was tradition.

Gary and Melanie had set the date – October 25,

a Saturday. It gave them just over four months to prepare. They'd decided on a morning ceremony at Maybury's Civic Gardens, led by a local celebrant. With Melanie being a lapsed Catholic and Gary a lapsed Presbyterian, a church wedding just didn't seem appropriate. It made sense to have the nuptials in Maybury and not Melbourne; Gary had his extended family and a legion of friends down here. And it was tradition. If you were a Maybury Quartermaine, you got christened, married and buried in Maybury, end of story.

This was fine by Melanie. She wasn't big on tradition but she was happy to go along with it. Unlike Gary's, Melanie's family was small. She had a total of three blood relatives on the guest list, all distant cousins on her mother's side. Her father, Jack, had moved away after the divorce; Melanie didn't know where he was and didn't really care.

Melanie's aunts, like her mother, had all died young. In fact, both sides of the family had fared badly in the longevity stakes, most of them 'passing over', as the clairvoyants called it, before the age of sixty. Hopefully the Quartermaine genes would boost the odds for Melanie's children and they'd make it to seventy, minimum. And she'd teach them the piano, of course. A long, healthy life and the joy of making music, that's what Melanie wanted for her children. That and the farm.

Four months might have seemed like a short engagement, but as Gary had explained to Melanie the night before, there was a reason for the unseemly haste. It was all because of his grandfather, 'Iron-Bar Jack'. Jack had been dead for over fifteen years, but he was still a major player in Gary's life.

Jack Quartermaine had never liked his grandson. From the moment Gary was born, with those ridiculous curls, Jack could see that the boy wasn't a Quartermaine, he was a Drummond. He had his mother's temperament – too soft. 'A man's gotta be hard when he's running a property,' Jack always said. Hard enough to make the tough decisions. But there was still hope. Like every Quartermaine male child before him, Gary would undergo the Three Trials of Boyhood.

Trial Number One: Aged Four

Armed with a rifle, Jack took his grandson out to a field and sat him down on a rock. Looking around him, Jack eventually took aim and fired at a rabbit. Retrieving the unfortunate animal, he dumped it into Gary's lap. The rabbit shuddered for a moment, then lay there cold and still, its dark eyes glazing over. Horrified, Gary burst into tears. Jack shouted angrily at the boy and marched him home, forcing him to carry the dead rabbit the entire distance. Gary cried every step of the way, and no amount of yelling would make him stop.

Trial Number Two: Aged Six

Jack slaughtered a pig for the annual Carcass Competition at the Maybury Show. He strung it up to bleed and instructed Gary to stand directly underneath it, the blood dripping down onto the boy's head. Petrified, the boy stood there for a moment, then ran away screaming. He ran too fast for Jack to catch him. He ran across two paddocks and finally threw himself into a water trough, scrubbing his head with his hands till his blond curls were rinsed clean.

Trial Number Three: Aged Eight

Jack took Gary into the woolshed and picked out a lamb for the Sunday roast. Jack straddled the lamb, held up its head and explained to the boy how to slit the animal's throat. It should be an easy task for the boy. Even at eight, Gary was a strong lad with a solid build.

Jack handed Gary a butcher's knife and gave him fifteen minutes to do the job. Locking the boy inside, he wandered off for a smoke. He returned to find Gary squatting in a corner, carving his initials into the wooden floor. The Sunday roast was munching on some hay, alive and well, without even a scratch.

Jack had done his best to educate Gary, but clearly the boy was beyond help. Gary had succumbed to hysteria when handling vermin, he'd displayed an irrational fear of blood and he had none of the mental discipline required for slaughtering. Jack had to take action. The Quartermaine land meant everything to him and he was determined to protect it. He went straight to his lawyer and made a new will.

He left his estate of two thousand acres (plus buildings, machinery and stock) to his son Colin. A thousand acres would go to his grandson Gary when Gary reached twenty-five. He'd get the rest when Col died. But Gary would never actually own the land – he'd only keep it in trust. He could build on the land and make his living from it, but he wouldn't own it, so he couldn't sell it – which was Jack's greatest fear. A Quartermaine would never even contemplate selling the property, but Gary was a Drummond – a loose cannon.

After Gary's death, the estate would go to Gary's sons. They would own the land outright, with no strings attached. Jack was counting on the dominance of the Quartermaine gene; he was counting on Gary to sire another Jack or Colin. If Gary died without leaving any sons, the land would go to Fraser Quartermaine, Gary's cousin and Jack's great-nephew, from the Mount Malabar branch of the family.

There was one last condition, which Jack hoped would encourage procreation. Gary would hold the land in trust from the age of twenty-five until his death, but only if he was married. Gary must be married by twenty-five and stay married or forfeit the land to his cousin Fraser. Should Gary be widowed or divorced, he had six months to get himself a new wife or he was off the property.

Gary and Carla's divorce had been finalised on April 25, so Gary would have to marry again by October 25 that year if he wanted to stay on at Wyllandra.

Gary had explained all this to Melanie, who'd listened, ashen-faced, until he'd finished. Then she had held Gary close and told him that Jack Quartermaine was a deranged sadist who didn't deserve such a wonderful grandson. She could only assume that Jack had been hit on the head or deprived of oxygen at some point – the old man had clearly been mad. Gary had been anxious to reassure Melanie that he would have married her anyway, in the natural course of events. They just had to speed things up, in order to comply with the will. But Melanie wasn't worried; she knew that Gary's feelings were true and his intentions honourable. He'd been honest about the situation and she valued his candour. A lesser man would have kept her in the dark.

WYLLANDRA, MAYBURY

Gary was standing in a paddock close to the Big House, digging up a dead mallee root. Stripped to the waist and deeply tanned, he was sweating under a fierce sun. It was extraordinary weather for June. Maybury's weather had become increasingly unpredictable. 'El Niño,' the locals would mutter at the pub. 'Confuses the shit out of the penguins.'

As Rosalie, the wildlife ranger, had explained to Melanie, a week of hot weather in winter could trigger a false breeding season among the local penguin population. They'd all lay their eggs at the wrong time of year – eggs that wouldn't survive once the cold set in again. The weather could also pose problems for migratory birds. There were numerous colonies that called Maybury home for a good seven months of the year. They included short-tailed shearwaters, known as mutton-birds, wading sandpipers and red-necked stints. They'd leave Maybury in April, heading for China or Siberia, or, in the case of the mutton-birds, the Arctic Circle, and they'd all come back in springtime, around late September. Last September there had been wild, unseasonal storms, making it difficult for the birds to land. After the storms, Rosalie and her crew had searched the beaches, collecting any injured birds and taking them to the wildlife infirmary, where they were nursed back to health.

Melanie had never really thought about the weather. Up to now it had only affected what clothes she wore or whether she'd take an umbrella. People in the country thought about the weather differently. It affected not only the wildlife but the soil and the crops and the stock – everything, really. Melanie liked that about Maybury; she liked the fact that people would sit in the pub and talk to their mates about seasonal shifts and confused penguins and actually worry about it. It made everything seem more interconnected. Which, of course, it was.

Melanie walked down from the house, carrying a glass of cold orange juice. She'd be driving back to Melbourne in a couple of hours. She had a few days' work at the hospital and a gig at Donovan's with the Morangos. She handed Gary the juice and he gulped it down, nodding his thanks. She noticed that he seemed a little tense today.

'Reckon I'll leave it a while,' he said and handed her the empty glass. 'It's getting a bit hot.'

'Very sensible,' she remarked. 'You know, "Mad dogs and Englishmen . . ."'

'Yeah, they're stupid bastards,' Gary leant his spade against a nearby fence.

'No, they "go out in the midday sun".'

'Yeah.' Gary frowned at her. 'That's why they're stupid bastards. Jeez, Mel, I'm not completely ignorant.'

'I'm sorry, I just didn't think Noel Coward had made it down to Maybury.' Melanie tried to make a joke out of it but Gary wasn't playing.

'Well, darlin', he got here a long time before you did.'

'All right,' she replied coolly, 'you don't have to bite my head off.'

Seeing the hurt in her eyes, Gary's frown disappeared. 'Sorry, love. I'm just a bit cranky today. I'm sorry.'

'S'all right,' said Melanie.

They started walking back towards the house. In a nearby paddock, Col drove past in his ute, which was piled high with posts and fencing wire. Melanie waved to him but he didn't wave back.

'Huh, I guess he didn't see me,' said Melanie, as the ute disappeared over the hill.

'He saw you, darl'. Don't worry, he saw you.' Gary put his arm around Melanie's waist and they continued walking.

'Is everything okay?'

'Not really,' replied Gary. 'Dad just paid out some money. He'll be in a stink for a while.'

'What, did he buy another horse?'

Gary gave a short, bitter laugh. 'Nope. He paid for my divorce.'

'Oh.' Melanie wasn't sure what to say. 'Right.'

'It's just the settlement. Old news,' muttered Gary. ''Course, I'll pay him back. It'll just take a while.'

'But Col's got plenty of money, hasn't he?'

'Sure,' said Gary, 'but he doesn't want to spend it on my divorce. Pisses him right off.'

They climbed the verandah steps together and walked into the house.

Gary felt bad about snapping at Melanie. He'd had a row with Col that morning, the payout stirring up some old issues. And here he was taking it out on his girl. It was a pretty miserable send-off. He resolved to make it up to her. Taking a couple of towels out of the hall cupboard, he steered her towards the bathroom. They made vertical love in Gary's cavernous shower – there were six nozzles installed, so you could be blasted from all directions – then diagonal love across the bedroom couch and horizontal love on the bed, then back to the shower.

Eventually Gary got dressed and went out to the kitchen. He put the kettle on for a farewell cuppa, then he opened the fridge and took out a stack of vegetables, including six cauliflowers, a dozen sweet potatoes and several kilos of spinach.

Melanie put on her travelling clothes: the now-faded 'Bjorn Again' T-shirt that Marshall had given her three Christmases ago, a pair of baggy blue shorts and her old pink ballet slippers. She carried her vinyl suitcase into the kitchen and dropped it near the kitchen door.

'You know,' said Gary, reaching for a chopping board, 'you should leave your stuff here with me. Well, some of it. Seems silly carting everything up and down all the time.'

'Yeah, I s'pose so.' She noticed the array of food. 'You a bit hungry then?'

'Nah,' said Gary, stripping the leaves off the spinach. 'It's not for me, darl', it's for the guests. I'm doing a dinner party tonight.'

'Oh.' Melanie felt a pang. The green-eyed monster letting fly with a good kick.

'It's a catering thing I do,' Gary squatted and rattled around in the saucepan cupboard. 'Fifty bucks a head – it's a good little earner.'

'Mmm. Sounds good.' Melanie rescued the whistling kettle from the stove. Be breezy, she thought, be light. 'Tea or coffee?'

'Tea, thanks, darl',' Gary opened the freezer, surveying its contents.

Melanie spooned some darjeeling into a blue china teapot and poured over the boiling water.

'So how does it work, this catering thing?' Fluffy. Breezy.

'Well,' said Gary, 'I provide the venue and the tucker, they hand over the money.' Leaning down into the freezer, he pulled out a dozen pork fillets, two legs of lamb and a side of beef, dumping it all on the sink. 'Let's see, meat . . . meat . . . and for entrée, we'll have meat.'

'You're such a carnivore,' Melanie teased.

Gary grabbed her playfully by the waist. Baring his fangs, he tapped his incisors. 'Listen, honey, these weren't designed for ripping into banana smoothies.'

Melanie laughed and returned his hug, hiding her disquiet about this sideline of his, wondering why he hadn't mentioned it before and chiding herself for being so territorial.

142

'So who's coming over tonight?' she trilled, reaching for the Panadol. All this breeziness was giving her a headache.

'Uh, tonight is . . .' Gary checked a calendar on the side of the fridge, 'school teachers. About fifteen of them.'

'Uhuh.' Melanie took her tea over to the table. 'So who else do you get?'

'Uh, let's see . . .' Gary sharpened a long carving knife. Melanie watched the muscles in his arms as he worked. 'Sporting groups, CWA, RSL. And the shire president – he'll book a dinner if he's got some pollies down from the city.'

'So, what – you cook for them?'

'Cook for them, serve the meal – you know, play the host.' He searched the pantry, moving aside bottles and jars. 'It's a bit of fun. I dress up in a tux, whack on some Mozart . . . Cripes, where'd I put the tarragon?'

Melanie sat drinking her tea, feeling covetous about their special table, which was apparently everybody's special table. Then she felt stupid for being so small-minded.

Sensing her mood, Gary came up behind her and started massaging her shoulders. 'You going to miss me, darl'?'

'Mmm, that's nice.' She sighed. ''Course I'm going to miss you.'

'Don't you go flirting with any of those doctor bastards.'

'All right. Only 'cause you asked so nicely.'

'Or those musician bastards.'

'Yeah, well, don't you go flirting with those teacher bastards.'

'Jeez, what a horrible thought.'

'Glad to hear it.'

He pulled her hair back into a ponytail. 'You know, you should try wearing your hair like this.'

Melanie frowned. 'Hmm, it's a bit severe.'

'You reckon?' Gary leant down and kissed the side of her neck. He pushed the T-shirt aside, revealing a lacy, lilac-coloured strap. He nuzzled it and mumbled into her shoulder, 'Have you spoken to Barry?'

'Yeah,' said Melanie, her body softening, 'I'm seeing him on Saturday. Sort out the decorations.'

Gary pulled the bra strap off her shoulder with his teeth. Then he unhooked the back of the bra and slid both hands under her T-shirt to cup her breasts. ''Cause anything you need, darl', Barry's your man.' He leant in closer and murmured in her ear, his breath warm on her neck. 'Except this. You want this, you call me.'

Melanie sighed, her body arching. Her head fell back onto Gary's chest, as his broad hands travelled down towards her thighs.

FIT 'N' FUNKY GYM, ALBERT PARK

Richard was humming to himself. A gentle bossanova – one that Melanie sang at the club. He was lying on a sun bed, soaking up the rays, determined to acquire that toiling-in-the-sun look, which wasn't easily attained in jazz clubs and reception halls. The solarium was his only hope.

Phew, sure is hot, he thought. 'Like a trip to Queensland,' they'd told him at the front desk. 'Cheapest holiday you'll get.'

I'd like a real trip to Queensland, he mused. Me and Mel, splashing about on the Great Barrier Reef. Wait a minute! Aren't I s'posed to be wearing goggles? Shit. No goggles. Right. Cancer of the cornea. Great. I know, I know, I'll just keep them closed. Tight. Tighter. Now relax . . . When's the beeper going to go off? This has got to be more than forty-five minutes . . . Richard, you're an idiot. Just relax, okay.

He started humming again, but before long he was back to worrying. These machines, he thought, they're pretty full on. I mean, what if it's cooking my internal organs? That could happen. Sure. Poaching them. Slowly, so you wouldn't know it. God, my sperm – it could be killing off my sperm! I won't be able to have kids!! No beep, where's the beep? What if the timer's broken?!

'Mr Cohen, time's up!' Someone was tapping at the door.

'Help! I can't make it stop!' Frantically Richard searched for a switch on the side of the machine. He kept his eyes closed tight. It was bad enough he was sterile, he wasn't going to be blind as well.

'Mr Cohen, are you okay in there?' More tapping and rattling of the doorknob, all to no avail. The door was locked from the inside.

'I'm trying to get out!' he shouted. This was no holiday in Queensland. He was trapped in a large irradiating coffin. There was clearly something wrong with the lid; it was slowly sinking in on top of him. Gritting his teeth, he inched his body sideways, sure that his chest was about to connect with the electrics and burst into flames.

'You all right in there, mate?!' Shit, thought the receptionist, her polite tapping now an anxious thumping. Should have warned him about the lid.

'BEEEEEEEEP.' The machine suddenly switched itself off, plunging the room into darkness. Richard slumped back onto the sun bed, dripping with sweat and wondering if he'd be allowed to adopt.

WYLLANDRA, MAYBURY

That night, at the Big House, the stereo had been cranked up to full volume. A raunchy blues number blasted out of the speakers. About twenty drunken women jostled for position around the kitchen table, screeching and hooting with delight at the star attraction. High atop the table was their host, Gary Quartermaine.

Wearing only a white bow tie, black leather G-string and long black riding boots, Gary danced provocatively among the empty wine bottles. He was solidly built, but it was solid muscle. His body was well-toned by a lifetime of physical labour.

He thrust his hips backwards and forwards, then side to side. He gyrated them seductively, doing a slow circle of the table, flaunting his taut buttocks. The inebriated revellers reached up to stroke his thighs and grab at his bum.

They shoved twenty-dollar notes down the front of his soft leather pouch.

Sitting in a corner of the room was Blodwyn Platt. Dressed in her dark, shapeless garb, with her cropped hair framing a gaunt face, she leant back in her chair and trained her eyes onto Gary. She watched him bump, she watched him grind, she observed the droplets of sweat rolling down his inner thigh. She didn't hoot or holler. She simply watched and said nothing.

SOMEWHERE IN OUTER MELBOURNE

The following night Richard and Melanie were riding in the back of a panel van, both wearing blindfolds. Everybody wanted Latino music these days, including the Boozy Crocodiles. The Boozy Crocs was a secret society made up of men who couldn't get into the Freemasons. Or the Buffaloes. They drank a lot, perhaps to dull the pain of their earlier rejections. The Crocs paid good money, but only if the band went along with all the cloak and dagger stuff – blindfolds, secret destinations, and so on. Bit over the top, thought Melanie. Still, she liked watching the men in their crocodile masks and their little black aprons, dancing the rumba in neatly ordered rows – it warmed the cockles.

Marshall and Patrick would wait up for her after one of these nights, insisting on a live-action replay. Once Marshall had nearly choked on his felafel during Melanie's rendition of the 'Boozy-Croc Mambo'. Singing loudly, she'd gone sashaying around the lounge room with a couple of vacuum cleaner attachments. Patrick had joined her, wearing his favourite apron, clacking a pair of salad servers together and baring his teeth with reptilian ferocity.

Richard and Melanie were packed in tight among keyboards and amps and the van's spare tyre. Two more vehicles followed behind, completing the convoy. They swayed gently with the rocking of the van until, eventually, Melanie nodded off to sleep. Oblivious to Melanie's slumber, Richard was lifting hand weights, talking about a documentary he'd seen – *Jazz and the Third Reich*. His arms and chest were tinted a deep orange, thanks to the liberal use of self-tanning lotion. He'd applied several coats of Poster-boy Bronze in an attempt to cover his solarium-induced sunburn and achieve a more manly hue. The end result, however, was more citrus than sex god. He was hoping that Melanie wouldn't notice.

'You know, Adolf Hitler really hated jazz. It frightened the living daylights out of him. 'Cause jazz , it's all about improvisation. And Hitler hated the idea of making it up as you go along. Gives people too much freedom, right?'

'Hmmph,' Melanie grunted, still asleep.

'So he made this rule that when you were improvising, you could only play a certain number of notes, right? For every note written on the page, you could only improvise so many notes off the page. You had, like, a quota. The guy was a loony.'

'Hmmph.'

'Just imagine it: the Gestapo's at the gig, having a few

beers. This is the Special Music Gestapo we're talking about. The Jazz Nazis.'

They hit a bump, Richard knocking his cheek with a hand weight, just missing an eye. 'Ow! Bugger,' he whimpered.

Melanie snuffled a little and continued sleeping.

'Anyway, you're up there playing, and the Nazis are counting . . . counting . . . and suddenly, "Too many notes! You're over the limit!" They go for their guns.'

Brrring. Brrring.

'Is that yours?' asked Richard. No response. The phone kept ringing. 'Mel? Are you okay?'

Melanie rolled over, snuggling up to a saxophone case. Still blindfolded, Richard felt around in a bag of leads, fishing out the phone.

'Hello . . . No, I'm sorry, she can't come to the phone . . . Yeah, sure, what's the message? . . . Uhuh.'

'Who is it?' Melanie yawned, stretching her arms above her head.

'I don't know, she's got an accent. She says – sorry, what was that?' Richard listened intently to the caller. 'Right . . . Uhuh . . .' Then he relayed the message to Melanie. 'She says, "When you show your legs on the stage, you look like a tramp."'

'Hi Consuela,' Melanie called out towards the phone.

'Hello, hello? She hung up. That's Consuela? You reckon?'

'Oh yes,' replied Melanie. 'She calls me all the time.'

'I don't get it.' Richard shook his head. 'I mean, what's her problem?'

Melanie rubbed her eyes through the blindfold. 'She thinks I'm sleeping with José.'

'Oh my God!' exclaimed Richard. Then, only half-joking, 'You're not, are you?'

'Yeah, him and Freddy Krueger, my two favourite guys.'

The van screeched to a halt. Melanie and Richard lurched forward then back, grabbing hold of each other for support.

Man, she's so warm, thought Richard. Her hair, it smells like daisies. Wasn't that a commercial? No, that was green apples. God, she's delicious. I should do something here . . . I could kiss her on the neck. Yeah. Just kiss her and pretend it was an accident. The forces of quantum physics impelling her neck towards my lips.

Melanie was surprised by Richard's embrace. He was stronger than she'd imagined. It felt comfortable, being so close to him. Familiar. If she let herself, she could just melt into his body. Christ, Melanie! Don't even think about it!

As Richard ripped off his blindfold and went to kiss Melanie's neck, the van doors were suddenly thrown open. Milos, Andy and Sarita were standing there in front of them.

'Don't you hate these gigs!' declared Andy.

Richard and Melanie scrambled out of the van, Melanie tearing off her blindfold and hoping that no-one had noticed her momentary clinch with Richard, or the colour of her cheeks.

Sarita threw a bag of whistles over her shoulder and strode out into the night. 'Come on, people. The Crocodiles await.'

NED KELLY MEMORIAL SCOUT HALL, RICHMOND

The following Saturday was a grey Melbourne afternoon. A group of boisterous men bounded out of the scout hall and onto the street. They hovered in front of the building, laughing and guffawing and punching the air. Among them was Richard, who had burst out of the hall with renewed vigour. After beating a drum and howling like a wolf for a couple of hours, he'd tapped into the raw, primal, collective male unconscious.

It was all thanks to 'Hounds from Hell', a series of workshops run by HUMP – the Health Unit for the Male Psyche. The unit was funded by several anonymous donors, rumoured to be members of the Boozy Crocs. The workshops were a harmless and effective way for men to release aggression. Or, in Richard's case, to find it.

Richard scanned the street, looking for Milos, who walked up behind him and punched him on the shoulder.

'Hey, Superfish!'

'Hey, coach!' Richard thumped him back.

'All right!' Milos punched him again.

'All right!' Richard thumped him back. 'Let's go, bro!'

They set off down the street at a brisk pace.

'You know, last night, I had a really wild dream about Melanie,' said Richard. 'Like, really kinky.'

'Yeah?'

'We were playing one of those product launches, you know, with the tap dancers.'

'Tropitang?'

'Yeah, Tropitang. Anyway, we're on a break and I go

into the change room and Melanie's there. She's wearing this white see-through dress, and she's naked underneath, and I lay her down on a bed of promotional T-shirts and we have this incredible sex.'

'This is not very kinky,' grumbled Milos.

'Then the tap dancers come in,' Richard continued.

'All right!'

'And they're naked, right. Except for their tap shoes and these pineapple rings they've got stuck on their breasts. So their nipples are poking through the pineapple rings . . .'

They turned a corner. At the end of the street a neon sign for Donovan's Den flickered into life.

DONOVAN'S DEN, RICHMOND

Melanie was already at Donovan's, the first one to pick up her pay, such as it was. Melanie hopped up onto a bar stool. She was wearing her driving clothes and her chestnut hair was pulled back into a ponytail. Reaching across the bar, she plucked a packet of cashews from the display stand.

'How much are these?' she asked.

'Don't worry about it,' said Brian.

'Thanks, Brian.' She tore the packet open. 'I'm going away today, just for a couple of weeks.'

'Down to the farm?'

'Yep.'

'So, you're running away from the band,' said Brian. 'That'll upset the punters.' Then he added with a smile, 'You've got a bit of a fan base, you know.'

'Yeah, sure,' said Melanie. 'Anyway, it's only for two gigs. Andy's found a replacement – Mitch Wheeler. He plays with that trio at the Sheraton. He's a great player, much better than me.'

'Yeah, but does he sing?'

'Um, I don't think so.'

'He doesn't sing and he isn't you. I rest my case,' said Brian.

'And there she is!' Richard called from the doorway. 'The beautiful Melanie, Queen of the Bossanova!' He and Milos gave a low bow, tugging their respective forelocks.

'All hail! All hail to the Sultana of Swing!' chanted Richard.

'All hail!' echoed Milos.

Melanie frowned at them. 'Have you guys been sniffing textas again?'

'No, sweetheart, just high on life!' Richard grinned, perching on the stool next to her and drumming his hands on the counter. Milos made a beeline for a shelf behind the bar, where Brian kept a stash of magazines. He grabbed a few and retired to a booth, in search of naked tap dancers.

'I s'pose you blokes want your pay,' said Brian.

'Ah yes, our pay,' replied Richard. 'Nothing like the sound of twenty-cent coins rattling around in your pocket.'

'You know, Mozart died a pauper.' Brian pushed a button on the cash register and the drawer shot out with a ping.

'Gotta go, fellas,' Melanie said before she leant across

the bar and kissed Brian on the cheek. She looked over at Milos, but he was engrossed in a centrefold.

She turned to Richard. 'See ya.' She gave him a peck on the lips, hopped off the bar stool and walked out.

'Hey, hey, right on the smacker!' said Brian.

'Forget it, Brian.'

'But mate, you're in with a chance.'

Richard was losing touch with his inner wolf and slipping into melancholy. 'Didn't you see it?'

'See what?' asked Brian.

'The ring. The engagement ring.'

Brian paused for a moment, choosing his words. 'Well, it can't be very big, I didn't notice it.'

'That's not the point, Brian. The point is, she's wearing it. She wears it all the bloody time. She never used to wear it. Nope – that's it. End of story.'

'Yeah,' said Brian, 'and whose fault is that?'

'It isn't *my* fault,' Richard protested. 'She just fell in love with somebody else.'

'She got tired of waiting for you, Mister Couldn't-pick-up-the-phone,' Brian said as he poured two shots of brandy and handed one to Richard.

'She doesn't go out with musicians,' said Richard. 'That's her policy.'

'It's a stupid policy.'

'Bloody stupid.'

'Exactly. And did you tell her that? Did you say, "Mel, your policy is utter crap"?'

Richard ran his finger around the rim of the glass, brooding. 'It wouldn't have made any difference.'

'Come on, man, you've gotta take her on! Tell her you mean business.' Brian shoved a rack of glasses into the auto-wash and flicked the switch, the machine clunking into action. 'Take a chance, for God's sake.'

'Yeah, right,' Richard muttered.

'No guts, no glory,' Brian intoned.

'You can talk,' Richard scoffed. 'I haven't seen you taking any chances.'

'I'm working on it.'

'Yeah?' Richard raised an eyebrow.

'Positive affirmation,' declared Brian, with the zeal of a convert. 'I saw it on "Oprah". You keep saying to yourself, "My soul mate is on a train and she's heading in my direction. She's holding a ticket with my name on it. She's on that train and she's heading in my direction."'

'So you've got an imaginary girlfriend on an imaginary train.' Richard drained his glass and plonked it on the bar. 'Good one, Brian. Gutsy effort.'

WYLLANDRA, MAYBURY

After a long, lazy breakfast of Gary's French toast, accompanied by home-grown mandarins and freshly brewed coffee, Melanie put on her jeans and a fleecy shirt and went outside to feed the chooks. Singing the Boozy-Croc Mambo, she danced around and threw handfuls of pellets onto the grass. The bantams and leghorns cackled away, fluffing their feathers and scratching the ground. She could swear they were moving in time to the music.

'Better watch it,' Gary said as he appeared behind her, putting an arm around her shoulder. He was dressed in his shearing clothes: T-shirt, bib-and-brace overalls and heavy work boots. 'They'll be asking for requests – eh, Millie?'

'Millie?' said Melanie. 'Have they all got names?'

'Yeah, Mum's idea, soft old thing.' Gary pointed to the hens in turn. 'That's Millie, the black one. Misty, she's the grey one. Betty. Gladys. Ah, I forget the others.'

'I like Millie the best.'

Gary took her hand. 'Want to walk me to the bike?'

They ambled towards the driveway, Gary stopping as they passed the cottage to pull some dead vines off the wall.

'I've been talking to Mum and Dad,' he said, 'about the cottage. I want to turn it into a b & b – wouldn't take much, be a good little earner. You could run it, Mel. It'd be your own little business – "Melanie's Cottage". What do you reckon?'

'Oh. Wow. Well, I've never . . .'

'You're a natural! You'd be the hostess with the mostest.'

'You reckon?'

'Mel, you're the PR queen. You could charm the fleas off a dog.'

'Thanks very much!' Melanie poked his arm.

'All right,' Gary said with a laugh, 'you could charm . . . the cockatoos out of the sky.' He put his arm around Melanie's waist and drew her towards him. Together they stood looking at the darkened, empty cottage. The rose-covered lattice fence, running along the left side of the building, separated the cottage and its environs from the sheds and the Big House. A profusion of wild lavender bushes surrounded the cottage like a shimmering purple haze.

'Think about it,' said Gary. 'It's a perfect setting – plenty of privacy – and it's far enough away from the house. We'll get heaps of bookings. They'll all say, "Book me in! I want to meet that gorgeous girl who's married to lucky old Quarters."'

'Yeah, the one with all the fleas,' said Melanie, and Gary laughed and gave her a hug.

They walked closer to the cottage, Gary running his hand along the rugged stone wall. 'You know, I built this place myself. Lived here a couple of years, then we built the Big House.'

That must've been with the first wife, thought Melanie, but she knew not to ask him about it. Gary didn't like talking about his ex-wives. After that first mention of them, at the beginning of the relationship, it seemed now the subject was closed. He felt that the past belonged in the past, and Melanie agreed completely. She had plenty of skeletons in her own closet, ten deep and packed in tight, and that's where they were staying.

Experience had taught her not to blather on about personal history. Tell your mates about it, by all means, but not your beloved. If you allude to one little incident, they'll start linking it to others, quizzing you gently on times and places. Slowly, inexorably, all your follies and indiscretions, all the regrettable, hideously embarrassing episodes begin to emerge, and before you know it, the past is barrelling towards you like a giant snowball, heading straight for the new, reinvented you and – bamm! – smashing it into a thousand pieces.

'I like the colour,' she cooed, caressing the cottage wall.

'Bluestone,' said Gary. 'Got a mate who's a stone mason. He showed me what to do.'

'That is so clever.' Melanie had always been impressed by people who could make things. She had no such talent. As the nuns always told her, 'Miss Francis, you couldn't sew a hem on a handkerchief.' And here was Gary, who had knocked a whole house together.

'I mean, how do you do that?' asked Melanie, admiring the well-constructed cottage. 'Just . . . build something like that, and it doesn't fall down?'

'And how do you play one thing with your right hand, and something different with your left?' replied Gary. 'Incredible! I couldn't do that in a million years.' He pointed to a nearby paddock. 'See there? After we do the cottage, I'm gonna build you a music studio. Right over there.' His eyes lit up. 'We could have a music festival! You could bring people from town – "The Maybury Latin Jazz Festival"! Hey, why not?!'

'Yeah, why not?' Melanie laughed, caught up in Gary's enthusiasm. Why not indeed, she thought. It's close enough to town. A chance for those grey-skinned Melbourne musicians to get some fresh country air.

Gary stroked her hair. 'I know it's a big ask, expecting you to move here. But we can bring some of the city down here. Best of both worlds and all that.' He embraced her and they stood for a moment without speaking, enjoying the warmth of one another's bodies. Then Gary checked his watch. 'Better go, I s'pose. I've got a few hours of shearing to get through.'

'I'll give you a massage when you get home,' said Melanie.

'Mmm, yes please,' Gary purred, resuming the hug.

Melanie slipped her hands into the sides of his overalls, and to her astonishment, she felt lace. She leant down to take a look.

'Gary, these are mine.' Melanie's eyes widened as she tugged at the black lacy briefs. 'You're wearing my knickers!' she exclaimed.

'Oi, careful!'

She ran her hands further inside the overalls, from Gary's hips down to his thighs. 'And my suspender belt! And my stockings!' Melanie's face revealed her growing concern.

'Yeah, I know.' Gary laughed. 'The things I do for money.'

'What?'

'Oh, it's stupid. I made a bet with Tom.'

'Who's Tom?'

'Tom Lewis – he's the wool classer. He reckons I'm not game, but you know me,' Gary said, winking lasciviously, 'I'm up for anything. Right then, better go.'

He threw his leg over his trail bike and kicked up the stand. 'See ya, darl'.'

Melanie watched him as he sped along the track, behind the Big House and off towards the sheds. But before she could gather her thoughts, a voice was calling out to her.

'Coooeee! Could you give me a hand, dear?'

Halfway up the drive, Dorothy was doing battle with a flock of uncooperative geese. Melanie joined her and together they herded the geese back down the drive, across the road to Dorothy's, amid much honking and flapping of wings.

Melanie returned to the house, kicked off her gumboots and made a strong cup of coffee. She sat at the kitchen table, nursing the cup between her hands, looking through the window at the sweep of green paddocks. Marmite came waddling in from the verandah and slumped at Melanie's feet.

Marmite was the lugubrious springer spaniel who had greeted Melanie and Jacqui at the inaugural dinner party. He was a tan and white dog who was carrying a bit of weight. Gary had adopted him from a neighbour rather than see him put down. Marmite had no skills as a working dog – unlike Col's elite team of hyperactive kelpies – so he'd been assigned to Melanie. Marmite's job was to accompany her around the property. He'd walk her down to the letterbox; he'd walk her to the clothesline, lying near the cane basket as she hung out the washing; he'd follow her to Iron-Bar Homestead and collapse in Dorothy's kitchen, growling at the kelpies if they got too close.

Marmite went about his duties with a forlorn, occasionally contemptuous expression. 'Stay on the verandah,' Melanie would tell him. 'Sleep all day if you like.' But he'd haul himself up and start plodding, with a resigned look that said, 'It's all right, boss, it's my job.'

Marmite's grumpy face usually made Melanie smile, but not today. She was thinking about Gary and the lingerie. Was he really dressing up just for a bet? Sure, those blokes in the sheds – the classers and the other shearers – were always playing jokes on each other. They were just big kids really. Of course it was a bet. Look at all those professional football players who couldn't wait to pull on a pair of fish-nets and do their Rocky Horror routines – on national television, no less. It was just something that blokes did. Pretty harmless really, just not what she'd expected from Gary.

Snoring loudly, Marmite rolled over and landed on his mistress's feet, pinning them to the floor. Melanie continued drinking her coffee, keeping quite still so as not to wake her companion.

She chided herself for being so neurotic about Gary. So he'd pulled on a pair of her knickers – big deal. The lads had dared him. It didn't *mean* anything. As usual, she was worrying about nothing. What did Patrick say? 'Ninety-seven per cent of the things people worry about never actually happen.' In Melanie's case, it was more like one hundred per cent.

She started thinking about the cottage and Gary's idea about a b & b. He was right, it would make a great little business. Gary was such a positive, energetic man – she loved that about him. He was always planning the next big project, then rolling his sleeves up and making it happen. He didn't drift about in a perennial state of ennui,

161

wasting precious time, like a lot of city boys. And now his plans included Melanie; she was part of his thinking. They were 'forging a life together', as Barry had put it.

She'd met with Barry the day before, at the Barking Shark, to talk about music for the reception. The Morangos weren't available; they were busy on the twenty-fifth with a Salsa Kings gig – a function in Brighton. So, on Barry's advice, Melanie had booked a cabaret band from Mount Malabar – a better choice really, for a country wedding. It wasn't a cool, Latin-jazz type of occasion; it was a 'hits of the sixties, seventies and eighties' occasion, with plenty of barn-dancing and the occasional waltz.

Melanie sipped her coffee and smiled at the sleeping spaniel who was lying across her feet, warming her toes. 'Forging a life together . . .' She liked that.

MAYBURY

The following morning, a Saturday, Gary and Melanie rose early and pulled on their overalls. They joined Simon and Pip and the rest of the Maybury Tree Planters at a stretch of land near the Northern Highway and laboured for hours, digging, planting and mulching.

At around midday Gary was addressing the local craft club. Members of the club had assembled at the Jack Possum Primary School for their monthly meeting. Melanie watched from the side of the classroom as Gary took the floor and spoke expansively on a range of local matters. She was impressed by his performance. Gary might be corn-fed and wholesome but he was nobody's fool. For one thing, he knew how to tap into government funding. As one of the locals had remarked, if there was rural assistance available, Gary could track it down, 'like a pig to truffles'.

This year the craft club wanted money for their Christmas party and Gary had a plan. As Melanie scanned the room, she realised that the craft club comprised almost exactly the same members as the tree planters.

Gary took a scrap of paper from his pocket and, consulting it, scrawled on the blackboard:

PROJECT:
Xmas booze-up on beach

WHAT WE CALL IT ON GRANT APPLICATION:
Site-specific workshop with marine themes
exploring pagan rituals

WHAT WE GET:
Cash from Greater Eastern Regional Arts Fund!

The audience burst into rapturous applause. Gary had done it again. Melanie clapped politely, but for her it smacked of the Whippet, who was sitting down the back with her girlfriend, Maxine, looking suspiciously smug. Blodwyn was always sticking her bib into Gary's projects, Melanie had noticed. Annoying bloody woman, she was so interfering and school-teacherish.

The meeting adjourned and the matronly club president came rattling into the room with a tea trolley. Everyone chatted over tea and pikelets, discussing fabric dye and glass-blowing and how to make a ten-foot dolphin out of wine bladders and string.

.♣.

Later that day, Melanie clung to the side of a trailer; it was filled with hay and numerous locals. Gary had invited the craft club/tree planters to a family sausage sizzle at Wyllandra. The children had insisted on a hay-ride. They were now zooming across the paddocks at high speed, Gary at the helm on Josafina, and Melanie on the trailer as supervising adult. Gary kept turning the wheel sharply and aiming for bumps, eliciting screams of laughter from his airborne guests.

Melanie was coming up in bruises and there were hay seeds in her bra. She smiled valiantly, while secretly praying for rain.

.♣.

After a very long day of tree-planting, sausage-sizzling and other people's children, Melanie was relieved that she and Gary were finally off to bed. If she didn't get some sleep – and soon – she would probably have to kill someone. Gary locked the kitchen door and Melanie switched off the lights. But as they walked towards the bedroom, an old brown station wagon tore up the drive and the occupants disembarked. Gary switched the lights back on and threw open the door.

'Come in, you old bastards!' Melanie heard Gary call out.

She leant against the wall in the corridor and sighed heavily. So much for getting away from it all. There was more peace and quiet in the city. 'Hey, darl'!' Gary called to her from the verandah. 'Look who's back!' Melanie dropped her head onto her chest and started tugging at her hair.

Brendan, Rosalie, Simon, Pip, Blodwyn and Maxine descended on the kitchen. Melanie, attempting to dredge up some enthusiasm, emerged from the hallway to greet them. She thought all the furious hugging was a bit much. They'd spent the whole day with these people, for God's sake. Resigning herself to more socialising, Melanie put on the kettle and reached for some cups. Blodwyn joined her, moving around the kitchen with a proprietorial air. Much to Melanie's annoyance, Blodwyn seemed to know where everything was kept.

By two in the morning, the second round of guests had finally departed. Gary and Melanie hauled themselves down the corridor and fell into bed. Melanie was exhausted. As she flicked off the lamp, the phone on the bedside table began to ring.

'Oh no,' she groaned, incredulous.

Gary reached across her and picked up the receiver. 'Yeah . . . Uhuh . . . Okay, be right over.' He hung up and got out of bed, pulling on his overalls.

'Don't these people ever leave you alone?' Melanie muttered.

'It's a dead cow.' Gary searched under the bed for his boots. 'It's on the road. We've got to shift it.'

'Is it *your* dead cow?' Melanie didn't hide her displeasure.

'It's Charlie Hamlin's dead cow and he needs a hand shifting it.' Gary snatched his keys off the bedside table and headed for the door. 'It's called living in a community,' he snapped, slamming the door behind him.

Melanie pulled the covers over her head. 'Well, *excuuuuse* me!'

DONOVAN'S DEN, RICHMOND

Melanie sat at the bar late on a Thursday night, talking to Brian.

'And this friend of mine,' she was saying, 'her husband likes to . . . well, he likes to dress up in her lingerie.'

'Yeah,' said Brian. 'So?'

'I mean, is that a normal thing to do? You know, for straight guys?'

'Well,' said Brian, filling a wooden bowl with pistachios, 'they don't broadcast it across the bar, but I gather it's not unusual.'

Richard was walking down a side street on his way to the club. He shifted his saxophone case from one shoulder to the other and looked behind him, peering into the shadows of the badly lit street. He could swear someone was following him. He slowed his walk to a crawl, trying to catch out the stranger who was skulking behind him.

Suddenly, he swung around and collared the man, shoving him against a brick wall.

'Hey!' the man shouted.

Richard recognised him immediately – it was the guy at the pool. The guy in the next lane.

'I got you, you bastard!' Richard yelled in the man's face.

'What?! What?!' The man looked frightened and utterly bewildered.

Richard kept yelling, tightening his grip. 'You've been following me for weeks! The pool, the deli, the club.'

'No, mate, not me!' The man squirmed, trying to free himself.

'You go back and tell them I don't sell drugs!'

'What are you talking about?' wheezed the stranger, gasping for air.

'Don't bullshit me!' Richard barked.

'Tell who? Tell what?'

'Come on, mate, you know who I mean – the Sciarelli brothers.'

'Sciarelli . . . they're a wedding band, aren't they?'

Richard looked at the man for a moment then released his grip. The man straightened up, coughing and checking his neck for any damage. He was of a slight build with a sensitive face. Not your standard thug, thought Richard.

'Well, who *are* you then?'

The man took out his wallet, plucked out a business card and handed it to Richard. 'It's Blake. Matthew Blake. Private detective.'

'Dig the Dirt Detective Agency,' Richard read the card

aloud then handed it back. 'You don't look like a private detective.'

'I do videos mostly. Weddings. This is just a sideline.' He took a packet of cigarettes out of his pocket and offered one to Richard.

'No thanks,' said Richard. 'Just tell me what you're up to.'

'Well, I'm trailing a suspect.' Matthew lit up and leant against the wall. 'My client is a nice Latino lady. She's married to a musician. Apparently he's some kinda stud, so, you know, the girls go for him.' He pulled a photograph out of his jacket and handed it to Richard. 'This is the female I'm trailing. My client reckons she's having it off with the husband.'

Richard looked at the photo and his face darkened. He slid the photo into his jacket pocket.

'Right.' He looked Matthew Blake straight in the eye. 'You can tell Consuela Torres that she's losing the plot. Melanie wouldn't touch that sleaze-bag with a barge pole.' Richard drew himself up to his full six foot two. 'And I'm telling you, mate, you go near Melanie Francis again – you even look in her general direction – you'll have me to deal with. You got that?'

The part-time detective scuttled away, adept at hasty departures. Richard strode proudly towards the club, his body pumping with adrenalin. He was bursting to tell Melanie about the incident. How could she fail to be impressed? Intrepid Hero Protects Maiden's Honour. Man with Sax Saves the Day. He'd give that bloody hayseed a run for his money.

Richard felt certain that the bond between him and

Melanie was growing stronger. Earlier that day, they'd spent a wonderful few hours together, playing at the retirement home in Croydon. They'd been going there on a fairly sporadic basis for the past couple of years. They enjoyed spending time with the residents and staff, who were a pretty colourful bunch. Melanie had once described the gig as a form of 'karmic investment', musing that, when she and Richard were old, maybe someone would come and play for them too.

Richard threw open the door of Donovan's Den and scanned the room. Sitting at the bar was his damsel in distress. But she didn't look too distressed. In fact, she was showing off her engagement ring to a friend of Brian's. Richard's heart sank. He was clearly operating in a parallel universe and Melanie was oblivious to the risks he was taking on her behalf. He'd collared a stranger in the street, for God's sake, and here she was, gushing over a stupid ring. He stood in the doorway for a moment, watching her chatting and laughing. He resolved not to tell her about his fearless display. She already had one intrepid hero, she didn't need two.

Inside the club, a group of young women were ensconced in a circular booth. Squeezed into tiny dresses, they were throwing back shots of vodka and slamming their glasses on the laminate. Richard noticed them as he walked in. One in particular caught his eye: a strawberry blonde with generous breasts. He smiled at her, and she returned his smile with a slightly dazed expression.

A predictable strategy, thought Melanie, who'd witnessed the exchange. It was a ploy she'd used many times herself: the old wide-eyed, deer-in-the-headlights look, designed to heighten a man's sense of his own importance. Of course, it's harder to pull off in your thirties. Hard to look blank when you've lived a little.

Richard arrived at the bar and stood next to Melanie.

'Don't you think you should wait?' said Melanie.

'For what?' replied Richard.

'Oh, I don't know, the age of consent?'

'Ha ha.' Richard tugged her ponytail.

'No, no, you go for it, mate,' said Melanie. 'My shout, Brian. A spritzer for me and a packet of boiled sweets for my friend.'

'I'll have a beer, thanks, Brian,' said Richard. He glanced over his shoulder to assess the target area.

As Melanie trawled her handbag for coins, Richard picked up his beer and moved towards the girls' table. Melanie and Brian looked on as Richard arrived at the circle of bosoms and launched into Operation Charm.

'Man on a mission,' said Brian, setting down the spritzer.

Melanie reached for the bowl of pistachios. 'You know, Brian, it's funny,' she said as she started pulling off the shells, 'you expose your body, the men come running. You expose your mind, they can't get out of the room quick enough.'

TIVOLI GARDENS, ALBERT PARK

Richard awoke the next day with a start, his brain in panic mode.

Shit! Chart! Shit! Woodwind . . . Year Twelve . . . Today! Write chart. Shit! Go, go, go! He reached across to the bedside table, groping around for his watch. His head hurt from too much alcohol. He was dimly aware that he'd run out of aspirin; he'd get some more on the way to school.

As his vision started to clear, he realised that he wasn't alone. There was a woman lying next to him. A woman in his bed – a rare sight indeed. It was the strawberry blonde from the night before. What was her name? Rani? Renée? Sandy? She was lying with her back to him, naked and still sleeping, her breath gently rising and falling. Daylight streamed through the bamboo blinds, casting shadows onto her creamy skin.

He remembered now: drinks at the club, late-night supper at Cervantes, then back to the flat for more drinks. She'd been talking about a course she was doing. Mahjong or Marxism or marketing jonquils – something like that. He hadn't been listening, he'd been plotting his next move. But before he could say 'I know we've only just met, but would you mind terribly if I kissed you?' she was tearing at his clothes and straddling his hips, unleashing a torrent of youthful passion which hadn't abated till 3 a.m.

He snuggled up close to the young woman's body and nuzzled the back of her neck. Forget the new chart, they could work on revision. He kissed the tip of the woman's shoulder and she stirred a little, emitting a quiet sigh. Still half asleep, she reached behind her, sliding a warm, soft hand between Richard's thighs.

THE MAGELLAN HOSPITAL, EAST MELBOURNE

Jacqui and Melanie sat in their usual spot in the gardens, eating their take-away lunches. The hospital cafeteria now sold Japanese food, which caused some consternation among the hospital ducks, who preferred soft bread to sticky rice.

'You should come down to the club,' said Melanie to her friend. 'It's a good night, Thursdays – a nice crowd. You could meet a really nice guy.'

'No thanks, Mel. I hate clubs. They're not my scene.'

'Jacqui, he's a cat.' Melanie examined her California roll, wondering whether that was crab or tuna in the middle. 'Cats are very independent, they like it when you go out.'

'It isn't Leroy,' said Jacqui. 'I just don't feel like it.' She prodded at her tempura broccoli. 'I don't like going out at night, not by myself.'

'But I'll be there.'

'Yeah, but you'll be playing the piano.'

'Not all the time,' said Melanie. 'We do get breaks.'

'Yeah, but most of the time I'll be sitting by myself like a fool.' Jacqui tugged at a sachet of soy sauce. 'Anyway,' she muttered, 'I went out with a guy.'

Melanie looked up from her lunch. 'What guy? When?'

'A couple of weeks ago.'

'You didn't tell me.'

'You weren't around, you were at Gary's.'

'So, how'd it go?'

'Well, what can I say? It was an unmitigated disaster.'

'Oh.' Melanie frowned. 'Bugger.'

'I've dated some cheap guys in my time, but this one . . .'

'What's his name?'

'Ray,' said Jacqui. 'Ray something. I forget. He was temping as an orderly. I met him in the caff. He's gone now, thank God.' She gave up on the soy sauce and tossed it in the bin. 'Anyway, we go to this restaurant, right, with some of his friends – about three other couples.'

'Did he pay?'

'No,' said Jacqui, 'but that's all right. The thing is, after we've finished eating, he asks the waiter for a plastic container. He puts in all his leftovers, then he reaches across and gets my leftovers.'

'Maybe he's got a dog.'

'No. No dog. He says, "This is my lunch for tomorrow." He's serious.'

'Well,' Melanie said with a shrug, 'that's not so bad. Waste not, want not.'

'Then,' Jacqui continued, 'he asks the waiter for another container, right? Three people on our table have eaten soup. So he collects up the bowls and he pours all the leftover soup into the plastic container.'

'Oh.' Melanie grimaced.

'I'm so embarrassed,' said Jacqui. 'The waiter's looking at me, like, "You *know* this guy?" I thought, okay, so he's cheap and he's got dubious habits. There are worse crimes, give him a chance. So, he drives me home . . .'

'Your place?'

'Yep. We're sitting in the car and he leans over and looks into my eyes, and he says, "Jacqui, do you know the first thing I noticed about you?" I'm thinking, this is nice. Maybe he likes my eyes, men always like my eyes.'

'You do have beautiful eyes.'

'Thank you, Mel. So I say, "Tell me, Ray, what is the first thing you noticed about me?" And straightaway, he says, "Your nipples, Jacqui. They're huge. Your nipples are so big, it's kinda freaky. God, you could hang clothes on those nipples."'

'He didn't!'

'I mean, that *and* the soup. Come on!'

'When did guys get so weird?' Melanie poked the mystery seafood out of her California roll and fed it to the ducks, who were most appreciative. Anything but rice.

Melanie looked up at the willow trees that surrounded the lake. A flock of noisy parakeets was flitting about, engaged in some kind of squabble. A raven swooped down from a telegraph pole, claiming a half-eaten Mars Bar, which had been abandoned on the lawn. A steady stream of staff, patients and visitors walked back and forth across the gardens, going about their business. It was a regular day at the office. The sun was warm on her face, but Melanie was feeling troubled. She decided to bite the bullet.

'Um, Jacqui . . .' she ventured.

'Uhuh?'

'I was just wondering, have you ever been with a bloke who liked to . . . dress up in your underwear?'

'Ahhh.' Jacqui gave her a knowing look. 'So the farmer's wearing your knickers?'

'It was just for a dare,' Melanie added hastily. 'Well, that's what he reckons.'

'Listen, Mel. When he gets into *other* women's knickers, that's when you gotta worry.'

'Yeah. Right.' Melanie smiled, relieved at Jacqui's reaction.

'And if *you* don't want him . . .'

'Yeah, yeah, I know.'

DAME NELLIE MELBA SECONDARY COLLEGE, HAWTHORN

'*One*-two-three-four, *one*-two-three-four . . .' Richard marked time with his ruler as the woodwind players struggled to keep up. He was thinking about the girl in his bed. Zani. When she was taking a shower, he'd checked her purse and found her driver's licence – it was a relief to know that she was over sixteen. Twenty, in fact. Still, she wasn't much older than the Year Twelves.

He sliced the air with his ruler. '*One*-two-three-four, *one*-two-three-four . . .'

I should feel guilty, he thought. But he didn't. He felt exhilarated.

THE MAGELLAN HOSPITAL, EAST MELBOURNE

Melanie sat in a recliner rocker, playing with the lever. She was up in the staff support centre, where the couches were comfy and the views panoramic. The centre, on the fourteenth floor, boasted five psychotherapists, two acupuncturists and a waspish Anglican priest (not a patch on Father What-a-waste). A steady stream of harried workers emerged from the lifts, helping themselves to decaf and biscotti, relaxing in the couches with glossy magazines.

This was Melanie's first visit to the centre. She glanced at a brochure entitled 'Is your job making you depressed?' Working in the typing pool could certainly get you down: the morgue on one side, the psych ward on the other; stuck in the basement with no natural light. It was a feng shui nightmare.

But it wasn't about the job. She was there to talk about Gary. Usually she'd consult Patrick or Jacqui about matters of the heart. (Never Marshall. He'd repeat everything verbatim at the salon, where styling and gossip were inextricably linked.) But there came a point when you didn't want to bore your friends anymore. And friends, by their nature, weren't impartial. They took your side. They didn't have 'professional distance'; that wasn't their gig. Melanie was quite comfortable about baring her soul to strangers. She'd first sought counselling fifteen years earlier, when her mother had died, to help her cope with the grief. The sessions had released a torrent of accumulated rage, directed at her father, Jack. She'd been referred to Al-Anon and had attended the meetings for about a year. Like Melanie, many in the group were adult children of alcoholics. They learnt how to change old patterns of thinking, so they could live their lives more productively, instead of railing against ghosts and shadows.

Melanie's record with men had been, on the whole, pretty ordinary. Probably a by-product of the stormy father–daughter scenario, she often thought. At thirty-four, the years were slipping by and soon her fertility would start to wane.

With Gary she had a new opportunity and she was determined to make it work. She'd enlist the help of a professional – a relationship coach, someone to keep tabs on her progress and alert her to any self-sabotaging behaviour. The support centre was handy – only a lift ride away – and it was free to all staff, so really there was nothing to lose.

The receptionist ushered Melanie into one of the consulting rooms, where, after some form-signing and other preamble, the session got under way.

'So, tell me about his father,' the counsellor was saying.

Dr Agnes Gledhill, PhD, sat in a high-backed chair, peering at Melanie through her glasses. Her mop of silvery hair was cut into a bob, the blunt fringe dominating a small, round face. Aged in her late fifties, Agnes was a bird-like creature in a smart grey jacket and skirt.

Nice suit, thought Melanie, but the hair was a worry. Marshall called bob cuts the 'crash helmet look'. Marshall was desperate to cut Melanie's hair – cut it right off, that is. 'Darling, long hair is *too* passé!' But she'd only let him do a trim. Anyway, it wasn't that long, it was long*ish* – just down to the underwire. It wasn't like she could sit on it or anything . . .

'The father,' Agnes repeated. 'What's he like?'

'Yes, sorry.' Melanie tried to focus. 'Um, Col? Well,

he's, uh . . . he's a tough old fella. Farmer. About sixty. What you'd expect really.'

'How do you know what I'd expect?'

'Oh.' Melanie was taken aback. 'I don't, I guess.'

The counsellor spoke softly. 'Never presume, never assume.'

'Oh. Right. Sorry.'

'And never apologise.'

'Right.' Melanie started to fidget, playing with her engagement ring.

'You're Catholic, aren't you?' Agnes smiled kindly. 'Lapsed.'

'How can you tell?'

'Easy.' The counsellor flipped a page in her notebook, scribbling a couple of lines. 'The nuns always leave their mark.'

WYLLANDRA, MAYBURY

'In here, fellas.' Gary led the way as two removalists lumbered up the verandah stairs and into the bluestone cottage. They were carrying a new sofa, which was cocooned in plastic. A little wooden sign, 'Melanie's Cottage', hung over the front door. It was decorated with a rose motif – the same yellow noisette roses that covered the cottage walls and the white lattice fence in the yard. Col had carved the sign and Dorothy had painted it. It was the finishing touch.

'Okay, love, ready!' Melanie had been waiting outside, and Gary now ushered her in. It was her very first look at the new b & b. The renovation had been financed by Col; he knew the place would make money, and he wanted to consolidate the marriage by making Melanie a part of the family business. During the past five weeks, as a team of tradesmen hammered and drilled and took smokos, Melanie had promised not to peek. Now, with Gary beside her, she had the grand tour and was duly impressed.

The ivory paint on the interior walls made the rooms look brighter and bigger. The furniture was new, but it still managed to blend with the rustic look, and there were new curtains and blinds throughout. The floorboards in the lounge had been revarnished and a pot-belly stove installed, so guests could curl up on the sofa and listen to the stereo, or read or watch TV, cosy and warm. In the kitchen there were now built-in cupboards and a stainless-steel sink and splashback, plus a new gas stove, fridge, coffee machine and microwave. In the bedroom there was a new queen-size bed, with a rose motif carved into the headboard.

The highlight was the bathroom. Gary threw the door open with a flourish – 'Ta da!' The walls were covered with large mirrored tiles, floor to ceiling. There was a new shower recess and vanity unit and, dominating the room, a huge spa bath. Melanie thought all the mirrors were a bit much but the spa was a definite winner.

'King-size!' declared Gary.

'King-size? You could fit the entire royal family into that,' Melanie said, laughing.

'Plenty of room for splashing about.' Gary embraced her. 'And tonight we're going to christen the tub – bottle of wine, a few mozzie coils . . . We'll get the barbie out of the way, then it's just you and me . . .'

'Oi, Gary. Ya there, mate?' A gruff voice came from the lounge room.

'Righto, mate! On my way!' Gary kissed Melanie on the cheek and went off to pay the movers.

Melanie opened the cupboards, which were stocked with fluffy new bath sheets. She took a couple out and hung them on a rack near the spa. A vase filled with fresh lavender sat on the windowsill. She picked out a stem and breathed in the scent. For the first time in a long while she felt safe. Melanie wasn't kidding herself, she knew that life in Maybury would take some getting used to – being nice to Gary's friends, no twenty-four-hour chemist. But it was a small price to pay. Finally she was on track. No more city boys.

City boys had their charms, but they all had one fatal flaw – mobility. They used their mobility as an excuse to disappear when things started feeling too permanent. They'd get a sudden transfer with their job, or they'd go cycling around Australia with their mates from the soccer club, or they'd zip off to Scandinavia in search of their Viking roots, occasionally sending a postcard or a jar of pickled herrings.

Gary wasn't mobile and he had no desire to be mobile. It wouldn't occur to him to leave the land. Farming was in his blood, his DNA. Gary was a man who thought long term, and Melanie wanted to be part of a long-term plan.

She'd had enough of transience. In the past sixteen years, since first leaving home, Melanie had moved house a total of twenty-seven times. Now she could throw out the battered suitcases and the plastic laundry bags with the broken zips. She'd never have to move again.

Melanie opened another cupboard, this one filled with bubble bath and apricot massage oil, among other luxuries. Placing the oil on a bench near the spa and patting down the soft towels, she felt a rush of desire. She couldn't wait for the day to be over, when she'd have Gary Quartermaine all to herself.

An hour or so later, the woolshed barbecue was up and running. A function on a grand scale, it was one of Gary's 'good little earners', and it was all thanks to Bunnalup Ridge.

For years now busloads of tourists had been coming to Maybury to visit Bunnalup Ridge, a famous historical site just two miles out of town. In the 1890s a gang of bush-rangers had come to a sticky end at this now legendary spot. Hunted down by the police, they'd been forced to the very edge, where, refusing to surrender and face the hang-man's noose, they'd jumped off the ridge crying 'Freedom!' (or in some cases, 'Bugger!'). Local guides would re-enact these scenes with much face-pulling and waving of arms, to the tourists' delight.

'They were smashed to bits on the rocks! They buried 'em where they fell.'

'Paddy Cready, he didn't die straightaway, he crawled.

All the way to that billabong, then he fell in. And Captain Jack Possum, he sank like a stone, but his old possum hat, it floated right to the top. Their souls got trapped in the water. You can see their faces staring up at you. See 'em?! There! You can see the eyes . . .'

Some tourists believed they'd found human remains at the site, secreting small bones in their anoraks and transporting them home, where they were mounted in special glass cases.

But the story of Bunnalup Ridge was a complete furphy. The bushrangers' bones, so proudly displayed in Tokyo and Idaho, belonged to feral cats and ringtail possums. There were no desperadoes at the ridge, no cavalry in hot pursuit, no-one plunging to their untimely death. In fact, nothing dramatic had ever happened in Maybury, except for a storm in 1957 which wrecked the original post office – not much of a drawcard. So, in the winter of 1971, the Maybury Tourist Bureau launched a writing competition entitled 'Local Legends'. Gary's Aunt Marcia had dreamt up the bushranger story. It was brought to life in a range of colour brochures and duly disseminated. Myth had become reality, and everybody liked it that way.

After visiting the ridge, the tourist buses would swing by the shearing sheds on Gary's property, for a you-beaut Aussie barbecue, complete with performing sheep dogs. Today's group was Japanese. There were thirty teenage girls, escorted by a middle-aged couple. The girls were very excitable and squealed loudly at the slightest provocation.

'Pretty lady! Smile, pretty lady!'

Melanie was distracted by the clicking of cameras. She was standing at one of the tables, doling out paper plates and plastic cutlery. Through their bilingual escorts, the girls were invited to help themselves.

There was 'good Aussie fare' on offer, courtesy of Dorothy, who had a talent for large-scale catering. There was lamb-on-a-spit, pig-on-a-spit, barbecues sizzling with chops and steaks, tables laden with salads and jacket potatoes and pavlovas smothered in whipped cream and passionfruit. Dorothy manned one of the spits, carving off slices of meat which Blodwyn and Maxine then served. Brendan and Rosalie were pouring soft drinks into plastic cups and Pip was handing out green tea and instant coffee – it was all hands on deck. As the visitors filled their plates, Melanie tried explaining to the girls that pavlova didn't really go with steak – at least, not as a garnish – but they didn't seem to get it, so she stopped worrying and just smiled for the cameras.

All heads turned as a vision appeared at the crest of the hill. Sitting at the helm of a freshly-painted Josafina were Gary and Simon. Grinning broadly, they wore Akubra hats, tasselled suede shirts and trousers, leather chaps and long leather boots with elaborate metal spurs. More rodeo than woolshed, thought Melanie. Try shearing a sheep in that outfit and you'd probably kill it.

The tractor trundled down the hill towards the guests, who were now squealing themselves into a state of apoplexy. As Gary and Simon pulled up, the girls rushed over and clambered aboard, posing with the men as the cameras clicked and whirred.

One of the girls grabbed Melanie by the hand and dragged her to the tractor, urging her to jump up next to Gary. 'Here, you sit. Pretty man and pretty lady.'

Melanie squeezed alongside Gary, dodging the rim of his Akubra, which kept getting her in the eye.

A second girl quizzed Gary, 'She your girlfriend? Pretty girlfriend!! You happy man, yes?!'

Melanie could sense Gary's displeasure. Fair enough, she thought, we all need our moment of glory. This was Gary's gig, not hers. She slipped out of the limelight and went back to the clearing up.

While shoving debris into a garbage bag, she glanced up and saw Brendan Buchanan. He'd abandoned his post at the soft-drinks table and was walking towards her.

'Hi.' From behind his back he produced a gift box, tied with a red satin bow. 'For you.'

'Oh, Brendan. Thanks,' said Melanie, pleasantly surprised. She wasn't sure that Brendan even approved of her. After all, she was a mere Come Over marrying a Born and Bred. 'That's very sweet of you. What is it, an engagement present?'

'Whatever.' Brendan shrugged.

Melanie untied the bow, took off the lid and, removing a layer of tissue paper, she found her gift. It was a large red dog collar studded with metal spikes. She held it up to admire it.

'Oh. That's . . . lovely,' said Melanie, thinking how ridiculous it would look on her dog. It would suit a pit bull terrier, or maybe a snarling Rottweiler, but not a gormless springer spaniel like Marmite. Besides, he hated collars, he refused to wear them. 'Thank you, Brendan,' she said, smiling. 'I'm sure that . . .' Melanie didn't finish the sentence. Brendan was staring at her in a very peculiar and most unsettling way. Suddenly, he started to growl.

'Rrrrrrr,' Brendan made a deep, guttural sound. 'Rrrufff Rrruffff!' Then he spun on his heel and walked off.

Gary bowed to the chaperones, who bowed back and handed him an envelope filled with cash. The tourists reboarded the bus and headed off to the Maybury Koala Park, which currently boasted two koalas, three bobtail lizards and an elderly guineapig who had his own cage. Gary walked around the tables, paying everyone for their services. Then he came up to Melanie, holding up the remaining cash.

'And this is for my darlin' girl.' He put his arms around her. 'Buy yourself some of that frilly gear.' He drew her closer. 'Want bubble bath,' he whispered in her ear. 'You, me. Go to tub. Now.'

He threw Melanie over his shoulder into a fireman's lift, and she was carried, laughing and squealing and kicking her legs, all the way back to the cottage.

After an hour of spirited lovemaking, Melanie and Gary reclined in the spa, sipping a Brown Brothers red. The light in the cottage was dimming, as the day drew to a close. Melanie reached lazily for some matches and lit another candle. Gary's mobile started to ring, from under a pile of clothes. He groaned, then reached across to find it.

'Hello? . . . Uhuh . . . Whereabouts? . . . Okey dokey. See you in five.' He climbed out of the spa. 'Sorry, love, it's a dead cow. Northern Highway.'

'Another one?'

'Must've been a log truck. They're big buggers.' He pulled on his tasselled shirt, now crumpled and damp. 'They just roll over cattle and keep on moving. Like bloody tanks.'

'That's three cows this week.'

Gary grabbed his keys. 'It happens. Bad time of year. Back soon. Sorry, love.' He leant down and kissed her.

'Um, Gary.'

'Uhuh.'

'Brendan gave me a present today.'

'Yeah?'

'A dog collar.' Melanie said as she pulled her hair back, twisting it into a knot. 'It was a big red collar, with spikes sticking out of it. He gave it to me, and then he said, "Woof."'

'He said what?'

'He barked,' said Melanie, 'like a dog. But it was . . . well, sleazy, you know?'

'Woof, eh? Woof!' Gary started chuckling as he headed out. 'He's a bloody character, that bloke . . .'

WYLLANDRA, MAYBURY

The next morning, Melanie was putting on her clothes rather gingerly when Gary cruised into the bedroom with a cup of Earl Grey and placed it on the bedside table.

'Here ya go, darl',' he said with a smile.

Mel's back was still stiff from the night before, after falling asleep in the spa. Gary hadn't come home till midnight, then he had been up again at five, preparing for yet another social gathering. Unlike Melanie, Gary didn't need a lot of sleep.

'Food's all done. They'll be rolling up at twelve.' He cast a critical eye over the green velvet dress Melanie had pulled on. 'Um, Mel . . . are you going to wear that?'

'Yeah.' She paused and looked down at the dress. 'Why, what's wrong? Is it too short?'

'It's a bit . . . I dunno, a bit . . . formal,' said Gary. 'You're in the country now. You can relax.' He ducked under the bed and pulled out a pink cardboard box. Printed on the lid was 'Margalee's Boutique, Cranbourne'. 'Here you go.'

Melanie opened the box and found a large, baggy pantsuit. It was a dreadful fawn colour – some type of puckered polyester.

'It's nice. Thanks.' Melanie hated it. Damn that knee-jerk etiquette. She removed the slim-fitting dress and started climbing into the dowdy suit. Nope, too ugly, she couldn't do it. She never wanted to be this comfortable.

'Look,' she said, 'I'm sorry, Gary, but . . . it's just not me. I mean, it was a sweet thought, but . . .'

'Fine. Chuck it in the box,' Gary replied, sounding terse.

Melanie was worried that she'd hurt his feelings. Did he really think she'd like it? God, next he'd be buying her a kaftan. 'You can take it back, can't you?'

'Yeah, I'll take it back,' he muttered, heading for the ensuite in search of a comb.

Melanie pulled on her dress again. 'Is, um, Blodwyn coming to lunch?' she called, hoping for a miracle.

'Yep,' Gary called back.

No miracle today. 'You know, I don't think she likes me very much.'

Gary returned from the bathroom, still combing his hair. 'Melanie, she's shy.'

'Not around you.'

Gary pulled on a new shirt. The dark blue silk matched his blue eyes and set off his blond locks. He'd had a few of these shirts especially made – some tailor up in Melbourne.

'Listen, Mel,' he said as he finished doing up the buttons, 'Blodwyn doesn't have a lot of friends.'

Melanie bit her tongue, resisting the obvious reply.

Gary changed his belt for one with a bigger buckle. 'And she's a teacher. She's helping me with my reading.'

'Very noble of her,' Melanie muttered.

'Jesus, Mel!' Gary exclaimed. 'Blodwyn's *gay* – remember?! She's bringing her girlfriend to lunch, for God's sake.' He admired his outfit in the bedroom mirror. 'I can't believe you're jealous of a lesbian.'

'I'm not jealous.' Melanie lowered her gaze, looking very sullen. Then she picked up a brush and started dragging it through her hair. 'Is Brendan coming?'

'Yep.'

Melanie couldn't hide her disdain. Gary spotted her expression in the mirror and turned to face her.

'They're good people, Mel. Just spend a bit of time

with them. Get to know them.' He gave her a pleading look. 'Will you at least try?'

'Okay,' she mumbled, feeling a pang of guilt.

It was a noisy group around the table, the volume increasing as more alcohol was imbibed. The food was up to Gary's usual high standard and the mood was congenial. Melanie was starting to relax, and Gary was paying her plenty of attention in front of his friends, which made her feel good. Vicki, the pert hairdresser, and Mick, the kindly slaughterman were there – a welcome addition, thought Melanie. She had always liked the cheery young couple.

To Melanie's astonishment, Blodwyn was making a real effort to be polite, and after a while she and the Whippet were actually conversing. They were surprised to discover that they both had similar tastes – in movies, writers, favourite places in Europe – all manner of things. In fact, Blodwyn's girlfriend, Max, seemed rather unsettled by all the bonhomie.

Across from Melanie, the rotund, jolly Rosalie was showing the petite young Vicki a bottle of liquid soap, some herbal concoction.

'It's tea-tree body wash,' Rosalie explained. 'Brendan uses it in the shower after work. It's the tea-tree oil – it cuts through the grease on his skin.'

Vicki examined the bottle and passed it on to her husband.

'That'd be great for Mick,' said Vicki. 'You know, after a day of slaughtering – well, he needs more than soap.'

'Yeah, looks good.' Mick read the label on the bottle and nodded approvingly. 'And look here: "Not tested on animals."'

Everyone stopped talking and looked up at Mick, incredulous. He suddenly twigged and they all started roaring with laughter.

After dessert Melanie went into the bedroom to find a box of chocolates she'd brought from town. She'd left them in her suitcase. She opened the door to the walk-in robe and found Gary, standing over her opened case, clutching one of her nighties. He was caressing the satin fabric and breathing in its scent. Seeing Melanie, he attempted to cover.

'Here's my girl,' he said as he gave her the nightie. 'You gonna wear this tonight?'

Melanie paused for a moment. She looked at Gary standing there, with his golden curls and ruddy cheeks and anxious blue eyes. He looked like a child, fearful of her displeasure. She smiled at him gently.

'Well, if I don't wear it,' Melanie said softly as she handed the nightie back to him, 'maybe you'd like to try it on.'

The relief on Gary's face was heart-rending. He embraced her with such profound gratitude that she thought she was going to cry.

TIVOLI GARDENS, ALBERT PARK

That same afternoon Milos and Renata were lunching in their flat, joined today by Richard and Zani. Having declared herself a staunch vegan, Zani abstained from Renata's Czech speciality, *svíčková* – roast beef in a spicy cream sauce served with dumplings. Instead, looking virtuous and slightly aggrieved, Zani picked at the green bean salad.

'Is like my name,' Milos was explaining. 'You say it "*Mee*-losh". This is correct way. "*Mee*-losh". But some people they say "*Mill*-oz" or "*My*-lows" – I hate that.'

'Yeah, like with me, people say "*Zay*-nee". But that's wrong, it's "Zar-*nee*".'

'Zar-*nee*,' repeated Milos.

'It sounds like an Indian name,' Renata observed.

'Yeah, I think she was, like, an Indian goddess or something.' Zani prodded the salad with a fork, wondering if the oil was cold-pressed.

'You know, Milos doesn't just play the trumpet,' Richard said as he topped up Zani's beer. 'He's a swimming coach as well.'

'A swimming coach? Kewl.' Zani nodded, impressed.

'And Renata is a mechanic,' continued Richard. 'A true Renaissance woman. She speaks four languages, she cooks like a dream and she can fix your car.'

'But only Skoda!' said Milos, laughing.

Renata looked annoyed. Milos was always giving her a hard time about the Skodas. Of course she'd trained on Skodas. In her village, it was the only car on the road. She was doing her best with these Cortinas and Falcons, but the engines were in the front of the car, for a start. It took some getting used to.

Zani turned to Milos with an earnest expression. 'Milos, there's something I've always wanted to know.'

'About Skodas?!' Milos slapped his thigh and laughed heartily. Renata rolled her eyes.

'No,' replied Zani, 'about swimming.' She was frowning behind her strawberry-blonde fringe. 'It's like, you see all these, like, swimmers – you know, Olympic-type swimmers. And they're, like, going up and down the pool, up and down for hours and hours. I mean, like, every day, up and down. Well, like, what do they think about?'

'Ah . . .' Milos nodded wisely, then he started miming a freestyle action. 'They think "One-one-one."' He changed to backstroke. '"Two-two-two." Then breast-stroke. "Three-three-three."'

Richard and Renata chuckled while Zani remained earnest.

'I get it!' she exclaimed. '"One-one . . ." It's like a mantra, right? It's like a Zen thing! Kewl!'

Milos was rather miffed. It's not easy to make a joke in English, he thought. The least she could do is laugh.

'Zani is studying Eastern Religions at TAFE,' Richard explained.

'Oh, that's nice,' said Renata. 'And what are you going to be when you grow up?'

'A Point of Light,' declared Zani, unaware that Renata was having a lend of her.

'Ah.' Renata ladled more beans onto Zani's plate, ignoring Richard's pleading look. '"Point of Light" – is good money? You can get promotion, you can be Manager Point of Light, yes?' Renata was tiring of this neophyte with the bobbing eyebrow ring. This tedious child, who thought Václav Havel was a savoury dip and the Prague

Spring was a brand of bottled water. She missed having Melanie around.

THE BARKING SHARK, MAYBURY

Melanie swung by the pub to give Barry the final guest list for the reception. They sat at a table in the public bar, poring over designs for the wedding cake, which Barry was also preparing. There must have been something in the air, thought Melanie, as Barry sorted through his reams of paper. That morning Sarita had called her on the mobile, in a very excited state. She and Andy were getting married – in October, only a week before Gary and Melanie. While a little surprised that they were marrying so young, and with such haste, Melanie was pleased about the news. Sarita and Andy were great together. She'd insisted that they visit her on the farm as often as possible – bring the kids down, when they eventually had them.

Mention of children had sent Sarita into gales of laughter. 'Bit early for that,' she'd protested.

'Oh. Right. So you're not . . .'

'Oh, God no!!'

'No . . . no, I didn't think so. I mean, I wasn't sure. I just thought, well, y'know . . .'

'Yeah, it does seem kind of quick,' Sarita had agreed. 'The thing is . . . Andy and me, we found this fantastic house in Richmond. My folks said we couldn't live together unless we got hitched, so we're getting hitched. I mean, we couldn't lose the house.'

'Well, no,' Melanie had replied, thinking that there were probably worse reasons for tying the knot. 'So I guess Andy's okay about it?'

'Are you kidding? He's *dying* to get married – he's already counting the sleeps! God, Mel, he's such an old-fashioned guy. He's worse than Uncle Nazim.'

It had been an eventful couple of weeks for Melanie too; she'd been learning a lot about agrarian life. She'd spent some quality time with Col at Iron-Bar Homestead, observing the finer points of cattle farming. This was Col's focus, along with his racehorses, whereas Gary knew more about sheep – officially. Col seemed to know more about all of it, in Melanie's opinion, but she never shared this view with Gary.

Sex was a big part of farming. Melanie had watched as Col swung into action with his electro-ejaculator, a nifty device that was inserted into the prize bull's rectum – gently, unless you wanted a hoof in the forehead – and attached by a long lead to the car battery. Col had assured Melanie, over the hum of the engine, that the bull quite enjoyed the process – you could tell by the end result. Apparently artificial insemination was fairly essential with cattle. Mating *au naturel* could damage the heifers. Bulls didn't know their own strength.

She had learnt about tillage and planting, about field rotation and the summer crops of maize and parsnips, which were fed to the stock, along with enriched grains. She had learnt that cattle grain was more finely ground than sheep grain, because cows had different digestive systems. If the grains were too large, they'd pass right through and be devoured by the waiting crows. She had learnt that sheep, like goats, had harelips, so they grazed more efficiently than cattle.

One afternoon she'd helped Col scrub out the water troughs while Gary was off at training. A volunteer with the State Emergency Service, Gary held a ticket in cliff rescue and attended regular sessions to hone his skills. When Gary had returned, he and Col had joined forces to clean out the dam – a big job done twice a year. The men had used two tractors and a giant scooper to scrape the bottom of the dam, going laboriously back and forth. Gadget Boy would have loved it, Melanie had thought, watching from the bank. It was giant Lego in action.

She and Dorothy had also done some bonding. They'd cried together when Caruso, Dorothy's pet cockatoo, was killed by a roving tiger snake, and the following week when Melanie's pet calf, Ronaldo, got in with the herd and was taken to the abattoir by mistake. They'd laughed together at Dorothy's geese, who'd discovered Gary's mandarin trees and had devised a system for obtaining the fruit. The geese had worked as a team, running at the trees in formation and hurling themselves at the trunks. The fruit would fall and be duly gobbled up. The birds would then regroup and repeat the manoeuvre, proving Dorothy's theory that while pigs were smart, geese were smarter.

Sitting now with Barry, Melanie glanced at the menu – no pork, no pâté de foie gras. Check.

Two local women, about to exit the bar, suddenly recognised Melanie. They paused for a moment then stumbled towards her.

'You're Gary's fiancée, right?' said one, feeling neighbourly after too many bourbons.

'Uh, yeah, that's right,' replied Melanie. She couldn't place the women, but they did look vaguely familiar. Maybe she'd seen them at a tree-planting.

'We thought it was you,' said the second woman, slurring her words. 'I'm Sharon, this is Steffi.' Sharon had consumed even more bourbon than Steffi and was very shaky on her pins. 'We run the Ladies Pistol Club,' she continued. 'Maybe we can sign you up?'

'Oh, I don't think so,' Barry stepped in, much to Melanie's relief. 'Melanie's not your pistol-packing type. She's a musician, you know?' He spoke with some pride. A film projectionist for over thirty years, Barry was a self-proclaimed member of the arts fraternity. And he liked to bask in the reflected glory of fellow aesthetes. 'In fact, she's a *professional* musician.'

'Well, that Gary, he's pretty damned musical,' Steffi said with a wink.

'Yeah, he's got rhythm all right,' Sharon snorted. 'An' a big bloody instrument too!'

'Now ladies, that's quite enough.' Barry glared at them. Melanie looked confused.

'We don't call it the full monty round here, darl',' said Steffi.

'No, we call it the full Gary!' Sharon slapped Melanie on the back, then she and Steffi lurched towards the door, laughing and whistling. 'Go, Gazza baby! Take it off, baby, take it off . . .' They disappeared out onto the street.

Barry looked at Melanie apologetically. 'Just ignore them. They're vulgar and stupid. Another squash?'

'No thanks,' she replied. 'Um, Barry . . . is there something I should know?'

'Oh, it's just some silly high jinks they get up to.' He waved his hand dismissively. 'You know how it is.'

'Well, I don't, actually.'

'Look, it's probably one of those dinners Gary has up at the house. I gather things get a little rowdy. I'm sure it's nothing.'

Melanie didn't look too reassured.

Barry looked around him, then leant in towards her, lowering his voice.

'Melanie, dear, there are people in this town – stupid, parochial, small-minded people – well, they aren't too happy about a city girl taking their golden-haired Gary. So they'll say things to upset you, to stir up trouble. You must learn to ignore them. Treat them with the contempt they deserve. Now . . .' He picked up his pencil and, with a flourish, resumed his sketch of the cake. 'Three tiers with a gondola on the top.' He beamed, as the pencil flew across the page. 'Very Venetian! What do you think?'

IRON-BAR HOMESTEAD, MAYBURY

Melanie drove up Iron-Bar Road, heading towards Wyllandra. She spotted Gary in his parent's driveway and turned in there instead. Gary and Col were loading up Col's ute, about to leave on one of their regular trips to the Mount Malabar saleyards. As always, they'd be staying the night with the Mount Malabar Quartermaines, catching up on family business.

The two men waved when they saw Melanie approaching. She pulled up next to Gary, who leant in through the car window and gave her a peck on the cheek.

'Just in time, darl',' he said. 'We're just heading off. How did you go?'

'Fine, fine. We've been sorting out the cake.'

'Rightio.'

'Um, Gary, can I talk to you for a moment?'

'Sure, darlin'.' Gary turned and called to Col, who was filling up the ute from the bowser in his yard. 'Oi, Dad! Be with you in a sec, okay?'

Then he turned back to Melanie, leaning his arm up against the car. 'What's up?'

'Oh, look, it's silly,' said Melanie, 'but . . . well, I was at the pub, and these two women came up to me and started carrying on about you taking your clothes off. How you had a . . . "big instrument", or something.'

'What bloody women?' Gary bristled.

'I shouldn't have said anything, it doesn't matter. I'm being paranoid, forget about it, they were just mucking around.'

'Did you get their names?'

'Oh, I don't know. Sharon, I think, she was one of them. They're from the pistol club. They were just drunk, but then Barry said –'

'What did he say?' Gary snapped.

'He said . . .' Melanie tried to sound nonchalant. 'He said things can get a little wild at those dinners you have.'

'And how the hell would he know? Barry's a bloody fool, he's been watching too many old movies.' Gary's expression softened. 'Now look, love, I'm sorry those women upset you, but they're talking rubbish. Sure, things can get a bit loud when I'm having a party, and we might have a bit of a dance. But no-one called Sharon ever laid eyes on my dick, that's for sure.'

'I shouldn't have said anything.'

'I bet it's that Sharon Hawkes, she's always half cut by lunchtime. She probably sees elephants hangin' outta my pants.'

Melanie laughed and shook her head. 'I'm sorry, it was just –'

'Listen, Mel, you're gonna hear all sorts of rubbish about me round here. We're the Quartermaines. We own half the district and people like to gossip. Make trouble. So just ignore them, okay?'

Col honked the horn and his two hyperactive kelpies flew into the ute.

Gary leant in through Melanie's window and kissed her on the mouth. Then he kissed her again – soft, lingering kisses. 'I miss you already,' he murmured.

Col honked the horn again and Gary groaned.

'Okay, darl'.' He moved back from the car. 'I'll see you tomorrow night. Go and have a chat with Mum. She just made some scones.'

Gary went over to the ute and hopped in next to Col. They headed off down the drive.

'Everything okay?' asked Col. He was watching Melanie in the rear-view mirror as she walked towards the house.

'Fine,' replied Gary.

'Mel's a good girl.'

'I know.' Gary stared straight ahead.

'You wanna keep this one,' Col grunted as they turned into Iron-Bar Road. 'Sort yourself out.'

'Careful, Dad.' Gary's voice sounded tight. 'Don't push it.'

Melanie went into the kitchen and joined Dorothy for Devonshire tea. In a short space of time she'd grown close to Dorothy, who, despite appearances, wasn't your typical farmer's wife. She was a woman with a past – a past well documented in the leather-bound photo albums she kept in the dining-room cabinet. Melanie loved looking through the old pictures, which revealed a glamorous and distant world.

It was the world of Australian vaudeville in the forties and early fifties. The Dancing Drummonds had toured the country as part of a variety show. The troupe comprised Dorothy's parents and her two aunties, and, once she was old enough, Dorothy herself. The Double D's were famous for their 'blue' song and dance routines – tame by today's standards, but considered risqué at the time.

The young Dorothy was dazzling – a knockout. The photographs showed a vivacious, bright-eyed teenager with a shapely figure and a mane of cascading blonde curls. Col had been shearing in Queensland when he'd first seen her onstage. He had been instantly smitten. He'd followed the show around the country, taking odd jobs in whichever town they were playing, until Dorothy had finally agreed to marry him.

'Didn't you miss performing?' asked Melanie, spooning some whipped cream onto a scone.

'For a little while,' said Dorothy, as she poured some more tea. 'And I missed my family. But then Gary came along and nothing else seemed to matter. And, well . . . those days were different. You needed the protection of a good man. It probably sounds silly to girls of your generation, but that's how it was.'

'It doesn't sound silly at all.'

'Col made me feel safe. You see, being married can shield you from a lot of things. It can make the world a little gentler . . . sweeter. Do you know what I mean?'

'Yes,' said Melanie, stirring her tea, 'I think I do.'

'I know that Col can seem a bit gruff, but he's very good to me, and I know how to handle him. That's the trick with men – you've got to learn how to read them.'

'Now there's a challenge.'

'Yes.' Dorothy smiled. 'Gary will keep you busy. Half-farmer, half-showgirl.'

Melanie laughed. 'Well, it'll never be boring.'

Dorothy regarded her future daughter-in-law with a kind expression. 'You know, dear, he loves you very much. Gary's not perfect; he has his faults. He can be thoughtless at times – which is my fault, I spoilt him. But he's got a big heart, and when I see the way he looks at you, well . . . it makes me very happy.'

Melanie thought for a moment as she crumbled a corner of her scone. 'The thing is, I sometimes wonder why he chose me and not somebody else.'

'Nonsense, dear!' exclaimed Dorothy. 'How can you say that?'

'No, really. I'm hardly the pick of the bunch – I mean, for a farmer. I can't cook or sew, I don't know anything about sheep, and there's no way I'm going to join the pistol club.'

'You sound like me!' Dorothy smiled.

'Oh, come on, you're a brilliant cook, and –'

'And so is Gary,' Dorothy interrupted. 'So you won't need to worry. Mel, dear, I know exactly why he chose you. You're beautiful and bright and you make him laugh. You've got energy, dear, and a good head on your shoulders. That's what Gary wants. Not some dull-witted local girl who's never been out of the district.'

'Really?'

'You should hear the way he brags about you.'

'He doesn't.' Melanie shrugged off Dorothy's remarks, but was secretly pleased.

'And you get him to do things – like this radio thing of his. He's having a marvellous time.'

Since Melanie had first become involved with Gary, he'd been talking about the community radio station, 3GE-290, which he listened to every day. The station operated from the campus of Mount Malabar's large agricultural college, broadcasting to the entire Greater Eastern region. Gary had long been toying with the idea of trying out as a voluntary announcer, writing and presenting weekly reports on life in Maybury. He'd feigned only a casual interest, but Melanie could tell that he was champing at the bit. All he'd needed was some encouragement. So she'd sat him down at the kitchen table and together they'd drawn up some program ideas. Then she'd placed a few calls to the station on Gary's behalf. Before long, he'd clinched a weekly spot – 'Gary Gets Local' – presenting community announcements, the latest crop and stock advice from the Agriculture Department and interviews he'd recorded with Maybury identities. The show was well received and the station managers were already calling Gary a natural. He could transform any material – even the dry and dusty saleyard reports – into highly entertaining monologues.

'Well, he's got a great voice,' said Melanie. 'Plus, he's talented, of course, and he's very confident. He sounds great on the air. He was born to do it.'

'But that's you, Melanie,' Dorothy insisted. 'You gave him the confidence. He's always had a bit of an artistic side, but he's been too scared to show it in case he wasn't good enough.' She got up from the table and went to the sink.

'I mean, as much as I liked Carla,' Dorothy continued, refilling the kettle, '. . . and I don't like to talk about his exes and I won't do it again, but Carla saw Gary as a farmer, nothing more. She couldn't see that he had other talents – creative talents. She just wanted him to be a farmer and make money. That's where you're different.'

'Yeah?'

Dorothy put the kettle on the stove and lit the gas. 'You want him to be happy, and he loves you for that.' She turned back to Melanie and smiled. 'And so do I, dear. So do I.'

TIVOLI GARDENS, ALBERT PARK

It was dusk as Richard sat cross-legged on the floor of his apartment, wearing a karate outfit an old flatmate had given him – in lieu of rent, if memory served. In front of him was a row of candles and a few sticks of incense – jasmine–ginger. He sat with his eyes closed, listening to the tape on the stereo. Guided meditation – it was Zani's idea. Focus your mind, control your anger, think yourself rich – the usual patter.

'You're standing in the middle of a large circle . . .' Swami Seth from South Carolina had a breathy resonance to his voice – a voice of spiritual authority, complemented by the judicious use of a gong. 'The circle is made up of all the people who bring tension to your life, who bring anger into your heart . . .'

Richard saw the circle forming, as a thin line of jasmine–ginger smoke wafted up his nostrils.

'Now is the time to make your peace and move on. *Bonnng.* You turn and face them . . . one at a time . . .'

Richard turned to the first cab off the rank, his father Larry. The standard father–son issues, impossible to resolve, better to just forgive. He took Larry's hands and made his peace. The figure of Larry smiled at him and evaporated.

Then it was the rabbi's turn. Rabbi Goldblatz, who'd removed Richard's foreskin with all the skill of a weekend gardener, leaving him with a conversation piece. Thanks, mate. Still, it was time to let go. *Pffft*, he was gone, up in a puff of smoke.

Now for the music agents, Bill the Barracuda and his team of piranhas. Very dodgy operators. Bad payers, late payers – no payers, if they could get away with it. 'But Richie, it'll be good exposure!' They still owed him a fortune but he knew he'd never see it. Bye, fellas. *Pffft*, up they went.

The gong took a protracted solo.

Richard turned to the last person in the circle, his arch-rival, spawn of the devil and thieving scumbag, Gary Quartermaine. He took Gary's hands as the dulcet tones of the southern swami guided him through the healing process.

'All that anger is just fading away, as you take their hands in yours . . .'

Richard smiled at the figure of Gary, who smiled back. Smug bastard.

'The love, the forgiveness, is flowing from your hands to theirs . . .'

Richard squeezed Gary's hands until Gary was no longer smiling, he was grimacing.

'Flowing like a river of love . . .'

Richard continued crushing Gary's hands until he cried

out in pain, unable to escape. He could feel Gary's bones splintering, his tendons popping under the pressure.

'We are all points of light, flowing as one glorious, giant point of light in a universal river of light and love . . .'

Gary slowly crumpled to the ground and dissolved into a pile of sheep droppings. Richard exhaled with a loud sigh and lay back on the floor, a smile playing around his lips.

'Bonnnnnnnnnnnnnng.'

CORAL TREE LANE, SOUTH MELBOURNE

Marshall ran for the phone. 'I'll get it!'

'If it's Tom Cruise, tell him I'm doin' a roast and he's invited,' Patrick called from the kitchen.

'If it's Tom Cruise, darling, you'll be eating that roast on your own! . . . Hello, who is it? . . . Oh! Hello handsome!'

'Who is it?' called Patrick.

'Tom Cruise!' Marshall called back.

'Hi Marshall,' said Richard, on the other end of the line.

'Hi Richie-babes,' replied Marshall. 'I s'pose you're after that crazy gal. Or have you finally seen the light?'

'Leave him alone,' Patrick shouted over the sound of running water. He'd burned his hand on the baking tray and was holding it under the tap.

'Um, is she there?' asked Richard.

'Sorry, sweets,' said Marshall. 'She's zipped off to the country manor, don't you know. Off to see that big hunk of man, that –'

'Yes, all right. Do you know when she'll be back?'

'Ooh, once the big guy runs out of puff, I guess. And by the looks of him, that could take a while. Lordy, that big farmin' man!'

'Marshall –'

'He's doin' it all for our Mel! He's stokin' that boiler, he's plantin' those turnips . . .'

'Yes, all right, mate, I get the picture. Look, no message, okay?'

'Okay. You know, Richie-babes,' Marshall put on his husky Marilyn Monroe voice, 'I could show you some great exercises for your embouchure, if you know what I mean.'

'I heard that, you little trollop!' Marching down the hallway, Patrick snatched the receiver out of Marshall's hand.

'Trollop?! Who are you calling a trollop, you tired old tart!' Marshall pinched Patrick on the arm with some force.

'Ow! Be nice. I burnt myself.' Patrick looked very aggrieved.

'What, on the arm?' said Marshall, and pinched him again.

'Sorry, Richard,' said Patrick. He turned his back on Marshall to stop him from taking the phone. 'He's being very naughty. Look, Mel should be home in a few days. Why don't you come over tomorrow? We're having a bingo night.'

'Bitchin' bingo! Bitchin' bingo!' Marshall jumped up and down in the hall.

'Oh dear,' said Patrick with a sigh. 'He's been into the red lollies again.'

'Bitchin' bingo, Paul and Ringo!' Marshall pogoed towards the kitchen.

'Thanks anyway, Patrick,' said Richard, 'but I've got a gig.'

'Well, dear, you know where we are.'

'Yeah, thanks mate. See ya.'

Richard hung up the phone, at first despondent, then resolved. It was stupid, all this pining over someone he couldn't have. She'd made her decision, it was time for him to move on.

He started seeing Zani on a regular basis and slowly came to terms with his unrequited desire for Melanie. He became a familiar face at the Fit 'n' Funky, addicted to his daily blast of endorphins. The gym management had given him life membership in exchange for him not suing over the sun-bed incident. The exercise was good for his playing and it helped him keep up with his young paramour, a girl of boundless energy, if somewhat lacking in finesse.

THE MAGELLAN HOSPITAL, EAST MELBOURNE

Melanie and Jacqui were sitting on their favourite bench in the hospital gardens.

'Come on, Mel, a lot of guys like lingerie.' Jacqui picked at her vegetable samosa and tried to sound reassuring, even though she wasn't in the mood.

Jacqui looked rather bleary-eyed, thought Melanie. She'd probably been watching late-night movies again. Gary liked watching the tube at night – often till 2 or 3 a.m., long after Melanie had gone to bed. As she was dozing, she could sometimes hear him in the lounge room. Gary reacted noisily to the action unfolding on the screen, gasping with delight or shouting out warnings to the actors, much like the audience at a pantomime. He liked Marx Brothers comedies and had laughed himself stupid the other night watching Groucho and co. in *Monkey Business*, quoting the best jokes to Melanie over breakfast.

'I don't care about the lingerie,' said Melanie, nursing a takeaway coffee. 'I can see why guys like to wear it, when they're having sex or whatever. But I just don't like him wearing my clothes.'

'God, he's so big,' said Jacqui. 'How does he fit into them?'

'He goes for anything in lycra,' replied Melanie. 'Stretches it completely out of shape.'

'Oh.' Jacqui tried to picture it. 'Yeah, that could work.'

'I mean, when they say "one size fits all", they don't mean a six-foot cattle farmer. Not in a mini-dress.'

'Is Gary six foot?' asked Jacqui.

'Five ten,' replied Melanie. 'He lies.'

Jacqui sighed. 'So he likes a bit of colour and movement, what's the big deal?'

'In theory, it doesn't bother me,' said Melanie. 'I mean, why should it? But when it's actually happening to you . . .

I don't know. I guess I'm just used to guys who like my clothes on *me*, not on *them*.' She shook her head. 'It's hard to explain.'

'A lot of guys wear dresses,' said Jacqui. 'What about the men in Bali? They wear sarongs. Or the Scottish guys? They all get around in skirts.'

'Yeah, but they don't wear matching stilettos.'

'He doesn't hit you and he doesn't take drugs. You're doin' all right.' Jacqui was getting impatient.

'He wants me to look like a frump,' said Melanie. 'He's the peacock and I have to be the peahen.'

'For God's sake, Mel, at least you've got someone!' Jacqui blurted.

'Hey,' said Melanie, taken aback, 'you don't have to get stroppy.'

'I'm not stroppy . . . I'm just . . .'

Without warning, Jacqui burst into tears.

'Hey. Hey, Jacqui, what's wrong?' Melanie placed her coffee on the ground and put an arm around Jacqui's shoulder, trying to console her. 'Come on, tell me. What's the matter?'

'It's Leroy,' Jacqui whispered. 'He's dead.'

'What?!' Melanie gasped.

'A car hit him. Last night.'

'Oh God. Jacqui, that's terrible.' Melanie delved into her bag for a packet of tissues. Now she was crying too. Leroy had been part of their lives – part of their daily conversation. She couldn't believe he was gone.

'It was quick,' Jacqui whimpered, through the tears. 'Broke his neck. Not a mark on him. I don't know how he got out of the house. My neighbour saw it happen. She said the car hit him, he took a couple of steps and . . . he just . . . dropped.'

'Poor Leroy. Poor little soul.' Melanie peeled some tissues out of the pack and handed them to Jacqui, then took some for herself.

'You know,' Jacqui snuffled, 'I . . . I . . . had him in a . . . in a donor program.'

'Uhuh.' Melanie didn't know, but she nodded anyway.

'The Cat Lovers, they run it. Them and the vets. They . . . they . . . took his heart straightaway.' Jacqui succumbed to a fresh bout of tears. 'They already used it for a transplant,' she wailed, burying her face in Kleenex.

'Well, that's something, isn't it,' Melanie ventured gently. 'Knowing that Leroy is still alive, kind of. Well, a part of him anyway.'

'His heart . . . they gave it to another Burmese.'

'He would've liked that.'

'Yeah.' Jacqui dabbed at her eyes, frowning at the dark stains on the tissue. So much for waterproof mascara.

Melanie felt truly sorry for Jacqui. She was beginning to understand the powerful bond that can develop between a human being and their pet. She'd become very attached to Millie, the little black hen. Millie would trot around after her like a puppy, vying for her attention. When Melanie was out on the verandah steps, reading or just gazing at the view, Millie would hop up onto her shoulder and perch there, making soft, contented noises.

Jacqui sighed, weary from all the grief. 'It's just so strange, not having him around. Being alone.'

'I know. But you'll be all right.'

'You're so lucky, Mel. You're gonna be part of a family. That's how it's meant to be.'

'I guess.'

'It's true.' Jacqui took a small mirror out of her bag and held it up to her face, inspecting the damage. 'We're not s'posed to be on our own. We're social creatures, we're meant to live in a group. We're . . . we're herd animals.'

'Yeah, I know.' Melanie picked up her coffee and took a sip.

'Anyway,' Jacqui said, managing a faint smile, 'I reckon Gary would look pretty good in a pair of crotchless knickers.'

'Come to the wedding and you'll probably find out,' said Melanie, and she and Jacqui both laughed. Melanie was relieved to see her friend perking up a bit.

Melanie's mobile started to ring. 'If that's Consuela Torres . . .' Melanie shook her fist menacingly, making Jacqui smile. Melanie pulled the phone out of her bag. 'Hello?'

'Hello,' came the reply. 'Is this Melanie Francis?'

Covering the mouthpiece, Melanie whispered to Jacqui. 'It's all right, it's a bloke.'

Jacqui pretended to wipe her brow, as if she was relieved that it wasn't Consuela. As Melanie listened to the caller, the colour began to drain from her face. Jacqui became concerned. 'What? Who is it?' she whispered.

Melanie put her hand over the phone and slowly turned to her friend. 'It's Jack,' she replied, looking as if she'd just seen a ghost.

'Who?'

'Jack Francis,' said Melanie. 'It's my father.'

DONOVAN'S DEN, RICHMOND

'Last orders, ladies and gents. Last orders,' Brian called out across the bar. Then he resumed his conversation with Richard's strawberry-blonde girlfriend.

'So, Zani,' he said, 'do you like Miles Davis?'

'Who?' She frowned.

'She doesn't really like jazz,' said Richard. He was sitting on the stool next to Zani, with his hand resting on her thigh.

'Well, it's not for everyone,' said Campbell. 'Anyway, Zani's too young for that old fogey stuff.'

'Old fogey?!' Brian spluttered. 'Miles Davis isn't old!'

'No, he's dead,' replied Campbell.

'He isn't dead,' said Brian. 'He's eternal. His spirit lives on.' He shot Campbell a look. 'Which is more than I can say for some people. Richard, has she heard *Kind of Blue*? She'll love it. It's a classic.'

Richard thought for a moment. 'I think I lent it to someone.'

'Me. You lent it to me,' said Milos. Then he turned to Zani. 'I make you copy.'

All the men enjoyed fussing over young Zani, with her gorgeous hair and her body piercing and her crop tops. They liked how the other men in the bar sat watching them, casting envious glances. They basked in that envy; it was sunshine on a winter's day.

'So, what music *do* you like?' asked Campbell.

'Um, well . . .' Zani thought for a bit, twiddling her eyebrow ring. 'Ummm, I like reggae.'

The men erupted in a chorus of approval. Reggae, man – now she was talking. At last, something they could all relate to. Suddenly they didn't feel quite so old.

'Jammin', man, jammin',' Milos chanted.

'I saw Marley in seventy-nine,' enthused Brian. 'Fantastic!'

'Great musician.' Richard nodded.

'No way! Peter Tosh, he's the guy,' said Campbell.

'Oh, come on,' scoffed Brian, 'gimme a break.'

'Sorry. Tosh is the master,' Campbell insisted.

'Whaddya reckon, sweetie?' Brian turned to Zani for the casting vote. 'It's Bob, right? Bob Marley is the king of reggae.'

'Um, yeah . . . Bob,' Zani replied with a blank expression. Then she crinkled her forehead. 'Is he any relation to Ziggy?'

WARROORA, WESTERN AUSTRALIA

It was a balmy evening in Warroora, a tiny coastal town in the far northwest of Western Australia. Jack Francis ambled along the beach in his singlet and shorts. He was wiry and tanned, in good physical shape for a man in his late fifties. Jack worked as a crayfisherman in Warroora, where he'd lived for the past twenty years.

With him was his wife, Bronte, a woman in her late thirties. She was holding a child, the couple's two-year-old son, Jordan, jiggling him up and down as she walked, much to the child's delight. Tonight Jack's daughter, Melanie, had joined them on their regular evening stroll. She wore a cotton sarong and a long shell necklace that Bronte had made for her as a welcoming gift.

Melanie was enjoying the sunset, feeling pleased that she'd decided to come. She hadn't seen her father since the divorce, when she was still a child. Meeting him at the airfield the day before, she'd been surprised by the resemblance. Melanie was certainly her father's daughter, at least physically.

Bronte had told Melanie over coffee that morning that she'd been urging Jack to make contact with Melanie for years now. Finally he'd plucked up the courage, tracking down Melanie's mobile number through one of his ex-wife's friends.

As Bronte talked, Melanie had thought about Richard, who'd often suggested that she make peace with her father. Melanie had always dismissed the idea out of hand, claiming not to care.

'Well, you know what they say,' Richard would reply. 'Don't die angry.'

After recovering from the shock of hearing Jack's voice, Melanie had accepted his offer of a plane ticket, arranging to fly to Warroora the following week. She too was ready for some kind of reconciliation. And she wanted to do it now, before the wedding. Get it sorted. That way she could move on unencumbered to the next phase of her life.

Her half-brother, Jordan, had taken an immediate shine to Melanie, holding up his toy boat and his favourite blue crayon, chatting away happily in his own secret language. Bronte wasn't much older than Melanie, which took some adjustment. She was a bit dippy, Melanie thought. A bit of an earth-child dream-catcher type, but she was friendly and sweet and seemed genuinely happy with her life in this tiny, faraway place. She was certainly devoted to Jack, who Melanie barely recognised.

Jack was a proper human being now. He explained to Melanie that after the divorce his real estate business had taken a dive and his health had begun to deteriorate. He'd been diagnosed with angina and suffered two minor heart attacks, which was the wake-up call he'd needed. He'd turned his life around, leaving Melbourne behind and reinventing himself in WA. He'd stopped smoking and drinking, started exercising and applied himself to learning new skills in the crayfishing industry. That's how he'd met Bronte. She'd been working as a deckhand on one of the boats.

Jack was clearly remorseful about the way he'd treated Melanie when she was a child. They spent many hours together sitting by the Indian Ocean, shooting the breeze and getting to know one another all over again. Melanie showed him photos of Gary and the farm and the various bands she'd played in. He seemed so grateful that she'd come to see him, that she'd given him another chance.

This version of Jack would've made a terrific dad, Melanie kept thinking, as she watched him poring over photographs, looking as proud as punch. At least he'd do the right thing by Jordan.

After three days Melanie said her goodbyes. There were hugs and tears and promises to keep in touch. They wouldn't be able to make it to Melanie's wedding, Jack explained, because of the crayfishing season. But they'd be free in the off-season, sometime in the new year. They'd come and visit then. Melanie insisted that they stay with her at Wyllandra and get to know Gary. Her father had agreed, with great enthusiasm, but Melanie wasn't entirely convinced. Despite his apparent transformation, in Melanie's mind, Jack was still Jack, king of empty promises. She'd accepted him back into her life, but trusting him was another matter entirely.

Melanie boarded the plane and waved to Jack and Bronte and her dear little brother Jordan, who was blowing kisses from the tarmac. Melanie held up the bright blue crayon Jordan had given her, so he could see it through the plane's window. Even if she never saw her father again, she thought, even if he never called her, that would be fine. They'd made their peace. Anything else would be a bonus.

Melanie flew back across the Nullarbor Plain with a lighter heart and a few new stories to tell. Now, at least, she wouldn't die angry.

Bookings for Melanie's Cottage were filling fast. It was the ideal getaway: no aggravation, no traffic noise, just the breeze in the she-oaks and the distant lowing of cattle. The scent of lavender mingled with the aroma of warm sourdough bread, which Gary baked and Melanie delivered. She'd wrap the bread in a gingham cloth, placing it in a wicker basket with homemade butter, apricot jam, a jug of milk and a jar of Dorothy's Anzac biscuits. The cottage fridge was always stocked with freshly laid eggs and tomatoes and basil from the garden.

Some guests liked to hide away and enjoy the cosy setting. Others headed out to the coast, hiking or abseiling or going out on the boats to watch the seals and the Southern Right whales. The guests were always welcome at the Big House for a chat with Melanie. Over tea and banana cake, they'd admire the view and enthuse about Melanie's good fortune, living in such a beautiful place. 'And so close to Melbourne,' they'd always say. 'It's the best of both worlds!'

Melanie and Gary were the perfect b & b team: 'Mein Host' and 'Mein Hostess', as Simon had dubbed them. They'd stand on the verandah of the Big House with their arms entwined, farewelling their rejuvenated guests as they headed back to the city. For all her egalitarian sentiments, Melanie couldn't deny it, she enjoyed being lady of the house. She was part of a landowning dynasty now, and people treated her differently. After years of working in typing pools and shopping centres, being addressed as 'hey you', it was good to have some status.

Sitting at the kitchen table, Melanie put the booking sheet to one side and took out her diary. There were five weeks till D-day – October 25 – and she was right on track. She'd already handed in her notice to the hospital. She'd work part time for another two weeks, then finish up for good. That would give her three weeks clear till the big event. She'd divide the time between Maybury and South Melbourne. There were some gigs to play with the Salsa Kings, the packing to organise, and Patrick was sewing the wedding dress – a short, sixties-style design – no meringues. He'd need her around for fittings.

After the wedding she'd be leaving the Salsa Kings, because their schedule was just too demanding. She'd still play the occasional gig at the retirement home. She'd be staying with the Morangos, no question. She'd spoken to Mitch Wheeler, the pianist who'd covered for her in the past, and he'd agreed to share the Morangos gig on a fairly permanent basis, playing on alternate Thursdays. So for now, at least until the children were born, she'd be playing at Donovan's twice a month. She could stay overnight with the boys, or with Jacqui. Dorothy – her dream mother-in-law – had offered to run the b & b whenever Melanie needed to get away. This freed up her options considerably.

Gary had agreed with her decision to have a city life as well; in fact, he'd been very supportive. Maybe he was thinking about Carla, Melanie mused. How Carla had left him because living in Maybury all the time had made her feel too confined. Gary didn't want a repeat of that saga, and neither did Melanie. It was all a question of balance.

Yin and yang, plain and peanut. Gigs at the club, lunch at Cheroni's, gazing at the stars with Gary, sex in the bath. Brilliant.

LIVING LEGENDS RETIREMENT VILLAGE, CROYDON

The Living Legends Retirement Village was a leafy, well-appointed residence in the outer suburbs of Melbourne. Here, former practitioners from the music, film, TV and theatre industries (those who hadn't made a packet overseas) could enjoy their dotage, reminiscing about the glory days. The home was part-funded by Art-House and the Actors and Musicians Union, but largely financed by the federal government, in recognition of the artists' contribution to the community. As it stated on the brass plaque in the foyer: '. . . a lifetime of subsidising Australia's cultural development with their tireless labours, for meagre financial return'.

The Living Legends were a discerning lot; you couldn't fool them with a mediocre performance. Today Richard and Melanie came on straight after the belly-dancers, so the crowd was rather agitated. They kicked off with a Fats Waller medley, and soon the audience was singing along (extremely well, most of them) to some old favourites including 'Your Feet's Too Big', 'I Can't Give You Anything But Love' and 'Honeysuckle Rose'. When the set had finished, Nurse Betty Harriot arrived with the tea trolley and they all took a break before the next act – a recitation of Lewis Carroll's 'Jabberwocky' and several poems by Spike Milligan.

Nurse Betty and some of the female residents were fussing over Melanie's engagement ring, admiring the old-style setting, the sizeable blue sapphire and the little white diamonds surrounding it. The wedding was the topic of much conversation at the home, everyone agreeing that an artist should marry someone solid, someone with a good income – get some security. 'Snaffling a rich farmer' – a grounded, reliable man who clearly appreciated the arts – was considered quite a coup.

Holding his mug of Liptons, Richard watched them as they clucked over Melanie. He tried to look unconcerned. One of the belly-dancers joined them in the sunroom. Richard started flirting with her, in a very obvious manner. He was hoping to elicit a response from Melanie but she didn't seem to notice. She was too busy handing around the photos. There was more clucking – what a handsome man, what curly blond locks and good strong thighs, what a beautiful house, dear, and such a stunning view of the property. Heading for the tea trolley, Richard consoled himself with a hefty slice of strawberry gateau.

BUNNALUP HIGHWAY, MAYBURY

As the log trucks rumbled by, the tree planters were toiling on the highway's median strip. Melanie was in bib-and-brace overalls, her hair dragged back into a ponytail. She was down on her knees, stabbing at the ground with a trowel.

Nearby were a couple of local builders, Jezza and Eddie, who'd been sent to the tree-planting by their wives. Gary had been drumming up support on Radio 3GE-290, the Voice of the Greater Eastern, and a number of women, charmed by Gary's mellifluous tones, had volunteered their husbands' services. As they dug, Jezza and Eddie had a good grumble about the local laird. They didn't realise that the nondescript woman immediately to their left was Gary's intended.

'That Gazza. What a life, eh?' Eddie said as he tried to dislodge a rock.

'Whatever shit he falls into, he ends up smelling like a bloody rose,' said Jezza.

'Well, he's got Daddy there to hose him down.'

'Yeah, right.' Jezza removed the plastic wrap from a young eucalypt. 'See he's had the cottage done up?'

'Yeah?' Eddie succeeded in shifting the rock. He hauled it to one side.

Jezza lowered the sapling into the ground. 'You know, he told Geoff Birkin he built the place himself.'

'What – the cottage?' Eddie stopped working and looked up. 'The bluestone?'

'Yeah,' replied Jezza. 'You know he's turned it into a b & b.'

Eddie shook his head in disbelief. 'That lyin' bastard. I nearly did me back in buildin' that friggin' place.'

'He was tellin' Geoff Birkin how to pour concrete.' Jezza packed the loose earth around the base of the sapling.

'Gazza?!' Eddie scoffed. 'He doesn't know a friggin' thing about pouring concrete. Beer, maybe . . .'

'Yeah, beer and bullshit,' said Jezza with a laugh.

Melanie listened to the two men, keeping her head well down in case they recognised her. Apparently her image of Gary as a gifted stonemason would require some revision. The man was wobbling on his DIY pedestal.

Gary suddenly appeared and took Melanie's hand. 'C'mon, darl',' he said with a smile and helped her up off the ground. 'We've got to get ready for tonight.'

MAYBURY COMMUNITY HALL

The Maybury RSL Ball was an annual event, attended by guests from all over the Greater Eastern. It was a formal affair with live music, soft lighting and big hair – the sort of dance they never had at St Jacobs, thought Melanie, as she took to the floor with Gary.

Tonight she wore a long, silvery, sleeveless gown. It fitted snugly around the bodice, then flared slightly so she could move in it. Gary was resplendent in his tux. He was in fine form tonight, attentive and gracious. He escorted Melanie around the room, introducing her to more of his extended family, to the Cliff Rescue volunteers he trained with, to the out-of-town guests who'd been coming to the ball for years (some of them for decades). They all greeted her warmly and congratulated her on the engagement. Gary kept telling everyone what a lucky bloke he was, smiling broadly when they agreed and looking very proud. Unashamed of displaying his affection, he'd pull Melanie close to him and kiss the nape of her neck, or the tip of her shoulder, or the palm of her hand.

Utterly spoilt and quite radiant, Melanie was having a wonderful time. Gary made her feel like the Queen of Sheba and the belle of the ball, rolled into one. So what if he couldn't pour concrete.

Together they danced around the room as the band played a medley of Viennese waltzes. Gary moved with impressive grace. His mother had taught him well, thought Melanie. Unlike a lot of men negotiating the floor, he knew how to steer.

The other guests looked on, murmuring their approval.

WYLLANDRA, MAYBURY

The following afternoon, Melanie was out in the chook-house, armed with a large metal spade. Dressed in some grubby overalls and a pair of oversized gumboots, she was shovelling manure for the compost and cleaning out the laying boxes. She was ably assisted by her 2IC, Millie, the little black hen, who liked to help out where she could. Marmite was eyeing them both from the verandah. Now that Millie was watching the mistress, he could cut back on his companion duties and do a little more dozing.

Gary appeared in the kitchen doorway. Freshly showered,

he wore his new moleskin jeans and a metal-grey silk shirt. He sauntered along the verandah and down the stairs, heading towards Melanie.

'Darl',' he called. 'Oi, darl'! Mum says we need more towels in the cottage.'

Melanie whistled appreciatively at Gary's outfit. 'Very nice. Where are you off to, looking so handsome?'

'Book club. Simon and Brendan are picking me up.'

'Right.' Melanie pushed the hair out of her eyes and squinted into the sun. 'You know, I like books, I read all the time. Why don't I come along?'

Gary frowned. 'Because you'd make us look stupid,' he replied, as if Melanie should know better. 'That's the whole idea, it's a book club for people who don't know much about books.'

'What about Simon?' asked Melanie.

'What about him?'

'Well, he went to uni, didn't he?'

'Yeah,' said Gary, 'but he didn't read any books. So darl', what about the towels?'

'You get the towels.' Melanie packed fistfuls of hay into the boxes and Millie cackled her approval.

'But Mel, the guys are coming. They're going to be here soon.'

'So, do it when you get back,' she replied. 'I'm not a servant, Gary.'

'Of course you're not a servant!' Gary flashed one of his charming smiles. 'You're my darlin' gorgeous girl and I want to give you a great big hug – except you're covered in chook shit.'

'Well, you did ask me to dress down.' Melanie spoke with some bitterness.

'You're in a good mood,' said Gary quietly.

Melanie leant against the spade. 'Listen,' she began. She'd decided that now was the time to broach a difficult subject. 'I don't want to hassle you, and you know . . . you know that I love you very much, but Gary, have you been into my cosmetics again?'

'God, Melanie!' said Gary, as if she was being completely unreasonable. 'It's just a bit of fun.'

'But you use all the expensive stuff.'

Gary kicked a pebble along the ground and said nothing.

'We've talked about this,' Melanie continued. 'There's plenty of cheap stuff in there, you can have that.'

'Cheap stuff,' Gary muttered under his breath.

'If you want the good stuff, you go and buy it.'

'Jeez, Mel, my one little luxury, you begrudge me even that.'

'But Gary, it's *my* little luxury.'

'Oh and my needs don't count, is that it?'

'Look,' said Melanie, trying to be conciliatory, 'you give me some money and I'll buy some expensive stuff for you – just for you – all right?'

'Not the same,' said Gary. He sighed heavily and looked at her with a hurt expression, as if to say she didn't understand.

And he was right, Melanie didn't understand and she didn't really want to try.

Brendan pulled up in the station wagon, blasting the

horn. Simon and Rosalie sat next to him, both of them grinning and waving. Leaving Melanie to the chooks, Gary walked off to join his mates.

Melanie threw down the spade and stomped into the house. She took a can of iced tea out of the fridge and plonked herself down at the table. Life was hideous and vile. Manual labour in the back of Bourke, with a bunch of Neanderthal neighbours who couldn't grasp the concept of solitude. Christ, they couldn't even read a book by themselves, they had to form a bloody club!

And what was she to them? A legal necessity. As far as Gary's mates were concerned, Melanie was the requisite spouse, nothing more. A way for Gary to hang on to Wyllandra so they could keep drinking his booze and cluttering up his house.

She decided to discuss it all with her counsellor at the next session – get some perspective. Melanie hadn't told Gary about her sessions with Agnes. In Melanie's experience, men usually flew into a panic when they heard the word 'counsellor'. They assumed that you were painting them in a bad light, giving them a bad report card. You were talking about them with a total stranger and they weren't privy to these conversations. It was a threat to their personal control, an erosion of power. Women saw it differently. It was just a chat. A chat to make sense of it all, a way to nut out solutions. It wasn't about apportioning blame or pronouncing judgment. But Gary may not understand that, so there was no point upsetting him.

Taking a long drink of the iced tea, Melanie started to calm down. It was only a bit of make-up, she thought, rolling the can between her hands. It's not like he's an axe-murderer or anything.

She hauled herself up from the table and went to run a bath. She'd be up in town tomorrow. She'd go for a swim, go shopping with Patrick and Marshall, maybe buy some new CDs – and nobody would talk about the price of beef.

TIVOLI GARDENS, ALBERT PARK

After fetching the mail, Richard picked his way across the lounge room. It was littered with slabs of chipboard, buckets of glue and piles of 'found objects', as Zani called them. There were slivers of glass and chunks of driftwood and somebody's old gardening glove, among other treasures. Eastern Religions had fallen by the wayside, replaced by Tactile Design.

The night before, Richard had sliced his foot on a broken abalone shell, which had lain camouflaged on the lounge-room floor. Limping through the debris, dripping blood, his other foot had become glued to some newspaper. Then he'd slipped on a mound of wet clay and fallen heavily onto a wire cutter. At that point, Richard had lost his cool. He'd shouted at Zani. He'd told her to clean the bloody place up before he was crippled for life. Zani had shouted back, calling him a sad old bastard. He'd retaliated with lazy bloody cow, and they'd ended up having sex. The usual pattern.

Richard flopped into the couch and looked through the

mail. The phone bill had rocketed, thanks to Madam Scam at Fone a Future. He decided to buy Zani a bag of runes which she could consult at her leisure. Toss the sticks, read the tea leaves, just stay away from the phone. Power was also up. The Snoopy night lamp, like the Olympic flame, could never be extinguished. Gas was up too, the oven now doubling as a pottery kiln.

He found a letter with no stamp, addressed to 'Richard Cohen, Love God.' He opened it to find a handmade card. 'Zani loves grumpy old Richard' was scrawled in brightly coloured crayon. Inside was a drawing of a saxophone. 'See you tonight, babe. You and the big shiny horn . . . Z xxxooo'

Richard smiled and put his feet up on the coffee table. He didn't really care about the bills or the extra house-work. Zani was sweet and playful and she kept him warm at night. Richard enjoyed making love on a regular basis – it was a great comfort to him. And while Zani wasn't the woman of his dreams, she had made him the envy of all his friends.

THE MAGELLAN HOSPITAL, EAST MELBOURNE

'You look tired,' said Agnes the counsellor, backing into her ergonomically designed chair. 'Tell me about it.'

Melanie cut to the chase: there was a problem. Gary was trying to usurp her femininity and claim it as his own. She knew it wasn't very PC, but try as she might, she couldn't get her head around it. She resented this appropriation of what she saw as her natural role.

'I'm the girl, doesn't he get it? That's *my* turf.' Melanie stabbed at her sternum with an index finger. '*I'm* the damn girl!'

Agnes observed Melanie for a moment then leant in towards her. 'You know,' she spoke quietly, in measured tones, 'I don't like to say this, but you're in danger of becoming a gender bigot.'

'A what?'

'You're ignoring the complexity of the human condition.'

'I'm not a bigot.' Melanie was stung by the accusation. 'I just want him to stay out of my clothes.'

'Let me explain.'

Melanie frowned and kept quiet.

'On the one hand,' said Agnes, 'you've got gender. On the other hand, you've got sexual identity. These are two different things. A lot of biological females choose a masculine identity – they're butch, if you like. And that's their prerogative. In the same way, Gary might have been born biologically male, but if he wants to assume a feminine sexual identity, that's his right too.'

'But I don't –'

'It hasn't been easy for Gary,' Agnes continued, 'growing up in that relentlessly male environment, with that unforgiving father. The sort of father who would punish and humiliate his son if he showed any sign of weakness.'

'Col can be pretty tough,' Melanie conceded. 'Mind you, the grandfather – he was a shocker.'

'So when Gary is hurting – spiritually, psychologically – what does he do? He employs a coping mechanism. He seeks consolation in the physical manifestation of his forbidden feminine persona.'

'He puts on a dress.'

'Exactly. And when he summons the courage to confide in you, when he reveals his dark secret to someone he thinks he can trust, what do you do? You undermine him. You belittle him. You treat him as some kind of threat to your precious female identity, whatever that is.'

Melanie frowned, pensive. 'I never thought about it like that . . .'

'No wonder men get confused,' declared Agnes, with a sweep of her hand. 'We tell them to be hard, then we tell them to be soft. We want them to charge into battle and slay the biggest dragon, then whip off the armour and empathise over sticky buns. Can you see why Gary might need to escape, take refuge in a little fantasy now and again?'

Melanie looked down at the carpet and chewed her lip. The woman had a point.

LIVING LEGENDS RETIREMENT VILLAGE, CROYDON

Melanie and Richard were playing duets in the sunroom, taking requests from the audience – 'Chattanooga Choo-Choo', 'Sentimental Journey', 'It's Only a Paper Moon', 'South of the Border', 'Basin Street Blues'. As Melanie took a solo on Felix, Richard glanced over at an elderly couple, Nigel and Emmaline, who were sitting on a couch holding hands. Both former tap dancers, they'd recently celebrated their fiftieth wedding anniversary.

Richard frowned to himself. When he was that old, Zani would still be a youngish woman. He'd be getting around on a Zimmer frame and she'd be off to netball training. And try as he might, he couldn't imagine spending fifty long years with Zani. What would they talk about? It was fine while they were having sex, but the pre- and post-coital conversations were pretty limited. When Richard was with Melanie they talked all the time, it was effortless. He could imagine them sitting on the porch, watching the sun go down, talking about music and politics and how well the grandchildren were doing at university . . .

'Mel, it's Gary!' Nurse Betty appeared in the doorway. She'd been watching TV in the front office and there had been a newsflash from Maybury. She raced over to the sun-room TV and switched it on.

A rescue was in progress, down on the Greater Eastern coastline, about six kilometres north of Maybury. The victim was a cousin of the Prime Minister's, apparently, which explained the extensive media coverage. The young amateur fisherman had walked across some rocks around to a quiet cove and found himself trapped by the rising tide. He was stranded on the shore at the base of Seal Cove cliffs, with the ocean closing in on him. The pilot of a light plane had spotted the man and radioed for help. A quick response was essential; not only was the sea rising, but the hapless angler was struggling to breathe. His anxiety had brought on an asthma attack.

As the news chopper buzzed overhead and the journalists flocked, the police coordinator at the top of the cliff was supervising the rescue. The State Emergency Service had been summoned. They sped to the scene, bringing ropes and stretchers and various anchoring devices. The team leader, or 'on-scene commander', as the junior reporter intoned, joined the police coordinator and put the SES team through its paces. The first aid officer, with breathing apparatus and emergency medication, was quickly lowered down to the stranded fisherman. She was followed by the escort, Gary Quartermaine, a local farmer. It was a slower, more painstaking descent as he was carrying a steel and canvas stretcher. The victim was placed onto the stretcher and duly secured.

'The commander is just metres away from me,' the reporter announced. 'He's on the two-way. He's on the two-way radio . . . he's talking them through it. He's calm, he's collected, he's a true professional, folks, and . . . yes . . . yes, they're getting ready for the lift.' The camera swung wildly between the team leader, the officer supervising the rope anchor and the three distant figures on the shore below.

As the stretcher was slowly hauled back up, Gary lay across its four supporting ropes, looking down at the frightened young man, talking to him quietly, reassuring him, while the first aid officer monitored the nebuliser. Finally, they were all back on the cliff-top and out of danger. A waiting ambulance whisked the victim away to the hospital at Mount Malabar.

As she sat in the Living Legends sunroom, watching

events unfold, Melanie's eyes filled with tears. After her initial horror at seeing Gary risking his life at the end of a rope, she was now bursting with pride. As the staff and residents clucked noisily about her courageous beau, she took the mobile into the foyer and tried to call him, but his phone was switched off. She left him a message, telling him how incredibly proud she was, that she'd see him at Wyllandra the following night, and that he should call her as soon as possible. Then she went back into the sunroom, where they were watching another version of the news-flash on a different station.

THE MAGELLAN HOSPITAL, EAST MELBOURNE

It was Melanie's last day at the hospital. Her colleagues had arranged a combination farewell tea and bridal shower in the tearoom. Sitting among the wrapping paper and chocolate crackles, Melanie thanked everyone for their gifts: the lead crystal vases, the cutlery set, the 'his' and 'hers' manchester and the inevitable penis-warmer, knitted by a giggling Maureen. All the women were thrilled about the forthcoming nuptials. They chattered away excitedly, continually interrupting each other.

'Go on, Mel, show us the photo.'

'Ooh, what a hunk! Has he got any brothers?'

'Ted and I saw him on the news.'

'You're so lucky, Mel. I'd love to live in the country.'

'Jacqui says the place is gorgeous.'

'I saw him on "Nightline". He was so brave. Did you know he's the chief of cliff rescue? How fabulous.'

'I thought he was the commander.'

'*And*, she's only two hours from Melbourne.'

'Is that all?!'

'You'll have to come up and see us. Bring Gary, okay!'

'Mel, it's the best of both worlds.'

The microwave pinged and Jacqui attended to the mini felafels. Sally from Finance squeezed the penis-warmer onto her chunky mobile phone and started mimicking the VA.

'You see, ladies, it's not the length that counts,' Sally drawled, in the VA's fruity voice, 'it's the width. The width – that's what really matters. And ladies, when you're doing the nasty, just go for it! Remember the golden rule: you've got to stay active . . .'

The others joined in the chorus, 'Stay attractive!'

The women suddenly froze as a shadow fell across the doorway. It was the dreaded Mrs Van Asch herself. Sally whipped the phone behind her back and Maureen nearly choked on her caramel slice.

With an imperious air, the VA strode up to Melanie and deposited a gift in her lap. Before Melanie could thank her, she'd turned and swept out of the room. Everyone gathered around Melanie's chair, all eyes on the package. Melanie pulled off the silver wrapping to reveal an expensive-looking cookery book, filled with glossy photos and haute cuisine recipes.

The book was called *Cooking for One*.

Melanie gasped. The sheer gall of the woman was remarkable. No false sentiment from the VA. She kept the guns blazing right to the bitter end.

With a look of astonishment, Melanie turned to her colleagues. After a few incredulous seconds, the entire group burst out laughing.

At lunchtime Melanie and Jacqui sat on their favourite bench, watching the ducks and the interns. Jacqui pulled a letter out of her bag. It was from the Burmese and Tonkinese Cat Lovers' Society. She showed it to Melanie.

'Look, isn't it cute?'

Melanie ran her thumb over the elaborate logo at the top of the page. 'I hope that fur isn't real.'

'They said I could meet the cat,' said Jacqui.

'Uhuh . . .'

'You know, the cat who got Leroy's heart.'

'Ah, right,' replied Melanie. 'The other Burmese.'

'Well, turns out it's a blue Burmese and Leroy was a brown Burmese, but I don't think he'd mind.'

'No.' Melanie smiled at her friend fondly. 'He wouldn't mind.'

'Anyway, they want us to meet up,' continued Jacqui. 'Me and the owner.'

'The owner of the blue Burmese?'

'Yes. But only if I want to.'

Melanie paused, trying to gauge Jacqui's true feelings on the subject. 'And do you want to?'

Jacqui looked very uncertain. 'I dunno, Mel, I'm kinda

nervous about it. You know, I'm just getting over it – losing Leroy and everything. It might bring it all back.'

'Well, you don't have to do it straightaway,' Melanie suggested. 'I mean, there's no rush, is there?'

Jacqui thought for a moment, then folded up the letter. 'Yeah, you're right. I think I'll wait a while.' Putting the letter back in her bag, she sighed to herself. Melanie always knew what to do. Life was going to be very strange without her.

FIT 'N' FUNKY GYM, ALBERT PARK

Richard lay in the sauna, sweating buckets. Plugged into his Discman, listening to Wanderlust, a hot Sydney jazz group, he didn't hear the door creak open. He didn't notice the two men approaching him until the towel draped across his conversation piece was rudely snatched away. The Discman went with it, crashing to the floor.

'Oi!' Richard sat bolt upright, shielding his groin with his hands.

Michael Sciarelli was sitting on the bench next to him, dressed in a three-piece suit. Johnny Sciarelli, similarly attired, was guarding the door.

'So, Mr Cohen,' said Michael, 'we meet again.'

'Look, could I have my towel?' asked Richard, feeling extremely vulnerable.

'We gotta talk, you and me,' Michael continued.

'Michael, c'mon,' interrupted Johnny.

'What?' snarled his brother.

'It's embarrassing,' Johnny pleaded. 'Give him the towel, will ya?'

'Please,' said Richard, 'just give it back.'

Disdainfully, Michael held the towel out to him. Richard grabbed it and wrapped it around his waist.

Michael leant in close. 'The word is . . .' He paused and scanned the sauna to make sure it was empty – a pointless exercise as they were clearly alone. 'The word is you're romantically connected with a young lady by the name of Zani.'

'Zani, yeah . . . I guess I am,' said Richard. 'Is that a problem?'

'She's our cousin,' revealed Johnny, with a hint of pride.

'Shut up!' shouted Michael. He wiped his neck with a handkerchief and resumed his menacing look. 'Ya see, Mister Cohen – Zani, she's our cousin.'

'You guys have a lot of cousins.'

'Tell me about it,' said Johnny. 'Christmas is the worst, you've gotta . . .' Johnny caught sight of Michael's expression and zipped his lip.

'Now, I'm warning you Mister Cohen . . .'

'Please, it's Richard.'

'I'm warning you . . . *Dick*,' Michael spat the word with some vehemence, 'you mess with our cousin Zani, you do one little itty-bitty thing to upset her . . .'

'Can we go?' Johnny was looking edgy.

'I'm not finished!' barked his brother.

'I've gotta take Auntie Emmy to the podiatrist.'

'Oh, for God's sake!' blurted Richard.

Michael and Johnny stared at him in disbelief.

'Hey, you talkin' to me?!' His suit now drenched in sweat, Michael was looking faintly ridiculous.

'No, I'm talking to the cast of *Swan Lake*,' said Richard, exasperated. 'Didn't you notice the tutus? Of course I'm talking to you!'

Michael and Johnny were too stunned to reply.

'It's pathetic – the whole schtick,' Richard continued. 'The whole . . . gangster thing. You don't enjoy it, either of you.'

Indignation was giving way to curiosity. The brothers kept listening.

'There's something else,' said Richard. 'Something else you guys want to do – it's just eating away at you. Am I right?'

'Hey, wait a minute,' Michael protested, rather weakly.

'Now you,' Richard directed Johnny, 'come and sit over here. Next to your brother.'

Johnny looked at Michael, who shrugged his shoulders. Johnny joined him on the bench.

Richard stood up and checked the knot in his towel. 'Right. I'm going to ask you a question. You have to say the first thing that comes into your head, okay?'

The two men nodded, apprehensive.

'You can't stop and think about it. It's gotta be your first reaction.'

They nodded again.

'Okay, here it is. Forget about what other people want you to do. Forget about what you think you *should* do. Just tell me, what is the one thing in the world that you really, really *want* to do? Tell me *now*! *NOW!*'

Michael and Johnny turned to each other, flustered. 'Umm . . .'

'I can see you thinking! Don't think about it, just say it! The one thing you *really* want to do . . .'

'Ahh . . .' The brothers were panicking now, the pressure getting to them.

In a booming voice, Richard counted them down, 'Three! Two! . . .'

'MUSIC!' Michael and Johnny blurted their answer in unison. Shocked, they turned and stared at one another. Could this be true? Had they been harbouring the same dream all these years? To know the thrill of making music – maybe play in a band like their revered cousins? With a cry of joy, the brothers embraced. Then they started to weep, with great blubbering gulps.

Richard stood back and smiled, savouring this moment of epiphany. Then he grabbed his Discman and made for the door. No point in pushing your luck.

WYLLANDRA, MAYBURY

As a pre-wedding celebration, Gary had arranged a special evening for Melanie. He wanted her to meet some like-minded locals, so he'd invited a group of musicians, dancers and sundry artists, plus Barry from the Barking Shark, to join them for dinner on Sunday night. Most

of the fourteen guests were former city dwellers –
'Stopovers', as Brendan called them. They had been won
over by Maybury's assets – the green hills, the beach, the
clean air and, most importantly, the cheap housing. Here
they could live on a shoestring and create in peace, travelling to Melbourne for launches and performances.

Over dinner they traded stories and drank plenty of
good wine. Moving to the lounge room, the guitarists
played some foot-tapping zydeco tunes while the others
danced. Gary joined in on the bongo drums, laughing out
loud when he lost the beat but persisting till he found it
again. Watching him, Melanie smiled to herself. Gary was
having a blast. She scanned the room – these were her
kind of people. None of the usual suspects, thank God.

Nursing their coffees, they talked about joining forces
and generating more activity. They could run programs for
the kids at the two primary schools: instrumental music,
movement, speech and drama. And some classes for adult
beginners: tap-dancing, painting, creative writing. They
could start a community choir – gospel choirs were popular, they'd probably get a good turn-out. Barry proposed
a weekly performance night at the Barking Shark, where
he'd provide the sound system and put on the food. They
could have stand-up comedy nights, original bands and
pub theatre. But it was Gary's suggestion, the Maybury
Latin Jazz Festival, that got the most support. The location was ideal, and with the right promotion it could be as
big as the Bellingen Festival or even Wangaratta. Melanie
offered to get the ball rolling. Brian Donovan could help
them out with some contacts up in Melbourne.

As Melanie circulated with a fresh pot of coffee, Gary rocked back in his chair and surveyed the scene. He turned to Phil Duncan, an ex-Brisbanite who played a mean slide guitar.

'The way I look at it,' said Gary, 'us farmers and you arty types, we've got a lot in common.'

'How's that?' asked Phil.

'Well, we're all primary producers,' said Gary. 'We all actually make something.'

'Yeah,' said Phil, 'and we all hate the middleman.'

'Too right,' said Gary.

As Melanie passed by on her way to the kitchen, Gary reached out and caught her by the wrist. Drawing her towards him, he gently kissed her fingertips, then the palm of her hand. Gazing into one another's eyes, they silently agreed to send everyone home.

When the last guest had departed, Melanie told Gary that she had a surprise for him – it was waiting for him in the bedroom.

Since her last session with the counsellor, Melanie had been doing some thinking. Maybe Agnes was right, maybe Melanie was being a little intolerant. If Gary wanted to dress a certain way, if it made him feel good, who was she to deny him? Part of her hoped it was just a phase, a need for reassurance. It was probably a reaction to the divorce. In time, all would be well. Until then she'd try to relax and play along. Who knows, she might even grow to like it. They could make it their special game, their secret indulgence.

She had tracked down a boutique in Richmond, a store

for the larger lady. She was after something special, Melanie had told the salesgirl. Something short and sassy for her big-boned country cousin.

Gary delved into the plastic bag, pulled out his gift and immediately got an erection. He tore off his shirt and jeans and pulled on the red slinky dress, admiring himself in the full-length mirror next to the bed. Melanie had to admit, there was something about a rock-hard penis straining through lycra . . .

Gary raced over to Melanie and embraced her, kissing her passionately. Then he threw her onto the bed, hitched up his red lycra dress and made very masculine love to her, well into the night.

FIRST AID TRAINING CENTRE, FOOTSCRAY

If you want to meet eligible men, there are three things you should try: join a golf club, join a wine-tasting club or enrol in a course – one that attracts blokes. That's what Jacqui had gleaned from *Bedz 2 Big*, a new singles' magazine. After scouring numerous pet shops and cat shows, Jacqui had decided that she could never replace Leroy. And the truth was, she didn't want another cat. She wanted a fella. She couldn't afford to play golf, and wine gave her asthma, so she enrolled in a first aid course. It was a practical course that would appeal to the male of the species. Plus it was short – a three-day intensive – so if the pickings were slim, you could cut your losses and move on.

Jacqui arrived at the first aid training centre and consulted the noticeboard. According to the list, there were eleven men and eight women in her class. The odds appeared to be in her favour – until she met the eleven men. They were all pit workers from a remote mining town – big, hairy, monosyllabic men who hadn't seen a woman in months. Their delight at being rolled into coma position by unknown females was matched only by their excitement about the plastic dummies – all blue-eyed blondes called Annie.

As Jacqui sat on her knees breathing life into a half-mannequin, several men gathered around the base of the plastic torso, all puppyish and starry-eyed, as if they were living out a dream. Jacqui wanted to explain to them that putting her mouth onto a piece of training equipment did not constitute a 'girl-girl' thing, but she decided against it. The state these guys were in, just saying the words 'girl-girl' might unleash a riot.

At the end of three days Jacqui could tie a sling, identify a box jellyfish and roll a hundred-and-twenty-kilo man into coma position while keeping him at arm's length. She collected her certificate and said a quick goodbye, declining eleven invitations to the pub where the lads were staying. While she had no doubts that the Panting Slag was a 'top spot', and the high praise for their battered saveloys well deserved, she really did have to go home and wash her hair. Several times.

Richard had shut himself in the walk-in robe, dodging empty coat-hangers as he practised his arpeggios. The door suddenly opened and there stood Zani, brandishing a pair of football socks. She dropped them into the bell of his saxophone.

'I can still hear you,' she snarled.

'Well, put in some earplugs,' he replied.

'It doesn't work. I'm *trying* to do my project.' Zani's eyebrow ring was bobbing up and down energetically.

'Ah, yes,' said Richard wryly. 'More found objects.'

'Are you making fun of me?'

'Not at all,' he replied, as calmly as possible. It really annoyed her when he kept his cool.

'Yes you are, you're making fun of me.' Zani's fuse was lit. 'And you've got that look again.'

'What look?' said Richard. 'Oh, you mean, "Gee, it's hard to practise when people keep shoving things down your saxophone" – that look?'

'I hate you, Richard,' Zani said, glaring at him.

'No you don't.' Balancing the sax on his knee, he adjusted the mouthpiece.

'I'm going back to my project now,' she snapped.

'Good,' said Richard. 'I'll know where to find you. I'll just follow the mess.'

Zani planted her hands on her hips and barked at him. 'My tutor says we create order out of chaos.'

'Well, you've got the chaos bit right,' said Richard, wetting the saxophone reed and slipping it into place.

Zani was very angry now, but she couldn't find the words to express it. Her face got hotter and redder. 'You're mean,' she hissed. 'You're a mean old bully!' She turned and stomped out of the cupboard, slamming the door behind her.

Richard emptied the socks out of his saxophone and blew extra hard.

WYLLANDRA, MAYBURY

Melanie stood in the king-sized spa, giving it a good scrub. She caught her reflection in the mirrored tiles – she looked tired. It had been a long day with too many visitors. In the city you can put on the answering machine and stay in bed, but in the country you can't ignore people that easily. They know where you live. They land on your doorstep with lamingtons and homemade pickles, expecting a hearing. They stay for hours, even when you've got a b & b to run, legs to be waxed and a wedding in ten days' time.

Maybe it was cold feet, but Melanie was feeling a little claustrophobic. She couldn't be anonymous down here. People were always watching her – talking about her at playgroups and craft mornings, most likely. It was the Quartermaine name, like Gary said, but understanding why it happened didn't make it any better. She polished the taps with a damp cloth. You're being paranoid, girl, you need a holiday. Thank God for the honeymoon – two weeks in a five-star hotel, destination unknown. Gary had told her to renew her passport, so she knew it wouldn't be Queensland. She was pinning her hopes on France.

Gary was having a busy few weeks. Now that he was a community radio star, he was always speaking at functions. This week it was the Show-jumping dinner, the Vintage Tractor Club barbecue and the Prison Board fondue night. Plus he and Simon were setting up more SLUDGE groups, promoting tree-planting in the wider district. This involved 5 a.m. starts and long road trips. Often he didn't get home before midnight.

There was a tap at the window. Dorothy, holding up a basket of washing she'd pulled off the line. Great, more ironing. Melanie smiled and nodded. After the wedding they'd hire a cleaner – no two ways about it. She couldn't be a scintillating 'Mein Hostess' with all this housework.

Another tap on the window. Brendan. He winked, saluting her with a socket wrench. Melanie ducked and kept scrubbing. Her bonding efforts with Gary's friends hadn't quite extended to Mister Fix-it.

She heard the tractor turning into the driveway. Gary had been working over at Col's today. She was looking forward to a night alone with him. Tonight was totally free – no meetings or social obligations of any kind, and no guests in the cottage.

She climbed out of the spa and opened the bathroom cupboard, looking for the apricot massage oil. The tractor stopped for a moment. Gary must be checking a gate, thought Melanie. It started again and rolled up into the shed.

After searching the Big House, Gary tried the cottage,

finding Melanie in the bathroom. He looked rather anxious. Hardly surprising, she thought, given the hours he'd been keeping.

'Darl',' said Gary, 'I've been thinking.'

He did his best thinking when he was driving the tractor, Melanie knew this. He'd come back home with a raft of new ideas, bursting to talk about them. She perched on the edge of the spa and Gary leant against the door frame.

'It's just that . . . well, I'm worried about you, Mel.'

Melanie paused. 'Why's that?'

'Well, you seem to have a problem with . . . with things dying.'

'No I don't,' replied Melanie, a little surprised.

'I know it's 'cause you're a city girl,' Gary continued. 'You're not used to things dying. I'm not crazy about it either. But I've been here all my life, I know how to deal with it.'

'Gary,' said Melanie, very calmly, 'I'm okay about it. Really.'

'Remember when we lost those lambs, when the crows picked out their eyes? And when the snake killed Mum's cockatoo, remember? And when your calf got sent to the abattoir by mistake? You see, Mel, you're getting all upset when I'm just talking about it.'

'No I'm not,' she sniffed.

'You see, darl',' he said as he sat down next to her, 'being on a farm, it's about the cycle of life. Animals get born, they live and they die.'

'I know.' She nodded.

'They die 'cause something else kills them, or they get sick, or they get turned into food. Right?'

'Right.'

''Cause if you're living on a property, you've got to come to terms with that.'

'I know.' She shrugged.

'You sure you're okay?' Gary took her hand.

'Yeah.' She smiled to reassure him. 'I'm okay.'

'That's good, darl', that's really good. 'Cause . . . I just ran over your chook.'

'What?!' Melanie gasped.

'I didn't see it, Mel, honest!'

'Which one?! Where . . . where is it?!' Melanie leapt up and pushed past him, running out of the cottage.

Gary followed her outside. 'It's down the drive. Well, part of it is. There's a bit on the tractor. I'm sorry, Mel. It just ran out in front of me.'

Melanie raced over to the shed and scanned the tractor tyres. There, stuck in the tread of the left tyre was a clump of distinctive black feathers, covered in blood.

'Millie!' she cried. 'MILLIE!'

🐌

Melanie assembled the corpse of poor Millie and buried her friend near the lavender bushes. It was a solemn and solitary ritual. Gary had been sent off to his parents in disgrace. She finished cleaning the cottage and put on another load of washing.

At six o'clock she took a long, hot bath. Gary was back but he'd been banished to the other side of the house. She

249

could hear him moving around, setting the fire, clattering about in the kitchen. She put on her dressing-gown and wrapped her hair in a towel. She was trying hard not to think about Millie. Melanie sat on the four-poster bed – an engagement present from Gary – and turned on the radio. Chris Isaak, *The Baja Sessions*. Yum. Lying back, she propped herself up on the pillows and rubbed some moisturiser into her hands. She was starting to feel vaguely human. There was a gentle knock at the door.

'Mel?' A contrite Gary.

She kept slapping on the cream.

'Listen, Mel, I'm sorry about the chook. I know you're a bit upset.'

'Her name's Millie.'

'Sorry – Millie. Look, Mel, it's been a shitty week all round. I've been away, you've been busy . . .'

'I want a cleaner,' she called.

'We'll get a cleaner. We'll get two,' replied Gary.

Melanie said nothing, enjoying the contrition. She liked that about Gary – if you asked him for something, he'd arrange it, no argument. He was very amenable, even if he did kill her chicken, the prat.

'I thought we could do something special,' said Gary.

I should bloody well hope so, she thought, reaching for the nail polish.

'I've got a surprise for you. It'll cheer you up. You ready?'

Champagne perhaps? Pears in red wine sauce? He'd probably been to the mini-mart to get her some chocolates. Or a video – something X-rated.

'Can I come in?'

'Oh, all right,' said Melanie, 'but only if you're good-looking.'

The door burst open and Gary stood there with his arms outstretched. 'Ta-da!'

Behind him were Brendan and Rosalie, Blodwyn and Maxine, Simon and Pip.

'Surprise!' they all shouted, attempting unison. Melanie was horrified, but Gary hadn't noticed. He was too busy bundling her out of the bedroom and down the hallway, following his friends.

The lounge had been set up with plenty of food and alcohol. There were board games and a pile of guitars and percussion instruments. The all-too-familiar visitors were pouring themselves drinks, gobbling snacks and starting the games.

'Look, Mel, we've got Twister!' said Gary. 'That'll be fun, right?'

Melanie could feel her throat tightening.

'Or Trivial Pursuit, yeah? Or charades,' Gary said as he mimed a rolling camera. 'We can play charades, right?'

'Charades!' the cry went up.

Melanie couldn't breathe. She ran back down the hall, through the bedroom and into the ensuite bathroom. Gasping, she turned on the taps and splashed water over her face until her breathing normalised.

Gary was right behind her. Was it asthma? Should he call the doctor? He wanted to drive her to the hospital in Mount Malabar, but Melanie insisted that she was fine. She was tired, she said, she just needed a lie down. He should go back and look after the guests. Eventually Gary's fears were allayed and, after tucking Melanie into bed, he returned to the lounge room for charades and chapattis.

Once he'd gone, Melanie jumped out of bed, threw on her tracksuit and scrawled a short note. Then she grabbed her keys and climbed out the bedroom window.

CORAL TREE LANE, SOUTH MELBOURNE

Patrick put down the receiver and shouted up to Marshall. 'Honkers, darling! We're going to Honkers!'

Marshall ran from the bedroom to the top of the stairs. 'I got the job!?' he asked, his eyes widening.

'You got the job, I got the job, we got the job!!' announced Patrick.

Marshall came flying down the stairs, shrieking with excitement. He grabbed hold of Patrick and squeezed him tight, spinning him around till Patrick got far too dizzy and begged for mercy.

Marshall suddenly froze. 'Oh my God!' He slapped his hands to his face. 'What am I going to wear?!'

Leaving Patrick to find his land legs again, Marshall raced upstairs to plunder the wardrobe.

Sitting in the counsellor's office with the calm blue walls and the fish mobile and the scented oil burner, Melanie picked at the grime under her fingernails.

'So,' Agnes spoke in her measured, professional voice, 'what exactly did you say, in the note?'

'Well,' replied Melanie, 'I said that I needed some time to myself and . . . I'd call him.'

'Uhuh.' Agnes nodded.

'I had to get out of there.'

'You have a problem with group situations,' said Agnes, more a statement than a question.

'When the group is barging into my house – yes I do.'

'You don't like sharing Gary.'

'Not all the time, no.'

'How does he feel about it?'

'The more the merrier – that's Gary.'

'Well, Gary's a country boy. He belongs to his community as much as he belongs to you. You don't understand this because you grew up in the city.'

'I understand plenty,' replied Melanie. 'I understand that it isn't normal to be surrounded by a big mob of people. Not all the time. He's got me, hasn't he? I should be enough.'

'That's the whole point,' said Agnes. 'You'll never be enough.'

Melanie fell silent. She knew when a lecture was coming.

'When you live in the city,' the counsellor continued, 'you don't need other people so much. If things get rough, there are places you can go. A big population means more infrastructure – government agencies and welfare bodies and a certain level of support. Right?'

'I guess,' said Melanie.

'But in the bush, you've got a small population, so there aren't the same resources. No formalised support structures. So what do people do? They make their own. They have sporting clubs and country dances and family days, because that's the glue that keeps it all together. It's called "social capital".'

'Yeah, but –'

'Life is fragile in the bush. People rely on each other. It's like they're all on a boat together, and if one end of the boat sinks, they all go down.'

'Yes, I understand that,' said Melanie. 'But Gary – he always has to be with other people. Always. It isn't normal.'

'It's normal for him,' replied the counsellor. 'He grew up in a communal environment, it's part of his wiring.'

'You think I'm being selfish.' Melanie started picking at her nails again.

'No, I don't think that. I think that maybe you need to adapt.'

'Adapt?' Melanie bristled. 'I'm always adapting, I spend my life bloody adapting! What about Gary? Why can't he make a few changes?'

'Of course,' Agnes said, shifting to a conciliatory tone. 'You're absolutely right. Gary's got to put in some ground work. He's got to talk to his mates and set down some rules. You're a couple, you need time together – just the two of you. His friends will have to respect that.'

Melanie sighed. 'I don't think Gary understands.'

'Give him some credit. He's an intelligent man. Talk to him.'

Melanie thought for a moment. 'Do you think that's why Carla left, because she couldn't stand the whole group thing?'

'Who knows. Maybe. Or maybe she wasn't as strong as you. Maybe she didn't have the skills to sit down with Gary and hammer out a compromise.'

The intercom buzzed, signalling the next appointment. Melanie rose to leave.

'One thing,' said the counsellor. She looked up at her client with a very different expression, one that Melanie hadn't seen before. The professional distance had evaporated. Agnes was talking woman to woman.

Melanie paused by the chair.

'It's always easy to leave,' said Agnes. 'Just pack your bags and walk away – anyone can do that.' Her eyes were suddenly sad. 'It's the easiest thing in the world.'

TIVOLI GARDENS, ALBERT PARK

'Will you please turn it off?' pleaded Richard, hovering around Zani. She was sitting on the lounge room floor, engrossed in her yoga routine, ignoring his requests.

'All right, *I'll* turn it off.' Richard made for the stereo.

'Stop! Don't you dare,' Zani shouted at him, contorting her pretty limbs into the next position. Then she added, serenely, 'I need the music. It helps me to concentrate.'

'It makes me want to kill people.'

'It's today's music, Richard. Get used to it.'

'It's not music. It's a repetitive bass beat that destroys your central nervous system.'

'Yeah, I guess that's why it's so popular.' Zani shifted from the lotus position to a headstand.

Richard grabbed his wallet from the table. 'We're out of milk,' he muttered, heading for the door.

CORAL TREE LANE, SOUTH MELBOURNE

'All the steps,' cried Leon, his elegant fingers ascending an imaginary staircase.

'Thirty-nine!' they all squawked back at him.

'Sunset Strip,' he intoned.

'Seventy-seven!' they rasped, the tension building.

'Garden Gate.' Leon's honeyed voice was showing the strain.

'Number eight!' they barked. Then 'BINGO!' shouted Marshall, doing a celebratory dance around the lounge room until he copped one in the eye from the low-hanging chandelier. He struggled dramatically towards the fridge in search of frozen peas.

Marshall and Patrick had invited Leon, JJ, Bryce, Abdul, Lauren and the rest of the Bitchin' Bingo crowd over to celebrate the Australasian coup. Patrick had secured a two-year transfer with Leo Dunne's, setting up the visual merchandise department in the new Hong Kong megastore. The lavish hair salon took up an entire floor, and Marshall had been appointed manager. The money was obscene.

'We can save a decent deposit, then come back and buy a really good place,' said Patrick.

'But we'll miss you!' replied Lauren.

The other guests concurred with a collective whine.

'It's ages away,' said Patrick. 'We're not going till January. Anyway, we have to get Melanie sorted first.'

'Ooh, the big wedding!' cried Leon.

'Small wedding. Maybe no wedding.' Melanie raked over her pad Thai with a plastic fork. She'd been very pensive since the session that morning with Agnes.

Patrick winked at Leon. 'Lovers' tiff. They'll get over it.'

'Now Melanie, you mustn't be silly,' said Abdul. 'A good man is hard to find, you know, and you're not getting any younger.'

'Yes, Melanie, he's right,' added JJ. 'How old are you now?'

'She's "older than Britney",' Patrick started, in a singsong voice.

'"...and younger than Madonna",' Melanie joined him to complete the chant, in their time-honoured ritual.

'Hey!' Marshall called from the freezer. 'Where's the vanilla bean ice-cream?!'

'Sorry,' said Melanie, with a guilty expression.

'She always eats ice-cream when she's depressed,' Patrick explained to the assembled guests.

'But we need it for the rhubarb crumble!' Marshall insisted.

'All right, I'll get some more,' said Melanie with a sigh, as she checked her pockets for cash and keys. 'Anyone want anything?'

'Ooh, a big beefy fireman, please,' called JJ.

'I'll see what I can do.'

As Melanie was leaving the house, the phone rang.

'Mel, wait,' Patrick called after her, 'it's for you. It's Gary!'

She stopped at the front door, then kept on walking, pretending she hadn't heard.

BENNY'S DELI, MIDDLE PARK

Melanie paid the cashier at Benny's all-night deli.

'Will you be wanting a bag for that?' he asked.

'Um . . .' She held the frozen tub in her hands, which were fast turning blue. 'Yeah, I think I will.'

'We do sell the string bags for eight dollars,' he reminded her, rather unpleasantly.

'Sorry.' She put down the tub and fumbled in her pockets. 'Um, I don't have it on me.'

Pursing his lips, the cashier shoved the ice-cream into a plastic bag, dropped it on the counter in front of her and turned away.

'We've got a compost heap at home,' she offered meekly, but the cashier was busy serving somebody else.

In a corner of the deli she spotted Richard. He was standing with his back to her, flicking through a magazine.

You couldn't miss Richard, she thought. He was usually the tallest one in the room – the guy with the gentle eyes and the dark brown curls and the goatee. She didn't like bushy beards or sleazy tashes, but a slim, neatly trimmed goatee could be a fine thing indeed, and it looked very fine on Richard. Shame about all the lying-bastard, male-musician behaviour.

Melanie walked quietly up behind him and whispered in his ear, 'Where's your raincoat, honey?'

'God! Melanie!' he gasped, clutching the magazine to his chest. 'You scared me.'

'What is it, *Busty Babes in Boobland*?'

Richard flipped over the cover. It was a music magazine. 'Ooh, *Downbeat*. You deviant.'

'Don't tell anyone,' said Richard, 'it's my guilty secret.'

'Did Andy send you the tape – the one with the ballad?'

'Yeah, I'll do the charts tomorrow and bring them to the club,' said Richard. Then he frowned. 'If I can get near the stereo.'

'Tell me about it,' said Melanie. 'If Marshall plays "Waterloo" one more time, it'll be his bloody Waterloo!'

'Now ABBA I could live with,' replied Richard. 'At least you get a few chord changes. But this techno stuff – it's excruciating. Thump-thump-thump. That's why they're all eating drugs, it's the only way to cope with the music.'

Melanie laughed and Richard glowed.

'You wanna come for a coffee?' he asked.

'I'd love to but I gotta get back.' She held up the bag. 'The boys want their ice-cream.'

'So when are they going?'

'A few months. January, I think.'

'Well,' said Richard, 'now that you're married off . . .'

'What do you mean?'

'Well, you're all set up with Mister Right. Now the boys can have a little fun.'

'Thanks very much.' Melanie's voice was tight.

Richard realised he'd struck a nerve. 'Mel, I'm joking.'

'I'm not some sad little spinster they're desperate to get rid of.'

'Mel, I said I was joking.' Richard tried to jolly her out of it. 'C'mon, chill out.'

'At least I've found somebody my own age,' she snipped.

'Sorry?' It was Richard's turn to be offended. 'Are we talking biological age – or reading age?'

'Oh and that's Einstein you've got hogging the stereo, I s'pose?'

'Yeah, well,' Richard blustered, 'she's good with her hands!'

'Yeah, well, so is Gary,' fumed Melanie.

'Well, great!' Richard snapped.

'Great!' Melanie snapped back.

'Well, aren't you the lucky one?!' His anger was rising.

'I'm so lucky I could spit!' She was shouting now.

'Fine!' he shouted even louder.

They both stood their ground, furious, glaring at one another.

'I have to go.' Melanie turned and stormed out of the shop.

Richard watched her leave. Then, his heart still thumping, he walked over to the till, putting his purchases on the counter.

'Will you be wanting a bag for that?' asked the cashier.

'Yeah, whatever,' Richard muttered, trying to figure out what on earth had just happened.

The cashier whipped out a plastic bag, stuffing the milk and magazine inside it. 'I hope you'll be recycling that, sir.' There was a distinct sneer in his voice.

'Yes, I will,' said Richard, collecting his change and taking the bag. 'I'll be suffocating myself with it later in the evening.'

THE CRYSTAL PRINCESS, CAULFIELD

The Sciarelli Brothers wore crisp white tuxedos and gleaming white shoes. Impeccably groomed, they exuded a patrician benevolence and quiet charm. They'd been stalwarts of the cabaret scene for decades, playing the tunes the punters wanted to hear. They played baptisms, bar mitzvahs, weddings, ordinations, funerals, children's parties, every kind of birthday from sweet sixteen to Queen's telegram. They played soccer matches, Grand Prix meets, house-warmings, divorce celebrations, and the rise and fall of the stock market.

Tonight was Jay de Nofrio's triple bypass celebration (he lived), and the party-goers were packed in tight, dancing to cabaret favourites. Dancing old-style, cheek to cheek, steps you had to learn – a quality gig, as the brothers explained to their two new recruits. The band had recently expanded from five players to seven. Joining the percussion section were their cousins, Michael and Johnny. Michael was on triangle and Johnny, the younger and more talented of the two, had been entrusted with the maracas. In time they would move on to more complex instruments, such as the cowbell or maybe the timbales, but as their older, wiser cousins advised them, music is an art, you gotta take it slow.

Michael and Johnny didn't mind. Just being there was enough. To be part of a proud family tradition – well, other than extortion. To be up there on the bandstand, to finally don the coveted white tux and the patent leather shoes. Best of all was the gold lettering on the jacket pocket – 'S.B.' The boys had arrived.

THE MAGELLAN HOSPITAL, EAST MELBOURNE

Melanie swung by the hospital on Friday and dropped off a present for Sally in Finance, who'd just announced her pregnancy. It was lunchtime so she bought a roll from the cafeteria and wandered into the garden, finding Jacqui in her usual spot. She joined her on the bench.

'I got a call from the donor guy.' Jacqui threw a hot chip to a belligerent seagull who'd been staring her out for the past ten minutes. 'You know, the guy with the blue Burmese.'

'Yeah?' Another seagull made a perfect landing on the

bench next to Melanie's right shoulder, receiving a piece of cheese for his efforts. The hospital ducks glared at their seafaring cousins with a mixture of envy and admiration. 'What did he say?'

'He wants to meet me so he can thank me.'

'That's really nice.' Melanie smiled. 'What's his name?'

'Oh, I can't remember,' replied Jacqui. 'It's foreign. Rostovar, Robespierre . . .'

'Rasputin?'

'Something like that. He had a really nice voice.'

'And he likes cats,' added Melanie. 'Sounds promising . . .'

'Yeah yeah.' Jacqui rolled her eyes.

Melanie's mobile started to ring. She pulled it out of her bag.

'Hello? . . . Yeah, hello, Consuela, what do you want? . . . Uhuh . . . Uhuh . . . No. No, I don't . . . No, Consuela, I don't think Zani is sleeping with José. She comes to the gigs because she's living with Richard, okay? Now, please, stop calling me.'

Jacqui shook her head. 'The woman's tragic. I almost feel sorry for her.'

'Loco, she's completely loco.' Melanie dropped the phone back into her bag.

Jacqui distributed the remainder of her chips to the waiting crowd. 'Have you heard from Gary?' she asked, trying to sound nonchalant.

'Yeah,' Melanie said as she dissected the contents of her salad roll. 'He keeps leaving messages on the mobile.'

'For God's sake, Melanie, you're getting married in nine days!'

'Eight.'

'Eight! You've gotta talk to him, sort it out.'

'I'll call him tomorrow, all right? After the gig. It'll be fine.'

'Good,' said Jacqui. 'Don't go shooting yourself in the foot. You always do that when you meet someone half-decent. What are we? Herd animals, remember?

'Yeah, I know,' said Melanie. 'It's just not the herd I had in mind.'

'I've seen worse,' said Jacqui.

Melanie threw a slice of beetroot to a passing wood duck – a sleek creature with a tawny-gold chest. He ignored the beetroot and trotted up to Jacqui, claiming the very last chip.

'Why don't you come tomorrow?' said Melanie. 'Sarita's mum does a mean curry.'

'I can't,' replied Jacqui. 'I'm going to the wine club. We're trying out a new sauvignon blanc.'

'I thought it gave you asthma.'

'It's okay, I take the puffer. Puff-sip, puff-sip – I get by.' She gave Melanie one of her looks. 'You *will* call him?'

'Yes, Auntie Jacqui, I'll call him.'

'I mean, you and Gary – it's never gonna be perfect. But who gets perfect?'

'I know.'

'D'you know what's out there, Mel? A bunch of goril-las with first aid certificates and Ray the Nipple Man. Those are the options.'

'I know, it's just that . . .'

'What?'

'I dunno, I have this gut feeling. Like my gut is trying to tell me something.'

'Yeah, it's telling you this.' Jacqui placed her hands over Melanie's stomach and spoke in a rumbling voice. 'Melanie, me want good food. Me want expensive booze. Me want financial security so me don't get ulcer.'

'Get off!' Melanie laughed and pushed her away.

'Bricks and mortar, my dear,' said Jacqui. 'Bricks and mortar. Don't blow it.'

Driving home from the hospital, Melanie felt like she was surrounded by couples. Young couples walking hand and hand, necking in bus shelters; older couples pushing prams or attending to toddlers; middle-aged couples strolling with their grown-up children. There were families in the street, families in their cars, all chatting and laughing and looking as if they belonged.

A row of billboards lined the street. 'She's precious. She's irreplaceable. Immunise now.' Those dewy-eyed babies got to her every time. An ad for cheap home loans featured a giant ram. Melanie smiled, remembering her first encounter with Gary, when he'd saved her from the demon beast. On one billboard there was a tanned, muscular male model wearing tight designer jeans and a ten-gallon hat. Smiling seductively, he was unzipping his fly. Melanie's eyes were drawn to his forearms and she nearly ran up the car in front of her. Eyes on the road, Mel, eyes on the road. She switched on the radio.

'Are you female . . . single . . . facing a childless middle-age? And what about your twilight years? Will you be falling prey to a sadistic unqualified nurse in a sub-standard government facility? Hey, ladies, it doesn't have to be you! Book yourself a berth at Ladies Who Lunch, the luxury retirement community for unclaimed treasures. Approved clients will –'

Melanie changed the channel.

'Tired of the rat-race? Find your piece of heaven in the country! Acre blocks are selling now at the Lavender Fields Estate. If you've got a hundred-thousand-dollar deposit, and you and your partner both work full-time and your combined income is no less than –'

She twiddled the dial and found music. It was Eddie Albert belting out 'Green Acres'.

'Aaarrghh!' she jabbed at the 'off' button.

DIG THE DIRT DETECTIVE AGENCY, NORTHCOTE

Consuela Torres was a valued customer; in fact, she was keeping Matthew afloat. His wedding video business was suffering, thanks to the proliferation of cheap video cameras operated by 'sheer bloody amateurs' – usually the bride's cousin. 'Bad lighting and crap audio,' he'd complain to his wife. 'That'll impress the grandchildren.'

Consuela sat next to him in the gloom, their faces illuminated by a television screen. They were sitting in Matthew's rumpus-room-turned-office, smoking dope and going through tapes. The footage revealed the secret life of one José Torres, Latino band leader and supplier of premium-grade marijuana.

Matthew moved across to the VCR, fiddled with the 'rewind' button and resumed his seat.

'The next bit – now we're coming to it . . . No, damn.' The office budget didn't run to a remote. He jumped up again and pressed 'fast forward'.

'Uh, here. Yeah, here we are,' he said as he pointed to the figure on the screen. 'There's José, and there – see, up on the left, behind the shed, in the blue dress. There she is!'

On the monitor, a woman in a large straw hat and a pair of dark glasses stepped out from behind a boat shed. Checking the coast was clear, she raced over to José and embraced him.

José kissed the woman, removing her hat. Her hair was concealed beneath a blue scarf. He kissed her again, *apaixonado*. Then they skipped off towards the shore and clambered into an abandoned rowboat for some furtive canoodling.

Consuela twisted a handkerchief around her fingers, tighter and tighter, her face darkening with rage. 'Who ees thees whore?!' she seethed. 'Thees . . . thees . . . *prostituta*! I 'ave to find out! I 'ave to know everytheeng!'

'Never fear, señora, Matthew Blake is on the case.' Matthew sucked on his premium-grade joint, inhaling sharply. 'I will expose this heartless home-wrecker.' He spoke while holding his breath as best he could, his eyes watering. 'I will tear off the mask of deceit and reveal the truth, because I am the Phantom, the ghost who walks.' Damn, this stuff was good!

Melanie stood in front of the bedroom mirror, putting on some lipstick. She moved back to admire her new dress, another creation from the House of Patrick. The satin bodice was emerald green and ruby-red tartan, the black skirt buoyed up by black tulle petticoats. Short and very cheeky – 'Celtic Carnivalé', Patrick called it.

She scouted around for her earrings, shifting a newspaper and finding her mobile phone underneath. She picked up the phone and checked her messages – all from Gary. She pressed delete.

'Melanie!' Patrick called from downstairs. 'The boys are here.'

Richard and Milos stepped into the hallway, looking handsome in their dark suits. Today it was both a gig and a party – young Andy and Sarita's wedding.

'Guitar and percussion,' Richard had said when he congratulated them. 'Great combination.'

'So is piano and sax,' they'd replied.

Richard walked into the lounge room, Milos trailing behind him. Milos was unusually quiet, thought Richard. He hadn't said much in the car coming over, and not a single joke about Richard's swimming.

'Hi Richie-babes!' Marshall greeted him with a peck on the cheek. 'Hi Milos! Don't you just love a wedding? Oooh! It'll be Mel's turn next!'

'Yes, all right, you.' Patrick gave Marshall a sideways look and seated the visitors on the sofa. It was a plush new sofa with an Aztec motif in earthy reds and browns.

'Do you like the couch? We get a big discount – thirty per cent,' Marshall chirped, putting on the kettle. 'We get all the latest designs. They're paying to ship it over, can you believe it? Ever been to Hong Kong, Richie-babes?'

Patrick leant in towards Milos. 'Are you all right, dear?'

Milos immediately burst into tears. Baffled by his friend's distress, Richard put a consoling arm around his shoulder. 'Mate, are you okay?'

'Milos, you poor sausage,' cooed Patrick. He darted to the foot of the stairs. 'Melanie,' he called, 'we need you!'

Patrick headed for the drinks trolley, Richard searched his pockets for a tissue, and Marshall tizzied about like a geisha, setting out cups and plumping cushions. Melanie descended the stairs in a flurry of legs and tulle. She looked over and saw Milos crying.

'Sweetheart, what's wrong?' She raced over and hugged him warmly, and together they sat on the couch.

'Melanie, what am I going to do? What am I going to do?' Milos whimpered.

'What is it?' She held him, speaking softly. 'What's wrong, come on . . .'

Milos lifted his head for a moment. 'Is Renata. Renata . . . she . . . she's gone!!' Then he burrowed into Melanie's shoulder and kept weeping.

'Ooh, these European men, they get so emotional. Don't you just love it?' said Marshall.

'Just make the tea, Gloria,' Patrick chided him.

After tossing back a brandy, Milos revealed that Renata had left him for a younger man – a sun-kissed sur-fie with blond dreadlocks and a gold tooth. One terrible,

269

fateful day he'd pushed his Corolla into Renata's garage. Their eyes had met over a steaming radiator and now they were living together – some holiday shack up on the north coast.

'And you know the worst thing? He eats . . . *take-away food*!' Milos started crying again. 'Has she no self-respect?!'

The doorbell rang and Patrick moved nimbly to the front door. It was Gary, all spruced up in his moleskins and sports jacket. He was carrying a large bunch of irises – a mixture of the purple Dutch iris and Melanie's favourite, the pretty, cream-coloured Louisiana iris.

Complimenting him on his good taste in blooms, Patrick led Gary down the hallway and into the lounge.

'Ooh, there's never a dull moment, is there?' Marshall gushed, seeing the handsome farmer with his big bouquet. 'It's like "The Bold and the Beautiful"!'

Gary and Richard acknowledged one another with a grunt.

'Gary, dear, can I get you some tea?' inquired Patrick, pulling up a chair for the new arrival.

'Uh, no thanks, mate. I just want a word with Mel, if that's okay.'

Gary and Richard were eyeballing each other, sticking out their jaws and pawing the carpet with their feet. Melanie whisked Gary up to her room before they started spraying on the curtains.

Marshall unwrapped the irises with a flourish and arranged the stems in an art-deco vase.

'Nice flowers,' remarked Milos, now on his second

brandy. He was trying to be brave and make conversation. 'A lot of flowers.'

'Yes,' trilled Marshall. 'Would've cost him a pretty penny.'

'Well, he's given the game away now,' Richard said as he poured some more tea.

'How do you mean?' asked Patrick, producing a plate of petits fours.

Richard chose a delicate pistachio swirl. 'It's a basic law of physics.' He leant back on the sofa and smiled. 'The size of the bunch is always directly proportional to the level of guilt.'

Gary sat on a chair, watching Melanie. She was standing at the dressing table with a pile of music charts, arranging them in playing order.

'I miss you, Mel. We all do. Dad's thumpin' about the place, even crankier than normal, and Mum gets all weepy . . .'

'Yeah, sure,' she said as she put the charts into a briefcase.

'It's lonely without you, Mel. It's bloody miserable, if you must know.'

There was a rap at the door. 'Melanie – two minutes,' called Richard.

'Okay,' she called back. She moved to the bed, knelt down and searched for her flat-heeled shoes, in case she wanted a dance at the wedding. 'I can't see how you'd ever get lonely,' she said. 'All your devoted followers, there at your beck and call, seven days a week.' She could feel her cheeks getting red.

'Is that the problem?' asked Gary.

Retrieving the shoes, Melanie stood up again. 'Well,' she began as she shoved them into a backpack, 'it's not like you need me or anything.'

'What? Don't be crazy, Mel! Of course I need you.'

'No, you don't – not really.' The tears were stinging her cheeks. Gary quickly rose from the chair and put his arms around her. She buried her face in his chest.

'Mel, they're just mates,' he said softly. 'A bunch of galahs I knock around with. You're the one that counts.'

'Yeah, sure,' came the muffled reply.

'Listen, Mel, you and me, we need some time on our own, right? Away from the mob at home. So . . . I'm going to rent us a place up in town.' He glanced around the room. 'A big place. We'll need plenty of room for the kids.'

Melanie gasped inwardly as a violent maternal pang hit her square in the abdomen and reverberated around her body.

'Half the time we can live up here, the other half down in Maybury,' said Gary. 'What do you reckon?'

Pulling away from the hug, Melanie went to the dressing table and plucked some tissues out of a box. Looking in the mirror, she dabbed at her tear-stained make-up. 'But when we're away,' she said, 'who's going to run the farm?'

'No problem, we'll get a manager. It'll be great. You can see your friends, play all the gigs you want . . .'

Melanie didn't respond, but she liked what she was hearing.

'And I can do some study,' he said as he moved up behind her. 'Up here at the TAFE. Something to do with English, I reckon. I like stories and reading and stuff. I was good at English at school – I didn't get to finish, 'cause Dad needed me on the farm, but I reckon –'

Another knock at the door.

'All right, I'm coming,' called Melanie.

Gary reached into his jeans pocket and pulled out a small key. He took Melanie's hand and placed the key in her palm.

'I got you a piano,' he said. 'A real one. Brand new.'

'What?'

'That's the key. But don't lose it – it's the only one, okay?'

'Gary.' Melanie was stunned.

'It's down in Wyllandra, sitting in the lounge room. You've got to bring down the key, open the piano and play me something beautiful.'

Melanie looked at the key. A real piano.

Gary stroked her face. 'I know you need some time, darl', I understand that. But when you're ready . . .'

'But Gary, that's the whole point!' said Melanie, suddenly agitated. 'We don't *have* any time. We get married next Saturday or you lose the farm. I feel like the entire Quartermaine dynasty is breathing down my neck, and if I don't . . .'

She stopped and looked down at her hands, fiddling with the key for a moment.

'The thing is . . .' She looked back up at Gary, her voice quavering. 'The thing is, sometimes I think the only reason you're marrying me is so you can keep the farm.'

Gary's shock was palpable. 'Jeezus, Mel.'

Seeing the hurt on his face, Melanie realised that she'd made a terrible mistake.

'It's just . . . it's just that . . .' she stammered.

'What, you think this is all an act?' Gary recoiled from her. 'You think I can just – what? – turn this on and off like a bloody tap. Is that who you think I am?!'

'No, but . . .'

'Well, *fuck* the farm!!' Gary was pacing up and down, enraged. 'Fuck the farm and fuck Jack Quartermaine. I'm sick of my bloody grandfather running my life! He's dead and he's *still* running my life and that's what the bastard wanted. Fraser can have the farm and good luck to him – he can take the fucking lot!!' Gary sat down heavily on the bed.

Tentatively, Melanie moved to the bed and sat next to him. 'You don't mean that.'

'Yes I do,' he barked.

They sat there for a moment, saying nothing. Then Gary's expression started to change.

'You know what? Maybe it's not such a bad idea.'

Melanie turned to look at him. 'What?'

'Leaving the farm. I mean, think about it. I'd be a free man. Nothing to feed, nothing to shear – wouldn't have to get up early.'

An idea struck him like a bolt from the blue and he leapt up from the bed.

'A caravan! We could buy a caravan, hitch it to the ute and just take off! Shit, yeah, I've always wanted to do that – go and see Australia! Go all the way round! Why not? Have a bloody adventure! We could go up and visit your dad!'

Melanie stood up and moved towards him. 'But Gary, you love the farm – and all the work you've done . . .'

'Doesn't matter, Mel,' said Gary. He was excited by the new vistas, the new road-movie possibilities. 'As long as I've got you, it'll be sweet. I can turn my hand to pretty much anything. We won't starve, you know.'

Richard knocked again. 'Mel, they can't start the gig without us.'

'I said I'm coming!' Melanie called. Then she looked at the piano key, unsure of what to do with it.

'Keep it.' Gary closed her hand over the key. Then he leant in and kissed her – a warm, lingering kiss.

Melanie could feel her body melting and half-wondered if there'd be time before the gig.

Gary took hold of her shoulders and looked into her eyes. 'When you're ready, Mel, you let me know.' He spoke calmly and quietly. 'I'll be waiting for you, okay? I'm like a stubborn old sheep dog – I never give up.'

As Gary left the room he ran into Richard, who was waiting to help Melanie with the keyboard. The two men glared at each other, lips curling, then went their separate ways.

THE DE SOUZA RESIDENCE, NARRE WARREN

The wedding took place at Sarita's family home, out in the distant suburbs. It was a garden wedding and thankfully the weather held out. There were pots of curry and trays of spicy delicacies, with gallons of Uncle Wency's guava punch to wash it all down.

Sarita was adorned in a red silk sari and veil, shot through with gold thread. She was laden with gold bracelets, necklaces and anklets that jangled when she moved. Andy looked equally fetching in his jacket, kilt and sporran. The other MacDougall men wore their kilts too, and the De Souzas wore traditional Goan wedding garb. It was a colourful bridal party, a joyous array of tartan skirts and silk pyjamas.

After the ceremony the band took to the stage, which was a makeshift affair decorated with sunflowers, gladioli and pom-pom dahlias. Music filled the yard, the guests twisting and shaking to a string of Beatles tunes, which were popular with both clans. Halfway through the set, they slowed the pace as Andy and Sarita danced the bridal waltz – which wasn't really a waltz, it was a ballad in four-four time that Andy had written especially. More like a bridal drift.

Melanie watched the dancing couple from behind her keyboard. They looked like they were floating – gliding across a sea of manicured lawn under a big southern sky. The sun was setting and the fairy lights shining in the trees made it all seem very dream-like.

Playing a long, sustained note on the alto sax, Richard had one eye on the chart and the other on Melanie. She was watching Andy and Sarita and getting all wistful, which made him extremely nervous.

As the evening progressed, the band moved into swing mode, with guest vocalist Uncle Nazim giving his own interpretation of a few Sinatra classics.

Melanie's hands were playing, but her mind was else-where. She didn't see the large, drunken man coming up behind her, lurching towards her, belly-first. He was struggling through a maze of amps and leads and shouting beerily, 'Pianna Man! Hey, darlin', play us Pianna Man! Come on, darlin'.' The man suddenly tripped and, with a loud cry, went hurtling towards Melanie's back – a massive projectile, threatening to slam her into the keyboard.

With lightning speed, Richard dropped his saxophone and threw himself at the flying guest, knocking him backwards and leaving Melanie unharmed. The music came to an abrupt halt as players and guests crowded noisily around the two men.

'It's okay, it's okay.' Richard lay flat on his face, raising an arm. He'd fallen into a pile of soft leather – storage bags for the congas.

The other man had landed on his back. Fortunately the alcohol had relaxed his body and the flowers had broken his fall. He lay on a mattress of dahlias and gladioli, warbling happily. Richard got to his feet and checked his hands – just a graze, thank God. He'd rather break both legs than damage his hands. The sax was still in one piece; there was a scratch on the bell, nothing more.

The band took five while the warbling guest was taken inside for a lie down, and the crushed flowers were propped back into place. Melanie was standing near the keyboard with Richard, giving him a thank-you hug. Then she went off to fetch him a drink and some pappadums.

Andy, Sarita and Uncle Nazim hovered around the stage, checking that Melanie was out of range.

'Nice save, man,' said Andy.

'So romantic,' added Sarita. 'You're a knight in shining armour. I think she was really impressed.'

'You know, in my village,' said Uncle Nazim, 'when somebody saves your life, you are connected to them forever.'

'Thanks, Nazim,' said Richard, 'but I don't think I saved her life –'

'Shut up, boy, I am trying to help you. Get with the program!'

'I appreciate what you're doing,' said Richard. 'But let's face it, it wasn't a cliff rescue. I'm not going to be on the news, am I?'

'Different scenario, same motivation,' Sarita said, nodding wisely. 'Believe me, she'll remember.'

At around ten o'clock, the fairy lights were being extinguished and the wedding party was moving off to Donovan's. Richard approached Melanie, who was packing her charts into a briefcase. He was hoping that his chivalrous gesture earlier in the evening might have earned him some minor brownie points.

'So, Mel, you coming to the club?' he asked.

Melanie snapped the locks on the case. 'No, not tonight. I'm a bit tired.'

'Heyyy! Come on, it's a big night. You'll get your second wind, you always do.'

'I'd really like to go,' said Melanie. 'But honestly, I've got to get some sleep.'

Richard could see that she meant it. 'Okay. I'll drop you home. As long as you're sure . . .'

'I'm sure.' Melanie picked up a white rosebud which

278

had fallen from Sarita's bouquet. She slid it into a button-hole on Richard's shirt. It was an intimate gesture, and he felt the blood in his veins heating rapidly. She looked up at him and smiled.

'Thank you, Richard. Thank you for saving me from the Pianna Man.'

'No worries, Mel.' Richard grinned. 'Anytime.'

CORAL TREE LANE, SOUTH MELBOURNE

By 11 p.m. Melanie had showered and changed and packed a suitcase. She headed downstairs and said goodbye to the boys, who were watching a video in the lounge room.

Patrick met her at the bannister. 'You're up late, Missy,' he said. Then he noticed the case. 'So,' he said, smiling his approval, 'you're off then?'

'Yep.'

'It's a long trip,' said Patrick fondly. 'Make sure you stop for a coffee.'

'I will.' Melanie put down the case and gave her friend a long, warm hug.

'Stop snogging him,' Marshall called from the sofa.

'Will not,' replied Melanie.

'Gary's a good man,' said Patrick. 'You made the right decision.' He pushed a strand of hair out of Melanie's eyes. 'I guess it's true what they say.'

'What?'

'When the fairytale's over, the love story can begin.'

'Oh, Patrick,' Melanie said, smiling up at him, 'that's wonderful.'

'It was on "The Bold and the Beautiful",' called Marshall.

'Don't care,' Melanie called back.

Marshall jumped up from the couch, came over and gave her a squeeze, then raced back to the TV.

'Sorry, Mel,' he called, 'Demitri's about to do Dallas.'

'You can hit "pause", you know,' said Melanie, but Marshall didn't hear her, he was too engrossed in the video.

Patrick picked up the suitcase and walked her to the door.

🥾

Melanie hit the road. The key to her new piano was dangling from the rear-view mirror, attached by a green ribbon. Heading south, she turned right onto the freeway. Then she wound down the window and slipped a tape into the stereo. Ricardo Lemvo and Makina Loca playing high-octane salsa. Singing along in her minimal Spanish, Melanie bobbed her head and shook her shoulders with great abandon, to the amusement of passing motorists, who honked their horns and called out to her.

Melanie didn't care. She was on a high, anticipating Gary's surprise at her unexpected arrival. And looking for-ward to all the reunion sex.

A caravan. A *caravan*?! Who was he kidding?! She knew Gary better than he did. He'd be lost without Wyllandra. He belonged there, it was in his blood – and now she belonged there too. Bugger the caravan, they were going to keep the farm. Anyway, she'd already seen Australia, now Australia could come and see her. She'd be down at Wyllandra with her gorgeous big hunk of farmin' man.

Melanie planted her foot and sailed along the freeway, leaving the city behind her.

DONOVAN'S DEN, RICHMOND

Standing at the bar, Richard made a call from Brian's private line. Andy and Sarita's relatives were getting very loud. Richard cupped a hand over his ear.

'Sorry for calling so late,' he said. 'I tried Melanie's mobile but she's got it switched off.'

'You'll have to speak up,' Patrick called into the receiver. 'Sounds like quite a party!'

'Yes, yes, it is,' Richard shouted back. 'Look, Patrick, is Melanie still awake?'

'Oh, well, actually, dear, you've just missed her.'

'Sorry?'

'She went out,' said Patrick. 'About ten minutes ago.'

'What – did she go to the deli or something?'

'Ah, no,' replied Patrick, trying to be delicate. He was fond of Richard and didn't want to hurt his feelings. 'Um, I don't think she'll be back for a while.'

'Oh,' said Richard. 'Right.' He could feel his heart sinking at a very fast rate, then hitting rock bottom. 'Okay.'

'Did you want to leave a message?' asked Patrick.

'No, no message. Look, thanks, mate. Sorry it's so late. Bye.'

Richard put down the phone and resumed his seat at the bar, ordering another whiskey.

Andy's dark-haired cousin Megan approached him with a rosebud, smiling flirtatiously. 'I think you dropped this.'

WYLLANDRA, MAYBURY

It was 1.17 a.m., according to the clock in her car, when Melanie hung a left into Gary's driveway. There were lights on, up at the Big House. Gary was probably up watching TV, she thought. As she drew nearer the house, Melanie's heart began to sink. There, in the yard, was Brendan's old brown station wagon.

'Pleaaase, not *tonight*,' she groaned, her disappointment soon turning to anger. It was one o'clock in the morning, for God's sake! Couldn't these people last five minutes without Gary? Didn't they have homes to go to? Then it occurred to her that she may have jumped the gun. Brendan would often leave his car at Wyllandra, she remembered. He'd leave it there overnight when he'd had too much to drink. One of his mates would drive him home, then he'd pick up the car the following day. There was certainly no sign of Brendan, thought Melanie, as she parked her car next to Gary's ute and looked across the yard into the well-lit kitchen. No drunken Neanderthal lurching about, raiding the fridge or plundering the pantry. Brendan would be safely at home, she concluded, with considerable relief. He'd be sleeping off yet another night of excess, wrapped in the soft, pink arms of his ever-forgiving Rosalie.

Melanie reached up and unhooked the piano key from the rear-view mirror. Then she hopped out of the car and walked towards the house, bounding up the verandah steps like a schoolgirl. As she crossed the verandah she nearly tripped over Marmite, who lay snoring on his blanket.

Arriving at the kitchen door, she threw it open with great abandon, ready for the noisy reception. Gary would probably scoop her up into a fireman's lift and make a dash for the bedroom.

'Gary!' she called.

The kitchen was empty, the sink piled high with dishes. Lazy sod. She smiled to herself.

'Gary?' she called again. No response.

She went into the lounge room, where the fire had burnt down to a pile of glowing embers. Stan Getz was playing on the stereo – a jazz CD she'd given Gary a couple of months ago. He played it so often he was wearing it out.

There, in the middle of the room was her brand new Ronisch – a state-of-the-art upright piano stained a deep mahogany. But it wasn't locked, it wasn't even closed. The lid was up and there was cigarette ash on some of the keys. Couldn't be Gary's, she thought. He doesn't smoke. Sitting on top of the piano were three half-filled wine glasses and an empty bottle of red.

Melanie walked down the corridor towards the master bedroom. The door was closed. As she approached, she could hear voices. There were people in there, talking and laughing. Gary's voice. A woman's voice – but it was deep, like a man's. And some kind of animal . . . growling . . .

Melanie reached for the handle and pushed it down. Slowly, soundlessly, she eased the door open. As she stood in the doorway and took in the scene that confronted her, Melanie's sense of time altered radically. It was like being in a car accident, when everything shifts into extreme slow motion, seconds becoming minutes, minutes seeming like hours. Melanie had entered the twilight zone.

In a far corner of the room, Brendan Buchanan was howling and barking like a dog. He was on all fours, chained to the wall. His considerable bulk was jammed into tight leather shorts, a string singlet and workman's boots. Around his neck there was a thick red collar with metal spikes – the one he'd given Melanie at the barbecue. The one she'd put in a drawer somewhere. He was straining at the leash, but he couldn't break free.

He was straining towards the four-poster bed – the one that Gary had bought Melanie as an engagement present. Gary was hiding in the bed. He was hunched up under the doona, squealing with laughter. One of his legs was sticking out. A large red stiletto was dangling off the end of his foot.

Standing with her back towards Melanie was Blodwyn Platt. She was next to the bed, standing right over Gary.

She was rigged up in a policeman's uniform, with a holster strapped to her shoulder and handcuffs hanging from her belt. Her short brown hair was plastered back with gel.

It was Brendan who saw Melanie first. He stopped barking and leered at her expectantly. 'G'day.' He appeared to be salivating.

Under the doona, Gary sensed that something was wrong. He threw off the bedclothes and leapt to his stilet-toed feet. Squeezed into the red lycra dress that Melanie had bought him, he balanced precariously on his spindly heels. Seeing her standing there in the doorway, he groaned in disbelief, the colour draining from his face. Melanie's eyes were drawn to his mouth. It was daubed with her special-occasion lipstick. Cinnamon Diva. Expensive.

Gary stayed frozen to the spot. Brendan pricked up his ears, canine-alert, and savoured the tension.

Now Blodwyn turned to face her. Seeing that it was Melanie, Blodwyn paused for a moment, surprised but not displeased. Then she reached for her shoulder holster and pulled out a rubber truncheon. More than a foot long, it was flesh-coloured, broad and decidedly phallic. Not your standard police issue.

Looking the ashen-faced Melanie straight in the eye, Blodwyn held out the truncheon with her left hand, hold-ing it at the base so it pointed directly upwards. Taking her right hand, she encircled the shaft with her long spindly fingers. Slowly and deliberately, she worked her right hand up along the baton's broad surface, relishing every centi-metre. From the base, up along the thick rubber shaft, all the way up to the bulbous tip. Her eyes still trained on

Melanie, Blodwyn brought the truncheon to her lips and kissed it, right on the tip. One delicate kiss. Then she smiled. It was a mocking, triumphant smile.

That was the last thing Melanie remembered seeing as she backed out of the room and ran down the corridor.

part three

CORAL TREE LANE, SOUTH MELBOURNE

Melanie drove back to the city on autopilot. There were very few cars on the freeway, and the journey slipped by without her really noticing. The boys were asleep when she got home. She moved about quietly so as not to wake them. The warm milk didn't work, neither did the brandy, so she knocked herself out with an ageing Temazepan she found in the fridge.

The next morning, Melanie woke to find that Patrick and Marshall had already left. She remembered they were going to Sunday brunch with Leon and the girls, so they wouldn't be back for a while.

She was still in a state of shock. Hyper-alert and strangely numb at the same time. She made some tea and sat at the kitchen bench, trying to focus her thoughts, trying to assess the damage.

She wasn't just losing a lover, she was losing her future life. Her blond, land-inheriting children had suddenly vanished, along with her illusions about Gary's honour, to say nothing of his taste in women. A voluptuous siren she could understand, but being cuckolded by the Whippet – it was the ultimate insult.

She thought about everything she'd done for Gary – the caring, the attention, the tenderness she'd lavished on him. She'd trusted him with her most intimate thoughts, she'd bolstered his self-esteem and she'd tried very hard to accommodate his 'idiosyncrasies'. She'd made him laugh, she'd planted his trees, she'd run his b & b like a well-oiled machine, she'd granted him exclusive access to her coveted breasts, but clearly none of it meant anything to Gary. He was happy to risk it all for some skinny witch with a dildo.

And as for Brendan, well, she wasn't even going to think about him, not yet. Her brain was already bursting with images of Blodwyn and Gary – the two of them thrashing about, Gary squeaking and squealing, the red lycra dress pushed up around his belly, Blodwyn jiggling about with her plastic appendage, urging him on in her best bass-baritone. Suddenly Ray the Nipple Man seemed pretty damn normal.

Melanie finished her tea and took a clean towel out of the linen cupboard. Standing under the shower till the hot water ran out, she tried to remember the drill for this type of occasion. 'Coping with a Crisis: Step One.' What was it? She turned off the taps and wrapped the towel around her body, hugging herself tight.

Now she remembered. Step One: Go to the Movies.

The Odeon was running their 'Shakespeare on Celluloid' series. It was ten o'clock on a Sunday morning and Melanie was the only person in the audience. This wasn't unusual at the Odeon, which was why she liked going there.

The room darkened and the projector clicked and whirred into action. It was the Oliver Parker remake of *Othello*, with Laurence Fishburne as the angry Moor and Kenneth Branagh as Iago.

The numbness had gone, replaced by a slow-burning rage. Melanie immersed herself in the saga of betrayal unfolding on the screen. She cursed the evil troglodyte Iago, as he hatched his wicked plan. Her heart went out to Othello, who couldn't see the viper in his midst, the viper poised to strike.

Iago made sense to her now. She hadn't recognised him at first, when she was fifteen and he was just a character in a school text. Now, twenty years later, she knew what Shakespeare was on about. Iago was Treachery. He was every snivelling creep she'd ever known. Every low-life scumbag who'd sold her down the river or trampled on her pride. Right now, Iago was Gary.

She bit into her chocolate bomb.

Othello, crazed with grief, suddenly realises his terrible mistake – he's been deceived in the vilest possible way. Iago has tricked him into destroying the one thing that brought any meaning to his life – his beloved Desdemona. There's only one course of action to take and Othello doesn't hesitate.

When Larry Fishburne plunged his sword into Ken Branagh's chest, Melanie cheered and punched the air. She cheered so loudly that the usher raced in to see what was going on. As Larry kept thrusting the sword, again and again, with increasing force, Melanie kept on yelling at the screen.

'Kill him again!' she screamed. '*Kill* the bastard! Rip out his throat! Yeah! Get him in the eyes! Now cut off his dick! Go on! Do it! DO IT! KILL THE FUCKING BASTARD!!'

Exhausted, she slumped forward and cried all over the seat in front of her. The rage was wearing off and the grief was kicking in. As the concerned usher gave her small sips of Diet Tropitang, a corner of Melanie's brain flickered into life. Like Othello, she would take action. Like Othello, she would have her revenge.

CHERONI'S CAFE, SOUTH YARRA

Carla arrived twenty minutes late, apologising profusely – some problem with a root canal. She sat down at the table and started rummaging through her handbag.

'Yep, enough for a latte,' she said, pulling out a twenty-dollar note and flagging down a waitress, 'my treat!'

Melanie was struck by the resemblance – green eyes, chestnut hair, noisy and outgoing – they could've been sisters. She was surprised that Carla had agreed to meet with her. Usually people like to close the chapter and move on.

She'd been easy enough to find. When Gary and Melanie first got together, Gary had mentioned that his second wife's name was Denton. Doctor Denton the dentist – it had stuck in Melanie's mind.

Their coffees arrived and Melanie reached for the sugar, depositing a spoonful into her cup (she could have sworn she saw Carla flinch). As the conversation progressed, it was clear that Carla had a few of her own demons to exorcise. Both women spoke rapidly, with a lot of gesturing, enjoying their confab of shared experience. It was great to find a fellow survivor, another escapee from the parallel universe that was Maybury.

'Book club? God, is that what they're calling it now?' Carla shrieked with laughter. 'Darling, it's an S&M thing. Brendan buys the stuff through a catalogue, stores it in his shed with the old washing machines and sells it to the locals. Hey, is he still doing the Chippendales routine?'

'Sorry?'

'Gary – those dinner parties of his. "Good liddle earner, darl'." Every Wednesday night when I was up in town. He thought I wouldn't find out, then one day I'm doing a clean and scale and my patient starts complimenting me on my husband's dancing. I thought she meant barn dancing, not lap dancing!' Carla started laughing again.

'So he *did* take his gear off!' exclaimed Melanie, incredulous. 'That lying bastard, he swore blind that he didn't.'

'Oh yes, he's very good at the righteous indignation. The question is, who *hasn't* seen Gary with his gear off? Not that I cared. He's an exhibitionist, he can't help himself.'

'So what about Blodwyn,' asked Melanie, 'is she the reason you left?'

'The skinny bird? Revolting woman, I wouldn't have her in the house. Always creeping about, putting her hands on my crockery. Look, he was probably doing her too, but that isn't why I left.'

'So it was Brendan?'

'Brendan?! God, no. Brendan doesn't have sex with anybody. He can't get it up, as they say in the classics. Too much LSD in the sixties. His cerebellum's shot to pieces.'

'But he was there . . . with Blodwyn and Gary.'

'Brendan's a voyeur, that's all. He likes to watch. Which is just as well.' Carla pushed the hair out of her eyes and leant back in her chair. 'Nope, I left Gary because of Tom.'

'Tom?'

'Tom Lewis. The wool classer.'

'Oh my God!' Melanie shook her head in disbelief. 'God, I had no idea. Tom Lewis. He was always so nice to me.'

'Well, you had something in common. Mind you, Tom wasn't the only one. Plenty of blokes in the Greater Eastern region have got to know our Gary. There's the guy who delivers the gas cylinders, the guy who runs the sale-yards in Mount Malabar, a guy who cuts keys at the Cranbourne shopping centre . . .'

'Cranbourne? He went up every few weeks.'

'Indeed.'

'But he was buying the groceries.'

'Well, they do call it the *Linga-longa* Carousel . . .'

'Oh my God,' said Melanie, her fears confirmed. 'So Gary is definitely bisexual.'

'Not *bi*sexual, darling,' said Carla. 'He's multi-sexual. Men, women, livestock, machinery, bits of piping he finds in the yard – he's into everything. The man's rampant, it's some kind of profound dysfunction. Didn't you notice the way he'd just disengage when he was having sex? The glaze would come over his eyes . . .'

'I thought he was just . . . lost in the moment,' said Melanie.

'Yes, *his* moment,' replied Carla. 'Nothing to do with you, darling. He's on autopilot when he fucks. He's probably thinking about poddy calves.'

'Oh, stop!' Melanie laughed, despite the quiet rage that was seething in her guts.

'You think I'm joking.' Carla signalled to the waitress.

'But if he's gay,' said Melanie, 'well . . . my flatmates are gay, they would have picked up on it.'

'Oh no, he's not gay. That's what's so weird about him. Him and Tom and all the other happily married men down there. More coffee?' She signalled to the waitress, finally catching her eye, then turned back to Melanie.

'You see, Gary thinks of himself as being profoundly heterosexual. It's just that now and then he'll have sex with other profoundly heterosexual men. Call him gay and he'd punch your lights out.' Carla lowered her voice as the waitress approached. 'I hope you made him use condoms.'

'Yes, thank God,' said Melanie. 'Force of habit.'

'A good habit, my dear, a very good habit. But you should have some tests, just to be sure.'

'Did you?'

'Every five minutes till the GP threw me out.'

Melanie smiled, but inwardly she was trying to get her mind around the idea that 'her Gary' – someone who'd professed to love her exclusively and eternally, someone she was going to reproduce with – had played Russian roulette with her health. And as for Tom Lewis – all the times he'd been over for tea and scones, and the whole time he was laughing behind her back . . . incredible! She couldn't remember any men delivering cylinders for the stove, only a woman. But, hey, she was probably up for it too.

The waitress took their order and departed.

'It isn't a question of sexuality,' Carla was saying, 'it's a question of honesty. I mean, if that's the way you're built, that's the way you're built. I don't have a problem with that. Just don't pretend to be something you're not. Don't pretend to be a faithful, monogamous heterosexual when you're a wildly promiscuous multi-sexual, you know? Just be honest, that's all I'm saying.' For a moment Carla looked vulnerable. 'He should've been honest.'

Nodding her head in agreement, Melanie decided to shift the focus from sex to money. She had often wondered how Gary could afford his extravagant lifestyle – the beautiful home, all the entertaining. The drinks bill alone must have been huge.

'Col pays for everything,' explained Carla. 'Col and the gee-gees.'

'So why did Gary need extra cash?' asked Melanie. 'You know, with all those dinner parties?'

'Good liddle earner, darl',' Carla hooted.

'And the barbecues for the tourists . . .'

'Oh God!' said Carla. 'Does he still dress up in that ridiculous Village People outfit? Mister Tassels!'

Melanie smiled weakly and Carla let out a laugh.

'But why do all that if you don't need the money?' asked Melanie.

'Because Gary, God love him, has to be the centre of attention. Any excuse to show off. He sets up these scenarios and casts himself in the lead role. "Gary the star", "Look at me, look at me!" It's pathetic.'

Melanie thought for a moment, trying to process all the new information. She was feeling quite dazed.

'But Col,' she began, 'he's always so tight with money.'

'Don't let him fool you,' said Carla. 'He's a squillionaire.'

'Sure, but he's pretty mean with it. Look at the place he and Dorothy live in – it's a hovel compared to the Big House. Why does he spend all that money on Gary?'

'Two reasons,' said Carla. 'One: he wants Gary to stay. A lot of country boys move to the city and Col's always been desperate for Gary to stay in Maybury and keep the dynasty going. Two: it's guilt money. Col has a guilty conscience.'

'About what?'

Carla paused. 'I take it he never told you about the first wife.'

'Only that she'd moved to Sydney. He didn't want to talk about it.'

'I'm not surprised,' said Carla.

The second round of coffees arrived and Melanie spooned some sugar into her cup. Two spoons – what the hell, she was having fun. Carla frowned at her.

'You know, that's like having a sugar mouthwash.

Never put sugar in your drinks, you might as well rub chocolate all over your teeth.'

'Yeah, I know.' Melanie looked suitably chastened. 'So,' she said, leaning in closer, 'tell me about the first wife.'

'Well,' said Carla, 'have you ever wondered why the place is called Wyllandra?'

'No.' Melanie thought for a moment. 'I thought it was an Aboriginal word.'

'Sandra Wyllie. Wyll-andra. It was Col's idea.'

'Sandra was the first wife?'

'Yes.'

'Oh. Right.' Melanie felt very miffed. She'd been living in a house named after a former wife and nobody had bothered to tell her. Still, it was increasingly clear that they kept quiet about most things in Maybury. Poisonous little community.

'Sandra was one of Col's jockeys. Or strappers or scrubbers – whatever they call them. Tiny wee thing. Gary fell madly in love with her. He was twenty-five. It was time to get married – keep the farm and all that – and there was Sandra. Perfect. Except for one thing.'

'What?'

'She was in love with Col.'

'What?! Col?!' Melanie gave a short laugh. 'You're kidding!'

'And Col was in love with Sandra. He was crazy about her.'

'Sandra was in love with Col . . .' Melanie shook her head.

'Well, they were both horse-mad, they worked together, she liked older men – it was bound to happen. Col convinced her to marry Gary. That way she'd be around all the time and they could continue the affair. 'Course, Gary didn't know about it. He didn't find out for years.'

'So . . . what about Dorothy?' Melanie felt a pang of sadness for her ex-future mother-in-law.

'Who knows.' Carla waved her hand dismissively.

Melanie saw that time and distance had given Carla an enviable detachment. She longed for the day when she too would be able to rattle off anecdotes about Gary and Maybury free from the anguish she was feeling now.

'Dorothy sees what she wants to see,' Carla continued. 'Nice woman, but she's trapped in the fifties. Anyway, the cottage wasn't good enough for Sandra, so Col built the Big House – all the mod cons. Anything Sandra wanted, Col reached into his pocket – in more ways than one.' Carla raised an eyebrow.

'What did Gary think about it?' asked Melanie. 'You know, Col spending all this money . . .'

'He was stoked. Life was great, he loved his wife – and here was Col spoiling them rotten. He thought Col was just showing his approval, that he was happy about the marriage. Then one day the ute broke down, Gary walked home and he found Col and Sandra going hell for leather in his own bed.'

'I know the feeling,' Melanie muttered.

'Don't we all, darling,' said Carla.

'Do you think it's because of Jack?'

'You mean the grandfather?'

'All the terrible things he did to Gary when he was a boy.'

'What terrible things?'

'You know, the "three trials of boyhood",' said Melanie.

'Oh yeah,' said Carla, 'that's right. How he dumped Gary in a tar pit and made him climb out, then he had to roll naked in a patch of nettles –'

'No,' Melanie interrupted her, 'I mean the dead rabbit and having to kill the sheep and the thing with the pig.' Then the truth slowly dawned. 'That was all bullshit.'

'Don't worry.' Carla smiled sympathetically. 'I bought it too. Poor old Jack. I heard he was rather nice.'

'So why did they call him Iron-Bar?'

'He had a metal pin in his leg – it was quite big. He got it in the war, I think.'

'Right,' said Melanie, now seeing Jack in a new light. 'But even so, he couldn't have liked Gary. I mean, all that business with the will.'

'He didn't *not* like Gary,' said Carla. 'He just didn't think Gary was cut out for farming – which he isn't.'

'Isn't he?'

'He's a crap farmer. Like Col always said, "That boy wouldn't work in an iron lung."'

'But he was always working. Heading off on the tractor . . .'

'And coming back hot and sweaty – yeah, funny that. It's Col who does all the work on the place, he runs both the properties. All Gary does is steal people's lingerie and go rooting in the sheds.' Carla scraped the froth off the top of her coffee. 'Great cook, though. That's the one thing I do miss.'

'And he's brave,' added Melanie. 'He rescued that guy off the cliff. Did you see it? They interviewed him and everything, he was all over the news.'

'Ah, yes, the quiet achiever,' said Carla with a wry smile.

Melanie felt a sudden pang. She still harboured feelings for Gary the hero, Gary the beau of the ball, versus Gary the low-life scumbag. She picked up her glass of water.

'To Iron-Bar Jack. Sorry, mate, I take it all back.'

'To Jack.' Carla clinked her glass against Melanie's, took a long gulp and plonked it on the table. 'So,' she declared, 'I was stupid enough to marry him, but at least I got a payout. What are you going to do?'

Melanie shrugged. 'I dunno.'

'You can't claim de facto,' said Carla. 'You didn't live there long enough. 'Course, you were engaged. You could sue him for breach of contract. But it's a long shot and he'd fight you tooth and nail.'

'God, I'm not going to sue him,' Melanie said, picking up the shortbread from her saucer and dipping it into her coffee. 'Anyway, who can afford a lawyer?'

'I hope you kept the ring.'

'Ohhh yes.'

'Good girl.' Carla nodded. 'But there's gotta be something you can do. Get him where it hurts.'

'Any suggestions?'

'You could pay someone to break his face. He's a vain bastard, that'd really upset him.'

'I've toyed with the idea,' said Melanie, 'but apparently there are laws about that sort of thing.'

'Pity,' said Carla.

'Yeah,' said Melanie, 'pity.'

In her vivid imagination, Melanie had done terrible violence to Gary and the odious Blodwyn. Her daydreams were filled with limb severance, howls of pain, removal of vital organs, pleas for mercy, withholding of mercy and subsequent death rattles. This gave her a tiny quiver of satisfaction, and it dulled her own pain for a moment or two.

She'd monitored the evening news for shark attack stories or boats lost at sea, or accidents on the farm – 'Farmer Drowns in Bucket of Sheep Drench', 'Farmer Locked in Silo, Suffocates in Avalanche of Wheat', 'Farmer Disembowelled by Runaway Plough'. Every morning she'd raced out to the lawn and scooped up the paper, rolled tight in its plastic wrapping, bursting with the promise of an overnight fatality.

Melanie wanted Gary dead. It seemed the fairest possible outcome. Why should the innocent party suffer all the grief while the wrongdoer skips off into the sunset? She thought about hacking up Gary's silk shirts and smashing his wine collection and trashing his beautiful kitchen. But that wouldn't work, he'd just replace it all. Thanks to Col, Gary had an endless supply of cash. It had to go beyond money. Gary had to lose something that was dear to his heart, something that couldn't be replaced.

An idea occurred to her. It wasn't the bloody, murderous revenge of Othello, but it would have to do. The rest

Melanie would leave to karma. With any luck, Gary and Blodwyn would be reincarnated as shit on the sole of someone's shoes. Hers, preferably. She liked to think that the constant pressure of living a duplicitous life would make Gary sick or drive him insane, but she doubted it. The man was born duplicitous, it was his natural state.

She consoled herself by picturing Gary, Blodwyn and wool classer Tom in a casualty ward somewhere, being surgically separated after one of their sexual exploits went horribly wrong. Or maybe the entire book club would get trampled by marauding cattle. She could see the headlines in the *Greater Eastern Gazette*: 'Of Beef and Bondage: Local Sadomasochists Bite the Dust'.

Melanie flicked through her little black book. It was time to call in a favour.

WYLLANDRA, MAYBURY

It was 4.15 on a brisk spring morning. Gary was up in Mount Malabar with his father – one of their regular trips to the saleyards. After Mount Malabar, they'd continue up to Cranbourne and do a big shop. While they were there, Gary needed to have some more keys cut, apparently. (It baffled Col that his son lost so many keys.) In Col's absence, the senior stablehand was running the training sessions. The 'troops' and the racehorses had already gone to the track, some distance from the homestead.

Under cover of darkness, a sleek sedan pulled up next

to Gary's letterbox on Iron-Bar Road and checked the address. Two men alighted, both strangers to Maybury. The car drove off and the two men moved quickly and quietly up the drive, sneaking past the Big House and over to the large tin shed.

They opened the shed door and climbed aboard Josafina the tractor. Starting her up, they reversed out of the shed and headed down the driveway, out onto Iron-Bar Road. Driving at full throttle, they took Josafina through the still-deserted township. They drove her past the bakery and the two pubs, then down past the pier and Bella's Seafood Emporium and the dinghies and yachts. Leaving the bay behind them, they wended their way up along the old coast road, higher and higher, towards Breakaway Point.

With the sun now lighting up the sky, the two men arrived at the edge of a perilously high cliff and slammed on the brakes. They nodded to one another, enjoying the magnificent view. The sunrise was more beautiful than any painting, and the smell of salty air filled their nostrils as the waves crashed heavily onto the rocks below. Putting the gears into neutral, they hopped off the tractor.

Both men were dressed in black with khaki balaclavas covering their heads. Their faces were hidden behind large, green crocodile masks. They moved to the back of the tractor and assumed the position. Summoning all their strength, their plastic snouts wobbling with the strain, the two men grunted and sweated and pushed Josafina right over the edge.

They stood there, on top of the cliff, and watched the

tractor fall. Down past the ancient cliff face she went, down past the swooping gannets and the screaming gulls, past the jagged rocks and all the way down into the briny, landing with a loud splash. The sun glinted on her cherry-red chassis one last time, as she sank into the bubbling waters of Bass Strait. The getaway car arrived, right on cue, and spirited the two strangers from the scene of the crime.

Sitting in his boat a mile out to sea, a Maybury fisherman watched Gary's Josafina plunge into the ocean and sink like a – well, 'like a tractor', as he'd later describe it to his wife.

Grabbing the mobile, he tried to call Gary, to alert him to the disaster, but Gary's phone wasn't answering – it must have been out of range. Later that day the fisherman tried again. It was up in Cranbourne, shopping with his father at the Linga-longa Carousel, that Gary finally learnt of the tractor's fate.

The news came as a terrible shock, like a sharp, heavy sword being plunged into his heart.

'Murder!! Bloody murder!!' Gary shouted, flinging out his arms with some violence. His mobile phone went flying through the air, landing, eventually, in the frozen chips compartment. Gary stumbled along the supermarket aisle, lurching into trolleys and knocking over a wall of tinned tomatoes until, finally, he collapsed into the arms of a matronly woman in a paper hat, who was handing out cubes of processed meat. 'Josafina. Josafina,' Gary whimpered. The saleswoman patted his hair and suggested he try the cabanossi.

Seeing the shameful spectacle that his son was creating, Col turned on his heel and quietly walked away.

.&

The following morning – Friday, October 24 – there was a solemn ceremony at Breakaway Point. Gary and the book club gathered high on the cliffs, right on the spot where Josafina's wheels had last rolled. Brendan and Rosalie wept audibly, Blodwyn murmured some hastily invented prayers about a man and his machine, Phil Duncan played a mournful slide guitar, and a group of gas-cylinder reps shuffled their feet uncomfortably.

Gary, looking drained and grief-stricken, made a slow sign of the cross. Then he dropped a wreath of lavender stems over the cliff, into the raging sea.

THE ERROL FLYNN MEMORIAL PUBLIC POOL, NORTH MELBOURNE

'Use your legs! Use your legs!' Milos was shouting instructions to his latest proteges, Michael and Johnny Sciarelli. It was lesson number one – kicking. The brothers were clinging, white-knuckled, to the side of the pool, churning up the water with their meaty thighs.

Zani was draped around Milos's shoulder, looking edible in a one-piece halterneck swimsuit – candy pink. She cheered her cousins on while fondling the coach's buttocks.

Brian Donovan opened the door of his brick-and-tile semi to find a stranger standing there. She was clutching a letter and looking very nervous.

'Are you . . . Brian Rostropovich?' she asked.

She was wearing a pair of dark glasses, so Brian couldn't see her eyes. Wisps of soft, caramel-coloured hair peeked from under the hood of her parka. She wore a knee-length paisley skirt and those schoolgirl black tights that Brian had always liked. He couldn't help noticing her well-turned ankles.

'Yes. I'm Brian. You must be Jacqui. Please, come in.'

Brian had adopted the name Donovan for business reasons. 'Meet you at Rostropovich's' just didn't have the right ring to it.

He ushered Jacqui into the lounge room, asking if he could take her coat. As she removed it, her hair fell out of the hood and down around her face. She was wearing a black cashmere jumper which clung to her breasts in a very alluring fashion. Running a hand through his thatch of grey hair, Brian tried to look formal and detached. He was closer to her now – she was wearing a floral scent with a hint of citrus. Subtle, not like some women whose perfume made your gonads shrink. What were they hoping to attract, bison?

Brian took the parka and hung it on the back of the door. Jacqui pushed the sunglasses up off her face and propped them on her head. Brian noticed that her eyes were a beautiful lilac-grey colour. But he only saw them for an instant – Jacqui was nervous and kept looking down at the carpet.

He led her towards the couch. There, lying on a burgundy cushion, was a pedigreed blue Burmese. Realising that her audience had doubled, the blue-grey feline stretched out her lithe little body and adopted a more luxuriant pose.

Gently, Brian scooped her up and showed her to Jacqui. 'This is Lucinda.'

Lucinda was a delicate cat with a pretty face. She reminded Jacqui of Audrey Hepburn.

'You can hold her if you like. She's very friendly.' Brian eased the cat into Jacqui's arms.

Tentative at first, Jacqui soon began to relax. Lucinda was rubbing up against her chin, purring loudly.

'Go on,' said Brian softly.

Slowly, Jacqui leant down and placed an ear to the cat's chest. There, inside Lucinda's rib cage, beating away with a strong, steady rhythm, was Leroy's heart. As Jacqui listened, the grief began to stir. She looked up at Brian, seeking some kind of reassurance. As their eyes met, they both felt the same exquisite pain. Two tiny arrows had met their respective marks.

Jacqui and Brian blinked, then continued gazing at one another, unabashed, neither able to believe their luck.

Consuela Torres sat in Matthew Blake's rumpus room, watching her paid informant stroke his chin.

'I have tracked down the mystery woman,' he revealed. 'The tart in the boatshed.' This was Matthew's favourite part. For a fleeting moment he was the centre of attention, the man with the goods. All eyes were on him. Well, two, anyway. He stroked his chin one more time for effect.

'They call her the "VA".'

Consuela stared back at him blankly. 'Who?'

'Mrs Vera Van Asch. Divorced, one son – he lives overseas. She works at the Magellan Hospital –'

'Hospital?' Consuela interjected. 'So! Thees tramp, she is nurse? Good. That's good . . . he's gonna need nurse, Meester Blake. He's gonna need many, many nurses and many, many doctors to put him to the one piece!'

'Well, she's not exactly a nurse, she's –'

Consuela grabbed hold of his wrist. 'What eef there are more?' she snarled. 'More of these . . . *prostitutas*?! We must keep looking! Always looking! I have to know! I have to know everytheeng!'

'Yes, señora.' Matthew nodded thoughtfully, trying not to look too pleased. Now he could get the car fixed and pay for his wife's trip to Broome. (Matthew was calling it a trip; his wife was calling it a 'fresh start', but never when Matthew was around.) He was already planning a sharp rise in fees. How far could he push it, he wondered, and still keep Mad Connie on board, shelling out all that lovely money? How far could he go without killing the golden goose?

'Yes, señora,' Matthew repeated, now wearing a suitably solemn expression. 'I really do think you're right.'

TIVOLI GARDENS, ALBERT PARK

Richard lugged Felix up the stairs, and Melanie followed behind with a carton of clothes. She was moving into Richard's flat. He'd organised a sub-let, so she could stay in the flat for as long as she wanted. The boys would be leaving for Hong Kong soon, and she couldn't keep the terrace house on, not by herself. Richard's place meant subsidised rent, courtesy of Art-House, and the luxury of living alone.

Melanie was feeling a lot saner these days. She'd replaced all the out-of-shape lingerie and her blood tests at the clinic had come back negative. She was coming to terms with her anger about Gary, and her dark, vengeful urges were abating. 'If you're out for revenge, dig two graves,' the ancient Chinese said. Melanie had realised that living well and being happy would be the best kind of revenge – and the least likely to attract a gaol sentence. Of course, news of Josafina's plunge into the briny had lifted her spirits considerably. Gloating over the wanton destruction of property may not have been very Zen, but it felt fantastic.

The Boozy Crocs had called Melanie from the getaway

car, reporting that Operation Belly-flop had gone off without a hitch. For days after the event, Melanie had been thinking about Gary's reaction – how he would have responded to the tragic news. She'd tried to imagine where he might have been when he'd heard about it, and what (or who) he'd been doing at the time. She wanted to be sure that she'd hurt Gary – that she'd wounded him in some way – even if it could never compare to the way he'd wounded her.

To her great delight, Melanie had soon received an eye-witness account confirming that Gary had indeed suffered mightily. The eyewitness was Lauren, one of Marshall's friends, a fellow hairdresser and regular guest at the Bitchin' Bingo nights. Lauren had phoned Melanie, at Marshall's insistence, to deliver a blow-by-blow description of Gary's performance.

On the day in question, Lauren had nipped out of her salon at the Linga-longa Carousel to pick up some frozen chips from the supermarket. As she was digging around in the freezer compartment, a rather attractive farmer type had emitted a blood-curdling scream, giving Lauren – and everyone else within hearing range – a very nasty shock. He'd then flung out his arms with some force, nearly clocking Lauren with his mobile phone. Melanie had listened intently to the account, savouring every last juicy detail. It must have been Gary. Apparently he'd kept saying the name 'Josafina'.

Marshall and Patrick had since taken to re-enacting the supermarket scene in the lounge room for theirs and Melanie's entertainment. Marshall would always play

Gary. He'd wear a tank top, boxer shorts and his fluffy toy sheep, which he'd strap to his groin with a couple of leather belts. Looking more demure in his tracksuit and a full-length apron, Patrick would play the saleslady, complete with paper hat and a tray full of samples.

'Murder! Bloody murder!' Marshall would shriek, shaking his hips to make the fluffy sheep jiggle up and down. Then he'd grab a large zucchini, raise it high in his clenched fist and start running at Patrick.

'No, kind sir!' Patrick would plead, batting his eyelids. 'Please, spare me! Here, try my cabanossi!'

'Mel! He's got sausage!' Marshall would squeal. 'A big stuffed sausage – with chilli! It's a "hunka hunka burnin' love"!' The scene would then continue with more sheep jiggling, Marshall's balletic interpretation of an exploding wall of tinned tomatoes and many jokes about pressed meat. Melanie would always feel better for watching it.

She was working at the Magellan again, two to three days a week. The VA had taken extended leave, for some reason, so life in the typing pool was now a lot more relaxed. Melanie was still playing gigs with the Salsa Kings and the Morangos, and Richard had got her some work with the Department of Education. She'd visit a new school each week, running workshops for Years Eleven and Twelve. Entitled 'School Notes', the scheme was designed to connect secondary students with working musicians – give them some insights into the profession.

She'd recently heard from her father, Jack. True to his word, he'd called to say he'd be visiting Melbourne in February, bringing the family for a holiday. He'd asked

Melanie to find them a hotel. She was looking forward to seeing Jack and spending more time with him. They could pick up where they had left off in Western Australia. And it would give her the chance to indulge her dear little half-brother, Jordan. She'd already planned a day at the Melbourne Zoo. They had a brand new baby giraffe, which Jordan would just adore.

Richard was now living in Hawthorn. With his knack for investing, Larry had cleaned up on the stock market and bought his son a three-bedroom apartment. At first, Richard had protested, but Roszika had sorted him out – 'Darling, please, are you crazy?!!'

The school had given him a promotion – a permanent job as senior music director. Plus he had the Kings and the Morangos and some lucrative session work playing for commercials. He'd even recorded a CD of his original compositions, but his elation over this achievement had been short-lived. The small jazz label Richard had signed with were screwing him to the wall. Citing 'hidden costs', they were withholding his royalty payments, in blatant breach of the contract. Further investigation had revealed there was a silent partner at the company and it was he who was causing all the trouble.

It was Bill the Barracuda, Richard's one-time booking agent. The Barracuda still owed Richard a packet from their earlier dealings and now the slimy bastard was stealing all his royalties. As a result, most of Richard's teaching salary was going straight to the lawyers. He was determined to nail the Barracuda, retrieve the master tapes and release the CD himself. If the lawyers couldn't fix it, there was always Michael and Johnny Sciarelli, thought Richard, in his more desperate moments. The boys could display their percussion skills by delivering a few sharp raps to Bill's cranium.

Melanie made them both some coffee while Richard assembled the futon. She was happy to be in her new home, with a brand-new bed, a view of the city and not a sheep in sight. Richard picked up the slatted base and unrolled it over the frame, thumping it into place. Melanie watched him, grateful for the help. He'd been quietly supportive during the post-Gary phase, at a time when his own relationship was ending – not that losing Zani was any kind of tragedy really.

Melanie had always said that musos should avoid entanglements with other musos, but Richard never challenged her about it. She often wished he'd grab the opportunity and make a case for himself. Show a bit of chutzpah. His passivity could be so frustrating.

Richard climbed to his feet and took the coffee cup that Melanie was offering. Together they crossed to the lounge-room window and looked down at the garden below. Richard had an idea for a gig there and asked her whether she thought there'd be enough space. He watched as Melanie assessed the size of the lawn area. He enjoyed standing close to her, listening to her talk. Another man might've taken advantage of the situation, preying on her post-break-up vulnerability, but he would never be that stupid. Richard knew all about the modern woman: she didn't want a man who acted like an animal. You must respect a woman's dignity and wait for an invitation, not charge at her like some randy primate. If Melanie did find him attractive, she would signal her interest when she was good and ready, at a time and a place of her choosing. That's how women liked to operate. It was Melanie's call.

SEVEN-MILE BEACH, TARALANGA

Up on the north coast of New South Wales, Renata was lying on a deserted beach. There were miles of white sand and only one set of footprints. She was reclining on a wide, flat rock, enjoying the heat of the sun, which was high in a cloudless sky. Clad in a black bikini, her skin had tanned to a deep honey-brown, her hair was streaked with gold highlights and she sported a gold metal ring through one of her eyebrows.

Hearing a voice, she propped herself up on one elbow and peered over her sunglasses. She saw a lone figure in the distance, running towards her with an athletic stride. It was Gavin, her surf-boy lover – he of the exploding Corolla. Wearing only a pair of boardshorts, his youthful body was taut and tanned and his white-blond dreadlocks were trailing in the breeze. There was an impressive scar on Gavin's chest – a skirmish with a tiger shark, he claimed. Renata chose to believe him, despite the surf club rumours about some chick with a bread knife. Gavin was holding up a container, raising it above his head as if it were a trophy. As her wave-conquering, shark-slaying Adonis drew closer, Renata could see that he was carrying a cardboard tub. It was filled with chicken – battered, deep-fried, takeaway chicken.

Renata looked up at the big, perfect sky and gave thanks to Saint Vitus of Prague for engineering such bliss. She'd light him an extra candle next time she was anywhere near a church.

DONOVAN'S DEN, RICHMOND

The jazz cellar was packed with noisy revellers. It was a double celebration – Christmas Eve and Brian's engagement. Brian Rostropovich Donovan was officially betrothed to fellow cat-lover Ms Jacqui McGlade. Everyone was delighted. Finally, the imaginary girl on the imaginary train had pulled up at the station, skipped along the platform and walked straight into Brian's life.

To mark the occasion, the Morangos had swelled from a cosy quintet to a fifteen-piece extravaganza. There was a loud, punchy horn section comprising alto and tenor sax, flugelhorn, two trumpets and a trombone, with a large percussion outfit to match. Two of the guest percussionists were still rookies, but what Michael and Johnny Sciarelli lacked in technique, they made up for in determination.

The band was playing a set of Bob Marley tunes. Zani watched adoringly from the audience, waving at her cousins and blowing kisses to her new squeeze, the multi-talented Milos. Patrick and Marshall were sitting at a table with the Bitchin' Bingo crowd, Marshall refusing to dance until they played something decent. Campbell, the resident regular, had shifted from his spot at the bar to join a table of medical typists. Campbell's wife, Eve, was with him tonight, holding his hand and chatting with the other guests.

Sarita's crew from Narre Warren were there, along with Andy's clan from Wonga Park. They were all up on the dance floor, cruising to the reggae groove. Brian and Jacqui were working behind the bar, finding it hard to serve and snog and watch the band all at the same time, but managing somehow.

During the next bracket, the band shifted gear into a funky Motown set. Marshall and co. were up and dancing now, and Eve and the typists had hauled a protesting Campbell to the floor. They were joined by five slim, silver-haired gentlemen in well-cut suits who looked strangely familiar to anyone who'd ever attended a wedding or bar mitzvah.

It was Richard's turn to take a solo. Melanie watched him play as she jammed along on the piano. He was in excellent form tonight. Urged on by the audience, Richard poured his heart into the gleaming saxophone, making it roar and squeal and moan.

As the sax solo built to a fever pitch, Melanie's eyes were drawn to Richard's arms. The muscles in his forearms were flexing and contracting as he played. Melanie couldn't stop looking at them. His forearms were remarkable – potent, assertive and yielding all at the same time. They were leonine and majestic, anarchic and vulpine. They were magnificent. They spoke to her. They moved her.

Richard had finished his solo. Standing back to let Milos take the floor, he noticed that Melanie was looking over at him. Curious, he smiled at her and she quickly looked down at the keyboard, her face turning a deep shade of crimson.

WYLLANDRA, MAYBURY

Blodwyn was sitting up in bed, wearing a red-and-white Santa hat and large mistletoe earrings. Propped up on some pillows, she was reading aloud from a children's book: a collection of Grimm's fairytales, lifted from the school library.

She was lying between two men – Gary on one side, Brendan on the other – and they were also wearing Santa hats. The three of them were freshly bathed and warmly dressed in striped flannelette pyjamas. The two men were curled up under the blankets, snuggling in close to Blodwyn's bony body. They listened, wide-eyed, to the story of Hansel and Gretel and the gingerbread house.

'. . . And they all lived happily ever after.'

Blodwyn closed the book, but Gary and Brendan protested, bleating like infants, 'Another one! Another one! Pleeease!'

Blodwyn gave them an impatient look then opened the book again. 'Honestly,' she said, waggling her finger at them, 'you two!'

The two men gurgled happily as Blodwyn leafed

through the pages, in search of new adventures. She kept glancing at her left hand, admiring the champagne diamond engagement ring and the shiny gold wedding band. Both rings were unusually wide, at Blodwyn's insistence. She didn't want anyone to miss them.

A shrewd operator, Blodwyn had played on Gary's grief over losing Josafina. It was Blodwyn who'd arranged the dawn service on the cliffs. After farewelling the tractor, she and Gary had gone back to the Big House for a consoling cup of tea. With Gary's defences well and truly down, it had been time to make her move.

Over a plate of melting moments, she had proffered her solution for the problem of the will. Barry had already organised the catering, and he'd made that wonderful cake – it would be such a waste. And if Gary didn't get married – well, he'd have to leave the farm.

'And let's face it, darling,' Blodwyn had said with a caring, sympathetic look, 'you wouldn't last five minutes in the real world.'

After a brief silence, Gary had agreed.

It was Gary Quartermaine's fear that had won the day for Blodwyn – his fear of trying to exist in the outside world without the privileges of birth.

They had married the next day – Saturday, October 25. The book club had rejoiced and Gary had got to stay on the property, accompanied by wife number three. Dorothy had taken a small pot of paint, walked over to the blue-stone cottage and changed the little sign on the door. Instead of 'Melanie's Cottage', it now read 'Blodwyn's Cottage'. Wyllandra had a new Mein Hostess.

Blodwyn Platt wasn't the catch of the century, but she was there and she was available on short notice. As Dorothy had said to Gary at the reception, patting his hand and speaking in a quiet, rather sad voice, 'She'll do, darling. She'll do.'

DONOVAN'S DEN, RICHMOND

Back at Brian's party, the Morango Big Band had moved from Motown Funk to sizzling Afro-Brazilian Mayhem. The percussion unit was taking an extended solo. The players were in overdrive, drumming up a storm on congas, bongos, timbales, cowbells, beer glasses, key rings and anything else they could get their hands on.

Richard stood on the bandstand taking in the scene, feeling quietly euphoric. Sometimes the music was so good, it made you feel that anything was possible. He looked over at Melanie, who was sitting at the piano, laughing at Andy's spoon-playing, which was always a total failure. God, she looked gorgeous tonight. She was wearing the little black dress that he liked – the velvet dress that showed off her neck and the shape of her breasts. He'd known the girl for years and she still made him crazy.

There was something different about her tonight. He'd noticed it when she was watching him during the solo. Something in her eyes – a hint, a glimmer. At least, he thought so. He couldn't be sure.

Through the corner of her eye, Melanie could sense Richard looking over at her. She avoided looking back, fearful that her gaze would stray to his forearms and she'd get all hot and bothered again. She couldn't afford to reveal herself, not any more. She had to be guarded, self-protective and cautious. This was the new Melanie. She wouldn't make it easy for anyone. If Richard Cohen wanted her – and she couldn't be sure that he did – but if he did want her, he'd have to gird his loins, gladiator-style, and march into battle.

Andy finished his spoon solo and, with Sarita, grabbed a handful of aprons from behind the bar. Tying them onto assorted guests – including Marshall and Patrick, who gleefully volunteered – they lined up on the dance floor and, to the beat of the congas, performed a group reprise of the Boozy-Croc Mambo.

Richard unhooked his saxophone from the neck strap and placed it on the stand. Leaving the horn section, he strode directly across the stage towards Melanie. Arriving at the piano, he leant against its battered frame and tried to look casually suave.

'You right there, Mel?' his voice was barely audible above the drumming and the clanging and the laughter of the crowd, as Andy and co. performed elaborate Boozy-Croc handshakes, flipping up their aprons in a can-can.

Melanie placed her hand on Richard's forearm. 'I'm great,' she replied, looking up into his eyes. Without really meaning to, she left her hand where it was, resting lightly on his arm. She was enjoying the warmth of his skin and didn't want to pull away.

Richard could feel all his nerve endings start to tingle. The slight pressure of Melanie's touch was something new to him. It was soft and tantalising and full of promise – very different to the way she usually touched him. It was all the incentive he needed.

He leant down and, very gently, kissed her on the mouth. Melanie responded warmly and eagerly, and they were both surprised by the rush of desire that flooded their bodies. Richard stood back for a moment to look at her – to look at her hazel-green eyes and flushed cheeks and that wonderful, familiar smile. Then he pulled her up from the piano into an embrace, and they continued kissing, *ardente, lascivamente*.

With a blast of sound, the rest of the band joined the frenzied percussionists. They played till the chi was coursing through their veins and the sweat was pouring from their bodies. They played till the room pulsated and the crystal sang and the crowd was swept up in the sheer joy of the music – their souls transported by the simple power of the beat.

acknowledgements

My thanks to Clare Forster, Ali Watts, Nikki Townsend and everyone at Penguin Books for making all things possible.

To Ron Blair, Colm Blake, Juliette Brodsky, Mike Bukovsky, Ingrid Butters, Avonia Donnellan, Kate Dunbar-Tapp, Bill Dunstone, Francis Grey, Bryce Kershaw, John Misto, Carol Odell, Sonja Patterson, Jan and Ian Peters, Helen and Marcia Powell; my mother, Laura Prodan, and my brother, Matt Prodan; Alison Salmond, Chris Spathis and Regina Zajusch for their inspiration, feedback and support.

Special thanks to Jane Morrow (Penguin), for her assiduous and sensitive editing, and to my agent, Anthony Blair (The Cameron Creswell Agency), for his invaluable guidance and care.